THE GOLDEN CHAIR

BOOK 1 IN THE ERIN REED TRILOGY

A.J. FONTENOT

The Golden Chair. Book 1 of the Erin Reed Trilogy. Copyright © 2019 by A.J. Fontenot. All rights reserved. AJFontenot.com.

Requests to publish work from this book should be sent to: Joe@ajfontenot.com.

ISBN: 978-1-6873571-1-3 (KDP paperback)

ISBN: 978-0-9981007-7-7 (IS paperback)

ISBN: 978-0-9981007-8-4 (hardback)

Cover design by Elena of L1graphics.

THE GOLDEN CHAIR

A man of courage is also full of faith.

— MARCUS TULLES CICERO (106-43
B.C.)

"Wherever you are, be all there."

— JIM ELLIOT (A.D. 1927-1956)

1

LAKE VOLTA, GHANA

THE SUDDEN, MUFFLED POPS CAUSED THEM BOTH TO jump.

Mofi had never heard gunfire before. And he wouldn't have known he'd just heard it now, if it wasn't for Tano beside him.

He sat up to look toward the sounds. Tano, wearing his signature tie-dye shirt, put a swift hand on him. And then, in a silent motion, pulled him behind the logs they were sitting on. It was so forceful, he almost lost his balance in the process. The afternoon breeze previously lulling them was now dead behind the logs.

"Mofi," Tano's face was taut. "Stay here," he said in a harsh whisper. He put his hands on each side of him, as if to emphasis his next point. "Do not leave until I come back."

Mofi watched Tano run the twenty or so yards, hunched over, to the two-story building. It was once a lodge, but had since been converted to the base of operations for the underwater logging operation on the coast of Lake Volta. Downstairs was mostly outdoor workspace, saws and heavy machinery. But upstairs was where the offices and airconditioned rooms were. Mofi watched Tano, still nimble for his age, jump, grab the railing, and pull himself up and over. And then, his tie-dye shirt disappeared over the second story's short balcony wall.

Mofi had been on the job exactly two days. Before this, he'd sold cell phone chargers at red lights in the metropolis that was Accra, Ghana's capital. It was hot, competitive work. And dangerous. Last week a boy fell asleep on the side of the road and was run over by a car. Not to mention, it didn't pay well. The money he was making logging was at least ten times what he made in Accra. Though, he sent most of that money back home.

This was different work, too. They were using big machines to cut the trees from underwater. And the trees that came out, once stripped, were good lumber. And unlike normal logging, this was relatively safe. Or, at least, it was supposed to be.

Tano came back, running with his head ducked low. He stopped behind the pile of logs where he'd left Mofi waiting. "They're dead," he said, drawing a deep breath. "All of them."

Mofi was processing his words, trying to understand. "Dead? Who is dead?"

"The others." Tano looked up at him. "He killed them."

"Why…what did—" Mofi began, but Tano cut him off, "Do you remember, yesterday, when the underwater machine found the cave?"

"Yes."

"I think I know what they found. I didn't understand it until just now. This is the *Volta Region*," Tano said, stressing those last words.

"Of course. I know."

"Where the Ashanti war happened," continued Tano, "with the British, a long time ago. Do you know the story?"

"Yes." Mofi didn't see how any of this was relevant right

now. "Everyone knows the story. But it's just a fable — Tano, what's going on?"

"It's not a fable. I thought it was. Everyone did. Until last night. I overheard them talking."

"Who?" Mofi interrupted.

"The big man. Keeler. We'd just finished our work in this area, and I asked him if he was ready to move on. He said 'no.' I asked him what he wanted us to do next. He said 'nothing.' That didn't make any sense. They'd always pushed us hard, to move fast."

Mofi continued to listen.

"And then, later, I heard him on the phone, saying they'd found something. He called it 'the artwork,' which was strange. There is no artwork way out here. And certainly not underwater. And then before I left, I heard him talk about 'an Ashanti man coming with a truck,' or something like that."

Mofi was listening, trying to understand.

"I only just pieced it together," said Tano.

Tano jerked around, looking back at the building. In the still of the now-breezeless afternoon, they heard a door shut. Looking carefully over the stack of logs they were hiding behind they could see the big man walking out onto the balcony.

He was looking for something.

"Mofi," Tano said, turning back to him, "listen to me carefully. There's not a lot of time. They'll have counted the bodies. They'll know we're still alive. Probably do already." He was speaking slower now, more deliberate.

"I need you to find someone and tell him everything I've just told you."

This was a strange request, because, as far as Mofi could tell, Tano hadn't just told him anything. And why *him*, he thought.

Tano pulled the leather strap hanging around his neck out from his shirt and broke it free. He put it in Mofi's hand. "Find my brother," he said. "Do you remember him, from when you were a boy?" Mofi nodded.

Tano's brother wasn't really his brother. He was a white man that came to stay with them in their village when Mofi was young. He didn't know many of the details. He only knew that he helped the tribe do something or other. But that's all he could remember. And even though he hadn't seen him in many years, he prided himself, as many Africans do, on his remarkable memory.

"But," started Mofi, "I don't know where he is. And why do you need me? Why can't you find him?" There were so many questions Mofi wanted to ask right now. Not least of them why someone, the big man, had just killed the other workers. And why, if Tano was right, he was now looking for them, too.

Tano glanced over his shoulder again.

"You'll find him," Tano said, looking back at Mofi. "He's back, working in the area."

Tano took a breath and with a deep calm, looked at Mofi. "I'm going to go over there. When I leave, you count to ten, and then run as fast as you can. Away from here."

KEELER

Keeler never much had a problem with killing. It's why he enlisted in the first place. And it's why, ultimately, he was discharged, 'dishonorably.' But there was always a steady demand for people who needed killing. He'd worked East Africa in the nineties. Latin America after that. And even a little bit in Russia. Though, in his experience, the cold was the worse killer. If he had the choice, he'd take the hot. Which was one of the reasons he was now here in West Africa.

As he walked out of the room, onto the second story balcony, he felt the breeze from the lake. From the second floor, he could see the water from Lake Volta disappearing into the mountain's edges. Trees, all these years later, still poking out from the water, like omens from a past life. And Keeler, as it turned out, was looking for life. Eleven down. Thirteen total. Two more to go.

Then, from the corner of his eye, he saw a blur of color, a man moving toward him, fast. Tie-dye shirt. Number twelve. Keeler turned, slipped a six-inch knife from its holder on his leg. As the man rushed him, he grabbed him under the arm and used the runner's own momentum to pick him off his feet. In a single, fluid motion, he slid the knife deep into the man's ribs. The colors on the shirt all becoming red. Keeler twisted his body around the man, removing the knife as he moved and planting it down deep into the man's neck. And then, as if choreographed, let him fall to the ground, making only the noise of an inanimate thud. Three seconds after the man had stepped onto the platform, he lay in his own blood, completely still.

Keeler looked around briefly to make sure there were no more like him waiting.

At that moment, he saw something else. Not close. Someone running through the logs. Twenty-five, thirty yards away. He raised his rifle, turned off the safety, put the scope to his eye, taking time to make the adjustments.

The runner's head now filled Keeler's view. It bobbed between the stacks of recently cut logs as it ran. Keeler was methodical, calculating. His black-gloved hand squeezed the trigger, knowing the shot wasn't clean. A miss. The man kept running. Closing in on the tree line.

An amateur would unload right about now. Use the fully automatic spray the weapon was easily capable of, thinking that more bullets would have a better chance. But that was sloppy. The truth was, one or two careful shots always had a better chance of hitting their mark.

Keeler let off another shot. The man slipped into the tree line. *Did he fall?* Keeler continued moving his scope forward, where he would be if he was still running. Then, *movement.* He missed. Too many trees. He was gone. Keeler swore under his breath.

He lowered his rifle and grabbed his walkie from his belt. "We have a runner. Just hit the tree line. I'm going to pursue on foot."

"Which way?" came the voice on the other end.

"Southeast."

"No," scratched the walkie in return. Even through the distortion of the long distance, Keeler could hear the softness in the other man's voice. *Not the voice of a soldier. Not the voice of a leader.*

The voice again: "If he's already at the tree line, he's got an advantage on you. He's a local. It'll take you too long. Besides, I need you to oversee cleanup. That's more important."

Keeler considered this for a moment. He knew exactly what he was capable of. And he knew exactly how long it would take him. He paused before responding.

"I'm sending a tracker."

The Patuka, as he was known locally. Roughly translated: the hyena. Every place had one. The opportunist whose loyalty to power was only topped by his greed. You didn't even have to find them. They had a way of finding you. A remora who spent his life feeding off of the shark.

This one just happened to be an excellent tracker.

Keeler pulled out his cell phone. Reception was okay at this height. He clicked the button for contacts; there were only three. He dialed and waited. "New job," he said into the phone. "Active now. Details to follow," and then hung up.

3

WASHINGTON DC

"This isn't adding up." Erin Reed stood looking down at a conference table in front over her. It was a scramble of papers, charts, and photos. She looked up at the minimalist clock on the wall — the kind that had only hands and no markers. *Almost time*, she thought.

Carl Ibsen, her boss and closest friend for the last nine years, stood across the table from her. "It's simple. A few people got too close. And…"

"And died," she finished.

"Our sources on the ground tell us this is an isolated case," he said. "It's Africa," he held up his hands. "This stuff happens."

"A bacterium," she said, "that hasn't seen the light of day in over fifty years is found. And within twenty-four hours everyone exposed to it turns up dead. That doesn't sound like a story to you?"

Nine years in, and she still couldn't shake the instinct. Something didn't smell right here.

At first, she thought it was just a holdover from her grad school days. *Find the truth*. That was what her journalism professor at Georgetown, Mark Allen, nailed into their heads. *If you're not doing that, you're not doing your job*, he drilled.

After school, Erin landed an impressive job working for the *Washington Post*. Part of that, she'd always figured, was because of her mother's history there. Her editor, a heavy Irishman by the name of Conall McGillis, worked with her mother in the early nineties. McGillis was one of the few people who had an even bigger file than Erin did on what really happened to her mother.

And then Erin took that trip to Trinidad.

The point she looks back on that changed everything, and not in a good way. It was a decade ago, but those six horrible days left her different. More different than she wanted to admit. And, not to mention, they nearly killed her. And it was those six days that ultimately caused her to leave the *Post,* and journalism, for good.

Shortly after that, Carl Ibsen approached her.

"A little bird told me you're looking for…," he hesitated, "a change of pace, let's call it." He said it like he knew more than he was leading on, but wasn't too interested in hiding that fact. But then…that was Carl. He wasn't cocky, he was charismatic. He had the kind of charm that didn't come from his looks. He was tall, but if you saw him on the street, you'd forget him. Maybe that's why he was so good at what he did.

"It's journalism," he told her. "Journalism with the kind of people behind you that can make a difference."

She didn't know what that meant.

"I own a media firm that focuses on a select few large clients."

"PR," Erin said.

"No, PR is manipulative. And rarely works. Besides, people see through that. We work with clients who are doing actual good in the world, and then we liaise with the wider media. You can think of us more as a feeder service."

"I'll tell you what," he continued, "you give me a month, and see if it's not a good fit for you. And then, if not, we go our separate ways. What do you say?"

Erin did need a job. And she had worked herself into a corner. Her experience was all in journalism. And, after Trinidad, she had to get out. But she was still in that awkward phase where she wasn't sure what she wanted to do next.

"Okay," she said. "A month."

It had been nine years since she and Ibsen had that conversation. The kind of years where you look back and wonder if it's really been that long. But in that time, they'd become a good team. And rushed, brainstorming meetings like this weren't uncommon, especially in their line of work.

"You know me," Ibsen said, resting his hands on the conference table. "I'm pro-press. I hired you, of all people, to head our major publicity campaigns. But look at the data," he waved his hand over the mess of papers in front of them. "This isn't one of those cases. Our first job is to keep our clients safe."

"That's what I don't get," she said. "The sample set is too small. We're only talking about a handful of people here. There's no way to know if we're getting close to a tip or not. The prudent option is to beat the *Post* to the punch. Even if it turns out to be nothing."

"Here are the facts," he said. "One of ITG's subsidiaries exposed some new virus—"

"Bacterium," she corrected.

"Bacterium," he said. "It killed a few people — sad — but our teams on the ground have no reason to believe it will go any further than it has. Next," he held up his thumb and index finger, "ITG's board is coming in and wants to be briefed on the implications. As there *are* no implications, we will tell them exactly *that*. It's an isolated case. And then, of course, we are watching it, blah, blah, and will keep them apprised of any developments."

Erin considered this. Specifically, she thought about what he wasn't telling her.

To his credit, Carl Ibsen's skills lay in curation. In 2005, Ibsen tapped his personal network and started R4 Worldwide, this PR firm. In the early days, they were just another struggling company doing public relations. But Ibsen was different. He was a visionary. He saw the world was shifting, and so he soon fired all of his smaller clients and decided to double-down on only the largest ones, becoming a boutique agency.

But, then, the financial crisis happened. And like many smaller businesses, R4, mortgaged to the hilt, was getting ready to file bankruptcy. No amount of charisma was going to change that. Except, it didn't happen like that. An obscure shipping mogul, Eli Bren, who Ibsen had done minor jobs for in the past, bought a controlling interest in R4. Bren, of course, got a good price on the deal. But then again, Ibsen didn't have much of a choice. He'd be relinquishing the reigns one way or another, to an investor like Bren, or to the bankruptcy courts. This way, at least, allowed R4 to stay alive.

At first, most things stayed the same. R4 was still a specialized PR firm. But soon they began handling a lot more work for InTrans Global — ITG, one of Bren's companies.

Bren had amassed a fair amount of capital over the years, and he was in the practice of buying smaller humanitarian aid organizations. It was actually Carl Ibsen's idea to use them for publicity for Bren's other, larger companies. It really came down to a matter of channeling the flow of information. Ibsen's PR brainchild was to use ITG's capital to support Bren's various charities, or NGOs. That way, when ITG showed up in the news, it was in relation to humanitarian work and not the typical selfish press releases their competitors were putting out.

"The ITG board is convening in…," Ibsen looked up at the clock on the wall, "twenty-eight minutes. Let's pull together what we have and not complicate it."

The conference room door opened behind them and Julia, Ibsen's executive assistant, walked in. She was a stereotype from top to bottom. But, to her credit, she was good at what she did. And she knew it, too.

"The final list for who'll be at the meeting," she said, handing Ibsen a piece of paper.

He took the paper without looking at her. "Thanks," he said.

"Most will be arriving here shortly," she told him.

He didn't respond as he was looking down the list in his hand.

She turned to leave.

"Oh," she said, turning back to him again, "and Paul Dannon's flight was delayed, so he'll be here, but cutting it close."

Erin looked at Ibsen. "You didn't tell me Paul is going to be here," she said.

"Uh huh," he said, not looking up at her. "Yeah, I guess ITG wants someone from SERA to weigh in. Just leave a few minutes at the end of your presentation for him to say something to the board."

"What's his opinion on all of this?" Erin asked.

"Honestly, Erin," he looked at her, "you know where I am on this. I try to talk to Dannon as little as possible."

4

PAUL

PAUL DANNON SLIPPED INTO THE BACK OF THE R4'S conference room. Erin was standing at the front, already presenting to the board. He found a seat in the back. He caught Erin's eye — which wasn't hard, as he was the only one not clad in navy or gray worsted wool.

He raised his hand slightly, giving her a little wave. *How long had it been?* he wondered. Seeing her there, grown now, brought back so many memories. Mostly memories of Gillian. He couldn't help seeing Gillian's brown hair and strong green eyes when he looked at her daughter.

Paul was never particularly close to Gillian, at least not after their childhood. But they both shared a certain love of the wild, the unknown. They were the kind of people who often didn't make good families. And the day Gillian died, seeing little Erin, so tough and so sad, even a quarter of a century later, it was still hard to think about.

But Erin's aunt, Olivia, had taken care of her. Olivia had taken care of them all. Even before Gillian died, when she'd work long assignments away from home, Olivia would keep Erin. Sometimes Paul wondered what it would have been like if he'd settled down and started a family of his own. Probably not too different from Gillian. Erin grew up strong. But no one should have to go through that.

Paul looked around the room, going through his outline as he did, getting his thoughts in order before he presented in a few minutes. He'd given hundreds of these talks. After he left the service, he'd started a medical procurement business. It was mostly networking and sales. Lots of boardrooms. Paul shifted in his chair. He thought after so many years he'd be used to these stuffy environments by now. The plush leather chairs and sea of dark suits. But he wasn't. Paul was made for the outdoors. It was as simple as that.

As Erin finished, Carl Ibsen stood to address the room.

"Paul Dannon," he introduced, holding an outstretched hand, palm up, in his direction. "Field director for Sustainable Environmental Resources for Africa, which many of you know as SERA. Paul's here to give us his perspective from the ground."

Paul walked to the front. He stood in front of a projector screen, for which he had no PowerPoint, and looked out into the small dark room.

"Ladies, gentlemen," he started, "it's always a pleasure to be here with you. As you're aware, for the last week, we've been closely monitoring the situation."

Unlike most charities, SERA was an NGO whose primary job was data — collect, analyze, and make projections to help local governments stay ahead of outbreaks, as well as to be a feeder to larger groups like the Center for Disease Control and Prevention (CDC) in the United States and the World Health Organization (WHO) worldwide.

Yes…Paul *was* well acquainted with the data, which is why most of what he reported tonight was a lie.

A few days ago, Paul began noticing discrepancies. Not the kind that flag reports. But the kind that only analysts with a pay grade too low to say anything will spot. For most of his professional life, he'd worked with humanitarian aid organizations in some form or another. What most people didn't realize is that NGOs are often fronts for corruption. There are, for sure, many good ones. But NGOs, by the nature of their work, deal with the unregulated, the donated. And it's often done in moments of crisis, when support is needed fast. So they become easy covers for the less-than-honorable.

Being in the special forces for nine years, followed by the competitive world of procurement, Paul had developed a sense for when someone was bluffing him. It's for this reason he's always built his teams around people who have direct access to the information. But Paul learned another lesson early on: don't play your hand until you're sure it's strong enough to win. Panama '89 taught him that. That was a hard lesson. One he still limps from.

The people he now stood in front of had each, in their own way, developed a sense of survival. Most of them becoming sharks in their own right. And despite their differences in approach, it was a world he understood well.

"So," Paul concluded to the board, "while we understand the concern for an outbreak, we do not expect it will be hard to contain."

Paul thanked them and walked back to his seat.

Ibsen stood and addressed the group. "Team, you'll have digital packets in your inbox by morning. Please review these, and, as more intel comes out, we'll keep you posted on it, as well as with any changes that affect our publicity plan." He pushed a button on a tiny remote and the lights came back on.

Erin picked up a small stack of manilla folders she'd brought with her and waited to shake the hands of several board members as they left the room.

Paul waited for them to file out and walked up to her.

"Paul," she hugged him. "It's good to see you. You haven't changed."

A little grayer, he thought, but he just smiled. "It's good to see you, too. How's your aunt?"

"Oh, you know her," she said. "Still…the same. Still safe. Still calls me each week to make sure I'm, I dunno…," she waved her hand dismissively, "still alive, I guess."

"Go easy on her. She means well."

"I know. Hey…" she said, brightening, "how long are you going to be in town?"

"Just the night. Back to Ghana in the morning. I left those kids unattended."

Jokes aside, 'those kids' actually *were* a concern sometimes. He trusted each of them. And they were competent in their work. Steller, actually. It wasn't that.

It was more the kind of people Paul naturally attracted. They were, in other words, people like him. People who didn't always bide the official rules as closely as each and every official would have them. And as a result, they sometimes got themselves into…situations.

"Well, that's what happens when you hire adrenaline junkies and Peace Corps dropouts," she said, smiling.

"Don't make fun of my dropouts," he said, pretending to be serious.

"Listen," she said, changing the subject, "I need to debrief with Carl, and we need to finish up a few things." She shifted her folders and looked down at her watch. "Do you have time to grab a drink in a few hours?"

"I'd love to," he said.

But in truth, this was another lie. It was becoming a theme for the night, he thought.

And…it was part of the reason they hadn't seen each other in so long. He couldn't help it. When he saw her, all the memories came with her. It's just easier to leave some things in the past.

Plus, more practically, he didn't know how far this thing went. The outbreak, if that's what it was. It was off. He was still investigating the specifics. So it was too early to know anything for sure. But if it was something, the last thing he wanted was her to get wrapped up in that. Again.

"Where are you staying?" she asked him.

"Oh…uh," he took a moment, trying to remember. "The Mayflower," he said. "Over on Connecticut."

"The Mayflower?" she gave him a raised eyebrow. "That's kind of swanky." She smiled. "I always pegged you as the tent type."

He let out a sincere laugh this time. The first since he'd landed back on U.S. soil. "You'd be surprised to learn how hard it is to find good camping grounds in downtown D.C. Besides," he said, jabbing a thumb over his shoulder, "I didn't book it."

"Okay, the Mayflower…," she said, looking up at the ceiling. "Oh, there's a little place not far from there. It's a dive called the Green Gail. And," she paused for effect, "I think you'll like it. It has a lot of…what's the word. Patina," she finished with a smile.

"Sounds like me," he said.

"I'll text you when I'm on my way." She turned to leave. Putting her hand on the door, she turned back to him. "Paul, it really is good to see you."

"You too, kid."

And, in a way, that was the truth.

5

IBSEN

Erin walked past a different dark, unused conference room and headed to Ibsen's office. R4 was a sparse combination of modern design and Silicon-Valley startup. It took up all of the second and third stories of their building. The downstairs was mostly open space. They had an in-house barista, Marc. Even though their building had a coffee shop on the first floor, open to the public, it was more for effect. Upstairs were offices and a few conference rooms, spread around a large atrium-style opening that looked out over the downstairs.

Erin turned the corner, passing her own office, going straight to Ibsen's. He wasn't back yet, so she sat at his small round table next to the window overlooking K Street. The little park across the street, usually a green spot, was mostly brown now, matching the season. And the sun, upon getting lower, had turned the little brown park bronze. Evening traffic was already beginning to build.

Ibsen walked in and without saying anything, walked past her. This was part of the routine. Moments earlier, Erin had been working with Performance-Carl. That was the energetic, charismatic visionary. But now, he was gone and Business-Carl had come. Business-Carl was contemplative, calculating, and, depending on which side of the deal you were on, cruel.

He looked out of the window, watching the cars.

"Carl," she started.

He didn't turn.

"I was thinking," she said, standing. "Let's play this up. Earlier today, I was reviewing the InTrans Global account. And most of ITG's publicity has been boring stuff, like new-vessel launches. Just industry news. But a newly uncovered dormant bacteria is discovered and a dozen people turn up dead in a short span of time — the media is going to jump all over that. There are already rumors of it becoming an outbreak. And because it's already so closely tied to ITG and the work they're doing in Ghana…," she trailed off, hoping he'd chime in.

He didn't.

"There's only upside for us," she pointed to the charts and reports she still had with her. "All of our sources are saying if there is an outbreak, it will be an easy one to contain. That puts ITG at the forefront of the solution. Easy win."

He turned, without looking at her, and began to move around the room, looking down as he paced.

"No…," he said slowly, finally. He looked up at her, more resolute now, "No. I want to bury this."

"Bury it?" Erin looked at him. "Why?"

"I talked with Jonah Lennox earlier today. He feels the—"

"You did?" she interrupted.

"It was…different issue," he waved dismissively. "He feels the political climate on the ground would not be helpful. Ghana's always been a stable part of West Africa. Controversy wouldn't be good for us right now."

Erin wondered for a moment if he'd heard anything she said. Or if he'd completely lost his mind. *'Controversy wouldn't be good for us'*... In the world of media, controversy was *always* good.

"This will get out, Carl. It's just a matter of who breaks it first. We have a chance to control it."

Ibsen walked back to the window again. He took a long moment before responding and then looked at her. "That's the way we'll play it for now. We'll monitor, but we won't build this up."

And, as if the two-way part of their conversation was over, he said, "Get a summary of our position down, and send it over to Julia. She'll handle the rest and get it out to the board."

He turned to look back out the window.

Erin picked up her collection of manilla envelopes and walked to the door.

"Erin…" Ibsen said to her, over his shoulder.

"Yes?" she said, more hopeful than she'd intended.

"Shut the door, after you."

6

THE POST

Erin exited the Orange line, walked up the stairs, and stepped out onto North Highland Street. It was a short quarter-mile walk through Arlington's office buildings and trendy lofts — a walk she made to and from work each day — that soon turned into smaller streets, lined with white-framed Victorian style houses. Each displaying its own neat lawn and Volvo.

Hers was a modest double, a two-story with no Volvo, and a lawn that was sometime-back replaced with shrubs and other low maintenance plants. She walked the cobble brick path and up the porch stairs, put her key in the lock and opened her front door.

Something about this part of the day always made her philosophical. Thinking about life. All of it. What had happened. What *will* happen. Maybe it was the solitude of the subway ride and walk that gave her mind a chance to slow down.

The almost-gone sun threw long shadows into her foyer. She flipped on the nearest light switch and made her way to the kitchen. The fridge had a few regulars. Bottled water, a cardboard holder with three long necks missing, and various store-bought microwave meals. She grabbed one of the latter and put it in the microwave.

She walked up the old wooden steps to her bedroom, took off her dark gray skirt and white blouse, tossing them away, and put on the same jeans and a new pullover. She walked back downstairs, emptied the microwave, and sat on the couch with her laptop and dinner. A nightly tradition.

Erin had reached a point in her career where she didn't always get a chance to check emails at the office. At least, not after the day got rolling. Plus, when she did, they turned in to a conversation. Checking them in the evening nipped all that nicely. And her empty house was all too happy to accommodate quiet work into the evening.

As she began to eat what was probably mashed potatoes, she looked through her email. A new message from McGillis, the editor at the *Post* who she submitted her articles to.

From: Conall McGillis <cmgillis@washingtonpost.com>
    Subject: water table pieces - tomorrow.

Finally, she thought.

Erin had spent almost two months tracking down leads and getting the right data. It started as an internal R4 project to align with one of ITG's new initiatives about building up lesser known water pollution associated with developing nations. The cash flow and jobs are welcomed, but what gets lost — or buried — in the shuffle is the collateral damage. The nearby villagers would get sick, or contract diseases, and because many of them were not in the practice of going to the hospital until it was, honestly, far too late, they'd get sick, and sometimes die. But by that time, the chain of events that caused the illness was long gone.

Ovie Thomas of the World Health Organization (WHO) had been working on this very issue for some time. "It's the socioeconomic conditions," he told her, "that play such a critical role in determining the types of contaminant that affect the groundwater." It's the groundwater, just a few feet below the surface, that taints gardens and contaminates drinking water, which then directly makes people sick.

"According to a World Bank report a few years back," he continued, "poor institutional frameworks are commonly identified with poor implementation of water policy, and the poor are almost always at greater risk from the adverse effects of poor resource management." Which is the exact situation developing nations find themselves in. They are doing the right things, putting in place the right laws and regulations, but until established, they are spread too thin to monitor, or even prosecute, the offenders.

"A practical scenario looks like this," an anonymous source told her. "Chinese companies, like Shongdang Mining, are heavily invested in Africa right now. And, to their credit, their reputation is good. They're licensed to oper-ate. But they'll set up a remote site, do their work, and move on. Because many African nations do not have long litigation histories, their regulations and permits have a lot of latitude. It's not that Shongdang is doing anything wrong, per se. It's just that there's no way to prevent the inevitable pollution from making its way to people living off the ground."

ITG—InTrans Global—had recently begun funding a clean-water NGO, and this internal report would be used mainly for shareholders. However, as is the nature with corporate culture, things change, and the project was no longer needed. By then, though, Erin had already done most of the investigating, so she shaped it up and sent it to

McGillis as an expert piece, a kind of op-ed for the industry. He'd apparently put it on the backburner.

"A lot of things go wrong in the world. Don't hear me wrong," he told her. "It's good stuff, but unless it's *new stuff* going wrong, it won't get the clicks." She knew all that.

But now he decided to run it. Must be slow in news, she thought.

She gave another glance through her inbox. Everything else could wait. She looked down at her watch and then sent Paul a text, "on my way."

She slipped on the shoes on the floor nearest her. She got up to shut the blinds at the back door, and, as she did, she thought she saw something outside move. It wasn't completely dark, with the inside light throwing shadows across her back lawn. But the glare on the window from the inside lights made it hard to see clearly. She stood still, looking for a moment. Seeing nothing, she grabbed her peacoat on the edge of the couch and left to meet Paul.

7

ACCRA, GHANA

Jonah Lennox sat at a small, round table with his back to the shore.

He watched the woman, local, hovering at the seaside cafe's bar, occasionally picking up old dishes, sometimes bringing new ones. She was half his age. Probably twenty, maybe twenty-one. And it showed. Not by her appearance, but in the way she held herself. Her mannerisms. And her slight hesitations. It was something he long ago learned to spot, just like it was something he long ago learned to shed.

Lennox turned away.

The next few days would be critical. He was here to think, and plan. He took a drink from the glass in front of him. The ice was gone. The trick, he'd learned back on his first job, was to visualize. Visualize all of the details, all of the variables. And then to play it, from start to finish, in his mind's eye. With all the variations and possibilities.

Confidence was about control.

And about ignoring distractions.

The Germans at the table next to him were drinking their beers and laughing. *Am herumscherzen.* They were loud. This is what happened to Germans when they came to a place like this. To the land where might is still right.

With his blonde, close-cropped hair and high cheek-bones, Jonah himself could be a German. And, at a time so long ago he'd almost forgotten about, he had been one.

The loud men looked at the woman, standing in the shade at the bar. "*Kellnerin*," one called to her, louder than necessary. She walked quickly to them. He spread his hands out to his friends' empty bottles, without speaking or looking at her. She began collecting their empty bottles.

"*Mehr Bier*," another said, as she was about to leave.

She hesitated for a moment, but quickly picked up the meaning.

As the girl hurried to remove the old bottles, Jonah sat with his right hand on the table, eyes trained on her, not attempting to hide his stare. As she bent over, she caught him looking at her and instinctively glanced away, before looking back. As if she were surprised by his directness.

He raised two fingers.

Hands full, she walked to his table, keeping his gaze.

"Would you…like a refill, sir?"

He looked at her for a moment, not answering. Then, his eyes dropped a foot or so. A move he also didn't try to hide.

She glanced away.

"En-yom-yam," he said slowly.

She paused and looked back at him.

"Your name tag," he said, "pinned to your blouse."

She giggled. "It's *EEN*-yomyam," she said, pronouncing it for him.

His eyes were on hers.

"It is good for me," she told him.

"I…," he leaned onto his elbows, "would hope so."

"No," she kept smiling, "it is my name. It means, 'it is good for me.'"

The loudest of the Germans at the table behind her, noticing they had no new beers, turned in his chair and took in the scene.

"*Kellnerin*," he blurted out. "*Wir haben Durst.*" Waving the back of his hand at her, he began to turn back around. She moved to leave.

"Wait," Jonah said in a low, cold voice. He was sitting back now, staring at the back of the German's head as he said it.

The German turned back around.

Jonah continued to look at him like he was an exotic pet.

"What is your…name?" Lennox said.

The German looked at him with small dark-set eyes. He brushed a hand in the air toward him and turned back around, picking up where he'd left off.

"Ludwig?" Lennox guessed.

This time Lennox first caught the gaze of a different German. A smaller man, who'd also enjoyed quite a few beers. It was a moment before the larger man realized Lennox was talking to him.

"No, wait," Lennox said, raising a lazy finger, "I've got it now. It's Richard, isn't it? You look like a Richard. Do they call you Rick? Ricky? Dick?"

The large German stood, knocking his chair over as he did. Turning to face Lennox.

The girl took a few steps back, not sure what to do next.

"Richard," said Jonah, in mock reprimand.

The man blocked out the sun as he stood over Lennox. He pulled one side of his sports coat open, showing the black metal butt of a pistol.

Jonah raised his eyebrows. "So…you fellas not here for the sights, then? Because," Jonah continued, waving his hand to nothing behind him on the beach, "you're really missing—"

The German's lips tightened. He huffed, reaching out to grab Lennox's shirt.

But in a movement that the alcohol surely wouldn't let him remember, it had all gone sideways. With more strength than his slender frame looked capable of, Lennox pulled the German's head down into the metal edge of the table. The other two Germans stood as the big one crumpled, a mess of dizziness and inebriation.

Lennox, still a hand on the big guy, looking as if he had more damage planned, paused and looked up at the other two.

They blinked, processing the scene, before holding up their hands. "*Nein…nein*," they surrendered.

Lennox released the big man, letting his head hit the bottom of the table with an audible thud. He reached down under the man's arm and grabbed the same black metal pistol, simultaneously causing the magazine to clack to the ground. In a single move, he'd separated the chamber from the body, tossing them both over the rail of the beachside cafe.

The girl, Enyomyam, still stood close by, her arms wrapped tightly around the empty bottles she was carrying. She looked to the men sitting and watching, then to the man crumpled on the ground, and then, finally, to Lennox.

Lennox sat back down, not quickly, not slowly, angling his chair now toward the beach. He took another drink from his glass. And said nothing.

The girl moved back into his field of view, taking a step closer to him. "My shift…," she said, "ends at one. Maybe… we cou—"

He held up a finger.

Her voice disappeared, as if with that small gesture he'd somehow taken it.

He continued to stare at the ocean as he took another

drink. He put down his empty glass and reached into his jacket pocket.

She waited, watching each of his moves.

He dropped a few twenty-Cedi notes on the table. And, without another word or look at any of them, stood up and left.

8

THE GREEN GAIL

Erin was hit by a wash of sound as she opened the door.

The Green Gail was an Irish bar. The inside was long with a bar along the left and round tables scattered throughout. The band was on a stage in the back, surrounded by large black speakers. The decor was mostly dark-stain from years of use, with occasional bright green accents.

Paul was sitting at the bar, his weight on his arms, an amber glass in front of him. Across from him, the bartender leaned on the counter, wearing a low-cut shirt, talking to him. Laughing. Flirting? It was strange to see Paul like that. Paul, her *uncle*. Well…not technically her uncle. But that was close enough. She wondered what he looked like when he was younger. She remembered seeing pictures of him when he was in the service. In that picture, standing sharp in uniform, like he could pick up three men. A long time ago now.

Erin walked up to the stool next to Paul. By now, the woman was at the other end, wiping down the counter. Paul hadn't looked her way yet.

"She's cute," Erin said, as she slipped onto the stool next to his.

Paul laughed a real laugh. He turned to face her.

"Yeah, she's cute," he said. Then holding up a hand and counting off his finger, "And I suppose if I had a daughter, she'd be…" he trailed off, thinking.

"…Just about that age?" Erin finished.

"Yeah," he smiled, "probably wouldn't work out." He picked up the glass in front of him taking a drink.

"About that," she said, "someone told me you were here, in D.C., this past March."

"I was…" he said before trailing off, as if he was considering how much to say.

Erin was about to press when the bartender came back.

"Anything for you, hun?"

Hun?

Automatic thought.

"Just, er…" she said looking over head at the forty different options.

How old is she anyway? Twenty-two, -three?

Erin gave another effort at scanning the list.

I probably have ten years on — Nope. She stopped the thought.

"I'll just…," she said, "give me what he's having."

"Comin' up, love," she said, shoving a glass under the tap and slipping it in front of Erin.

"Thanks," Erin said

The woman winked at her and walked away.

Erin sat, processing that when Paul started talking again.

"It was a short trip," he said.

"Trip?" she said, looking at him.

"Last March."

"Oh, right."

He took another drink.

She sipped her own.

"I understand, you know," Erin said.

"What's that?" Paul said.

"Time," she took another sip. "It doesn't really fix anything."

He was quiet for a moment.

"No… it doesn't," he said.

They both sat, not looking at each other.

"It was never you, you know," Paul said. "You were always a bright spot. After your mother died, it was…" he trailed off again. "What I mean is, I wanted to be there. I should have been there. Even before, when it was just you and her."

Erin never knew her dad.

To a lot of people, that was sad. But to Erin, it was just part of growing up. He was never around. She'd never even seen a picture of him. The one time she'd asked her mother about him, when she was in third grade, she'd told her she didn't know who he was. But even at eight, Erin was old enough to know that wasn't true. Gillian always had a way of being honest with Erin. Even if that meant not telling her the truth. Something even in her eight-year-old mind could sense it was for a good reason. And maybe that was it. Maybe that's what growing up without a dad, and then, suddenly, without a mom, meant. Maybe it meant you learned to see inside people quicker. Maybe, experiencing loss gave you a better sense of reality or something. Or maybe that's just what little kids who lose their parents tell themselves, a kind of self-soothing. To compensate for getting all that pain.

Erin pushed the thoughts out of her mind.

"Paul," she asked tentatively. "How close are you working with Jonah Lennox?"

Paul turned as he looked at her this time.

"Why?" he said.

"Well…maybe it's nothing, but…"

"What?"

"The data we've been getting has all been coming directly from his lab. Which, in one way, is not unusual. I mean, over the last six months, since we've been active in Ghana, the reports have always included data from his group. But I was reviewing the latest reports, and it doesn't add up. Specifically," she continued, "the data has all the warning signs of an outbreak. Yet, the reports we're getting from Lennox are saying 'nothing to worry about' — which is the same thing you said this afternoon to the board."

"Uh-huh," he said, facing the bar again, taking another drink.

"And then this afternoon, Carl told me he'd talked to Lennox," she said. "Today," she added for emphasis.

Paul looked at her again. His face was serious.

"He never gets involved in these things," she said. "You know Carl, he's all high-level."

Paul nodded slowly, sitting still watching Erin talk, waiting.

"But the real strange part was, when I suggested we get ahead of this — even if it turns out to be nothing — and work up a story on it…Carl had no interest. But," she said, "it was more than that. He actually *didn't* want me to do it."

"When did he tell you that?" Paul asked.

"Just after you and I talked, earlier today."

Paul sat back on his stool and looked up to a spot on the board with all the beers. He sat like that for a long moment before turning back to Erin. When he did, his words were deliberate. He looked around before speaking.

"Erin," he said. "Listen to me on this one. I don't have any right to tell you what to do. I never did. But," he paused, "keep a healthy distance on this one. There's a line on these things. And sometimes it's hard to see it. It's what...," he trailed off, his eyes darting to hers and then away again. "It's how it happened with Gillian."

Erin's thoughts were beginning to move faster now. *Was Paul worried?* Regardless of whether someone was a fan of Paul or not, 'worried' was not how they described him. Her head began to swim. *And mom? What did that mean?* She looked down at her mostly full drink. She'd hardly touched it. She looked back at him.

"Paul."

He didn't look at her.

"What are you not telling me here? What's going on?"

He turned to her and, barely above a whisper, looked her directly in the eyes. "SERA has been analyzing the data. But a week or so ago, we began to notice something...something not quite right."

Erin could hardly hear him over the band and bar-chatter. But she listened, focusing on every word.

"The bacterium, under the right circumstances, *could* be killing people like the report said. Except," he said, "it's not. The bacterium was an 'old' version Staphylococcus — what we often call 'staph infection.' In its modern form, it's still dangerous. But we have antibiotics for that. There is an advanced form, MRSA, which is antibiotic resistant, but the data — even what we're getting from Lennox — isn't that. However, putting all of that aside, staph takes more than 24 hours to kill you. A lot more. Depending on your immune system, the soonest would be a few weeks."

"I don't have enough on this yet, but..." he hesitated. "It doesn't take a very deep look to see that there's something else going on here."

"You mean something else killed those workers?" she said.

His eyes darted down and then back at hers. "I'm almost sure of that."

"What was it?"

"At this point, I really have no idea."

"Is it a 'who'?" she asked.

He didn't answer that question.

"But what I do know," Paul said, "is that, at least a few people in that conference room today, and maybe Ibsen, know more than they're letting on about this."

"Paul," Erin began, leaning back. "I know you and Carl don't see eye to eye on, well…anything, but—"

"Erin," he said.

"Look, Carl's an opportunist, yes. And if you cross him," she gestured with her hands, "he can be a bit vindictive. But *this*, what you're talking about, this is something else entirely."

Paul watched her.

"No," she said, "I know him. He wouldn't be involved in something like this."

"How sure are you about that?" he said, letting the words hang in the air.

She looked at him but didn't respond.

"I hope I'm wrong," Paul said.

As he said it, she noticed how tired he looked.

"I hope I'm wrong about it all," he said. "But, if I'm not, then the more you look into this, the more you push it and don't drop it, then the closer you are to getting into someone's crosshairs."

She turned away. Thinking. Remembering. A decade ago, when she'd gone to Trinidad to track down a missing source. The whistleblower. She was almost killed for finally doing the right thing. Almost killed to keep secrets secret. And in her dreams, Erin still remembered those six days when she thought the whole world had lost her.

Paul looked down at his watch and let out a deep breath.

"It's getting late," he said, "let's get out of here."

"Okay," she said, not really listening. Still processing.

"I've gotta go to the little boys room first."

Her eyes went up to his again, "okay," she said, "I'll meet you outside."

9

CONALL MCGILLIS

CONALL MCGILLIS SAT AT A MID-CENTURY METAL DESK. It had paper and folders stacked on it and on the floor around him, too.

What they never tell you is that 'senior editor' really means chief paper-shuffler. He did like his job. And in this environment, when people were going to Facebook and bloggers for their 'news,' and newsrooms were doing their best to keep any reporters on staff, he was thankful. But he missed the days of hunting stories.

He started working at the *Washington Post*, basically, as an errand boy, just four years after Woodward and Bernstein became newspaper legends for blowing the whistle on Nixon and the Watergate scandal. At that time, the paper, while growing rapidly, was still not the *New York Times*. A kid like him could get in without too much experience. In those days, it was all about endurance and perseverance…and grit.

What that meant for him, today, wasn't too much. Times had changed. And then they'd changed all over again. Today — tonight, to be more precise — he was working alone, as was often the case. It wasn't his workload making him do it.

McGillis was a born night owl. He just produced better when it was dark. As long as he made it back for the 10:00 a.m. A1 meeting in the morning, his boss (and her boss) didn't care about the hours he kept.

This is where McGillis was when Erin called. It buzzed from under the Wexford story's stack. He fished it out, and, without looking at it, answered, "Huh."

"Conall, it's Erin."

"Erin, article's already locked. You know. It's already scheduled to be in print tomorrow."

"Yeah, no — it's not that."

"You got something new?"

"Maybe… I don't know yet. Have you ever heard of a Jonah Lennox? East Africa."

"Jonah…Lennox…" McGillis put down the paper he'd been working on and rubbed his forehead. "Nothing right away. What's the connection?"

"He runs a research facility in Ghana."

As she was talking, he put the phone between his shoulder and cheek and started typing, looking him up online.

"They do a lot with humanitarian aid and health data," she said. "They haven't been in West Africa too long, though."

"I don't see anything online. No 'Jonah Lennox's' that matches that description."

"Conall, I was talking with Paul Dannon — you know Paul?"

"Paul… oh yes, your Paul. Right."

"Right, he's been in Ghana recently. And," she said, "this is strictly off the record at this point—"

"What is it?" he said.

"Well, there's a potential outbreak. A newly uncovered bacterium. It's killed a few people. And you know how R4 is.

That's the exact stuff we're looking for. But Carl is trying to bury it.

"Bury it?"

"It's not just that, the data I'm getting from Lennox's lab in Ghana is inconsistent."

"And so…"

"And so when I asked Paul about it, he got all serious and told me to keep my distance."

"Did he actually give you anything other than that?"

"Well, no. But I think there's something going on here.

"Erin."

"No, hear me out. Things weren't adding up today when I talked to Carl about it. But when I mentioned it to Paul, he got weird about it and told me he didn't want me to end up like Gillian."

McGillis stopped. That was it. This was why she was calling.

"How many times…," he started.

"It's not that," she said.

"Erin," he cut her off again. "You're a good reporter." And he meant it. Erin Reed *was* a good reporter. Some people just had it in them. Gillian did. And Erin did, too. Except for this. She was stuck on the conspiracy. "You're looking for something that's not here."

"Conall, you're the only one who has a bigger file than I do on Somalia '93."

"And that's what I'm telling you," he said.

"It fits," she said. "Mom was looking into NGOs being used as fronts for corruption, right?" He could almost see her holding up fingers to count off her points as she made her case. "The pattern in each of the cases was controlling some *outbreak*."

"That was over 25 years ago."

Clearly not listening, she barreled forward. "She was

briefing you daily from Mogadishu. If we go back through those dailies, I'm sure we'll…"

The dailies… he thought. No. He'd been through those files too many times. Whatever happened to Gillian, it wasn't in that file. But it wasn't just Erin. Gillian was his friend, too. And what happened over there, how she died, and how quickly everyone seemed to forget — which was understandable, as the entire Somali infrastructure was crashing down in 1993. But something was… No. It was over, there's nothing else there.

"No," he said. "The answer's no. You know I cared about your mother. I worked with her for almost twelve years. If you've got a new story, let me know. But don't make it personal, okay. Erin?"

"Yeah."

"Don't make it personal," he repeated.

"I'll keep you posted," she said, "Gotta go now."

She ended the call.

McGillis put the phone down. He propped his elbows on his desk and started chewing on one of his fingernails. A habit he only did when he was thinking about something he didn't want to. Despite himself, he was thinking about what Erin had said. There are a lot of theories in the world. But *journalists* deal in facts. It was a speech he'd given her before. And now, in his head, he was now giving it to himself.

He looked down at his watch. Just after ten. It was going to be a long night. He could feel it.

10

ASSOCIATED PRESS

ACCRA, GHANA (AP) — TWELVE MEN ARE DEAD AT Lake Volta at an underwater logging company.

A new strand of Staphylococcus (a bacterium commonly called Staph infection) was uncovered in the Lake Volta region of Ghana last week.

Some local health professionals are now concerned that many in the region who do not have access to antibiotics may be at risk.

Jonah Lennox, director of a research center in Ghana studying the new strand, believes there to be no cause for alarm.

"There is absolutely no chance," said Lennox, "that this is anything other than an isolated case."

Lake Volta is the home to the thousands of underwater trees, preserved since the Akosombo dam was built in 1965, which flooded the entire region and created the largest, by surface area, manmade lake in the world.

The new strand of bacteria was recently uncovered by Discovery Logging Ltd, an underwater logging company harvesting the fifty-year-old trees. The hardwood is still in good condition and highly sought in furniture manufacturing. The Ghanaian government takes a 20% cut of all trees harvested prior to exporting.

The Lake Volta region, in the south of Ghana, is largely a rural area, surrounded by farms and small village-cities.

The Ghanaian Ministry of Health was unavailable for comment.

THE VAN

PAUL LEFT THE RESTROOM AND MADE HIS WAY BACK through the bar, putting on his jacket as he walked.

He opened the door, feeling the bar-room stuffiness give way to the cold night air. He saw Erin, standing against a light post, facing away from him as she finished a call.

As he walked up to her, she turned to him, putting both hands in her jacket and shuttering as a whip of wind passed through them.

"I'm this way," she said, pointing with her elbow.

"I'll walk with you," he said.

The two of them walked in silence. There was a myriad of thoughts in Paul's mind as they walked. One of them was his gauge of the board. He was pretty sure none of them were in on what was about to happen. What *was* about to happen… He turned those words over in his head. Paul had been around long enough to recognize the scent of when something wasn't right. And he smelled it now. But it was still too early to know anything.

Officially, the ITG board had asked him to come, paying for his trip. But unofficially, his own assignment as it were, was to get ahead of whatever was going on. Paul was leaving in the morning, and he wasn't any closer to figuring out what Lennox was doing.

Lennox..., he thought.

And Ibsen... Why was Ibsen talking to Lennox, he wondered. Paul and Ibsen had their own rough history. And perhaps that's to be expected. They were cut from the same cloth. And, in a weird way, they both do the same kind of work — only from drastically different angles. Ibsen has always lived deep in the pockets of the well-connected, the well-*funded*. While Paul, he preferred the—

A big light jerked in front of him, ripping him out of his thoughts. His own shadow, and Erin's too, flashed onto the building next to them.

In the same moment, he heard the uneven whirling sound of an engine whose car has just taken a heavy bump. Like when a vehicle mounts a curb at speed.

He turned, over his shoulder the wild flash of two, square halogen headlines, rocked up and down dangerously as the panel van mounted the curb. It sliced down a no-parking sign as it did.

The van engine pushed harder, and without fully turning around, Paul pushed Erin, bodily.

Her body flung against a parked car, and she rolled onto its hood, falling over.

Paul slammed himself flat against the wall of the building, hitting it hard. He made himself as flat as he could, not closing his eyes as he did.

The van passed inches from him, and the air around it pulled him like a suction.

As the van rushed pass, Paul turned, marking it.

White.

Chevy.

Small tail lights...late nineties.

No windows.

No license plate.

The van's red lights bounced back onto the street, tires squealing, as it clipped a parked car. The scrape of the bumper seemed to echo around them. It rounded the nearest corner. And, as quickly as it had come, it was gone.

He stood looking after it. Stuck on that last bit… *No license plate.*

He jerked his mind back to the present. *Erin.* She'd already gotten up and was standing beside him, looking too at where the red taillights disappeared a second ago.

Both of them where heaving lungfuls of cold night air.

"You okay?" he asked.

She looked at him, not speaking, and then back behind them as if expecting another. And then she blurted out, "What," she said between breaths, "was *that?*"

He looked to her and then back to the spot where the van had disappeared.

"That," he said, steadying his breath, "was a warning."

She looked again in the direction the van had gone.

"Paul—" she started.

"Erin," he said, shaking his head, "I'm serious. Keep your distance on this one."

They both stood there for a moment. She pulled her jacket closer around her. He unzipped his halfway.

"Let's go," he said.

They walked the rest of the way to the Metro in silence.

Erin swiped her card. Paul started to buy a ticket, then hesitated.

"I'm okay," she said. "I don't think they let *vans* on the Metro."

He looked at her.

"It was a joke," she said.

"Yeah," he said, "right."

She looked at him for a moment longer. There was a controlled calm about her. It was shock. People in shock were optimistic, dismissive. She was… It really was like looking at Gillian again after all these years, he thought.

"I'm, er, heading back in the morning," he said. "Sure you're going to be okay?"

"Yeah."

"Then, I'll see you in…"

"A year or two?" she offered with a little smile.

Paul smiled, too. But it wasn't a real smile.

"Yeah," he said, "a year or two."

12

BEN

Ben Okello swore.

"So…" Gavin said, letting the question linger.

Ben looked at him and then back at the aging Land Rover. It was mid-afternoon, and the Ghanaian sun was still hot. Steam hissed out from between the metal in the front grill. The Land Rover sat pressed into a mess of trees and mud.

Ben put his hand behind his pink-dyed hair, resting it against his neck, thinking.

Paul has always been a reasonable man. He understands things happen. Especially out here. Then again, 'reasonable' is a relative term. Everyone has their limits. And so far, this week is shaping up to be one that might be testing those limits. And then… there was that thing in Belize a few years back. That was unfortunate. And really, to Ben's own defense, none of those vehicles were actually Ben's fault. It was more of a wrong-place wrong-time sort of thing. Ben pushed all of that out of his mind.

"Do you know how to use a winch?" he asked Gavin.

"A winch? Is that, like, a British thing?"

Sometimes Ben couldn't tell if Gavin was making a joke or asking a real question.

"It's the silver cable on the front of the car."

"Oh, er, no."

Ben looked at him.

"I analyze data for a living," he said defensively. "And," he added, "I didn't *technically* need to be here at all."

"I know, I know," Ben said, looking around. "See the tree over there, the big one?" Ben pointed to a mango tree about twenty feet away.

"Yeah."

Ben reached down and pulled the cord out of its tight coil.

"Take this," he said, handing the hook to Gavin. "Pull the cable with you, take it over there and wrap it around that tree. When you get it around, use the hook to clip it together."

"What are you going to do?" Gavin asked.

"I'm…," he trailed off, thinking.

The truth was, Ben was just doing what he did best. *Make it up as you go along.* To some, that was irresponsible. But not to Ben. For Ben, it was a skill. A survival mechanism.

Ben grew up black in Britain. That wasn't the same as growing up black in America… but there still weren't a lot of black people in Britain. Especially not in *Wales*, which is where Ben's parents moved in his formative years. They were doctors, and they opened a practice in an underserved area.

And, the son of two doctors, Ben was on the same track. Good grades, good school, and then, getting into the right med school. And if he hadn't pushed eject, that's exactly where he'd be right now.

Instead, for the better part of the last decade, Ben made his living traveling to difficult places, taking pictures, and then selling those pictures to concerned parties, like NGOs, or the occasional corporate client. The skill here was in the timing. These kinds of pictures have a shelf life. Getting there first, making all the right local contacts, that was everything.

And that's how he met Paul.

They'd started working together on a contract basis at first. But soon Paul brought him on, full-time. And over the last few years, Ben's work with Paul had expanded to more than photography. Mostly, he took over Paul's work when Paul had to travel.

Gavin slipped as he worked his way around the tree. He said something indistinct as he struggled to get his footing again. After he'd wrapped the cord around the tree, he clipped it. "Okay," he called out to Ben, "it's clipped."

Ben gave a quick tug on it from his end, and then sat behind the wheel of the Land Rover and pushed a button on the dash.

The winch began to hum, and the cable between the truck and tree tightened. Ben watched the cable.

The truck jerked and slowly started to move, sideways at first, and then it straightened up. Steadily it moved out of the muddy-tree mess they'd landed in a few minutes ago.

Once the Land Rover was sufficiently out of the mud, Ben hit the button on the dash again, and the truck stopped moving. He leaned out of the window and yelled, "unhook it."

Gavin unhooked the cord and walked back over. They both stared at the dirty, truck, letting the next, obvious question float silently between them.

"Do you…think it still works?" Gavin said.

Ben pulled the hood release and lifted the hood. As he stood looking over the dirt-colored engine, his fingers traced down until he pulled back and looked down at the front of the truck. A small but solid branch stuck out of the grill, a green leaf still attached to it.

"Reservoir," Ben said.

"Reservoir..." Gavin repeated, standing back, and looking down into the engine.

"It's the water tank that the radiator uses," Ben said.

Ben bent down and looked at the stick and then leaned into the engine and shook the radiator.

"Everything still seems solid. Except for that," he said, pointing to the branch sticking out from the grill. Ben reached down and pulled it out.

"So that's it?" Gavin said.

"Maybe," Ben said.

"We still need to fix the reservoir. And fill it back up with water. At least until we can get back to camp and fix it properly."

Ben turned to Gavin.

"Bring the spare water around, would you."

"The spare drinking water?"

"We'll need it for this more."

Gavin walked to the back of the Land Rover and pulled off a brown rectangular tank with a large X imprinted on it. He lugged it around to the front.

Ben leaned into the cab through the open passenger side window. Reaching down, he found a roll of duct tape.

Gavin made it to the front, lugging the heavy water tank.

"Wait, you're going to tape it?"

"You have a better idea?"

"I...," he started and then stopped. "Will that really work?"

"We only need it to work for just a little bit more," he said as he ripped a piece off with his teeth.

Ben leaned in and put the tape across the cracked plastic

reservoir container. He ripped a few more pieces. By the time he was done, it looked like a duct-tape Christmas present.

"Give me the water," he said.

Gavin heaved it up to him.

Ben slowly poured it in.

"Hold this," he said, pushing the water container back to Gavin, as he dropped to the ground, looking under the engine.

"Okay," Ben said, standing back up, "I think this might work."

"Wait, *might*?"

"Definitely, it'll work."

Gavin looked like he wanted to say something else, but Ben was already behind the driver's seat starting the engine.

"Come on, you wanker," he said under his breath.

The engine revved to life.

Ben let his hand hover just over the steering wheel, watching the temperature gauge.

"All right, love," he said. "I *knew* you'd do it."

He leaned his head out his window, "drop it, we're good."

After a moment, Gavin dropped the hood and then walked around and got in the passenger side. "And just so that we're clear," Gavin said, pulling his door shut, "when Paul finds out about this," he motioned to the front, "*I wasn't here*."

"Paul?" Ben said. "Mate, Paul *trusts* us…meaning," he said, lowering his voice, "we don't have to share every little detail. Right?"

Gavin looked at him.

Ben kept his eye on the temperature gauge on the dash as he pushed down on the accelerator, causing the back tires to kick up a cloud of dust.

13

SOME CHANGES

Erin left the Metro and walked, on autopilot, while her brain was elsewhere. Processing. Replaying.

Was the van aiming for Paul?

Why was Ibsen hesitating before?

What has she missed in the reports Lennox had sent over?

She put her key in the lock, turned the knob, and pushed her front door open. She reached around the corner for the lightswitch, throwing a blanket of light behind her out into her yard.

Erin lived in a safe neighborhood. It was one of those things she was, at the same time, thankful for and annoyed by. Thankful she didn't have to worry too much about break-ins, but annoyed by the sterile nature of neighbors whose biggest concern seemed to be who cut their lawn and when.

At that moment, however, as she closed her door, she had a different feeling. She felt, distinctly, that she wasn't alone. The hair on the back of her neck stood as she felt like she was being watched. Or…maybe, she thought, that was just a bit of paranoia from before, left over from almost being run down by a stranger in a van a half-hour ago.

As she shut her door, she felt her phone buzz. She pulled it out of her jacket pocket and saw a screenful of notifications.

A text from Richard — her on-again, off-again (currently off-again) boyfriend:

"thinking about you. we should give us another go."

Get back together via text… She shook her head. "Nope…" she said under her breath as she thumbed through her other notifications.

A text from Ibsen.

A missed call from Ibsen.

A *voicemail* from Ibsen.

As she clicked through to listen, another text from Ibsen came in:

"call me."

She tapped back to the missed calls, touching his name, and put the phone to her ear.

"Hey," Ibsen answers. "Where are you?"

"I'm—"

"I was thinking," he said, not waiting, "you were right, we should do this."

"Do…what?"

"The story."

He was hyper. More than usual. It almost sounded like he was on something…

"Where are you, Carl?" she asked.

"I'm here. Office. Was thinking about what you said. You were right. *This* is the way to go," he stressed. It almost sounded like he was trying to sell her on something. Like she was one of their clients. It was a switch she'd watched for years, one she was all too familiar with.

"Carl, wait," she said. "Just a few hours ago you were strong-arming this. And you're calling me at—" she stopped to look at her watch, "—ten-forty at night. What's happened?"

"Happened? Nothing. You were right," he said, still talking in rapid bursts. "Okay, listen, gotta go. Heading out. Go do it, okay. Julia's got your tickets. Emailed them to you."

"Tickets?"

"Yeah, Ghana. Just…," he said.

She could see him in her mind's eye, waving a hand, dismissing the details.

"…shadow SERA for a few days, write it up, we'll publish it somewhere later. And ITG will appreciate it."

Erin pulled the phone from her ear and tapped the speaker button and opened her email. A new email from Julie: 'Fw: Your flight confirmation from IAD to KIA.'

Erin turned off the speaker and put the phone back to her ear.

"…is good. Good call," he was still talking.

"So…wait. Now you want me to go to Ghana? Just like that."

"That's what we're talking about. Of course. It's good. You're good. See you in a few days."

"Okay but—" she started.

He was gone.

She stood in her foyer, still holding her phone and thinking through this strange call she'd just had. Carl had always been an impulsive person. But it wasn't like him to not have a plan. To shoot from the hip. For all of the show, he really was a good strategist. She couldn't help but feel there was something else she was missing…

Her phone vibrated again. She looked down. It was Conall McGillis.

"Hey," she said, her mind still floating in and out of the last call.

She heard a heavy sigh on the other end. "You're not going to believe this. I don't even believe I'm telling you…"

"What is it?"

"Lennox," he said. "After we hung up, the name kept nagging me. Or maybe it was your constant—"

"What is it."

"I pulled out the old files," he said. "I looked back through the daily briefs Gillian was sending me. It's been a long time, ya know," he said, starting to drift into the weeds.

"Conall."

"Anyway — I didn't find anything there."

Erin put the phone on speaker and leaned against the wall, pushing off her shoes as he continued to talk. She walked into her living room.

"Then," he continued, "I happened on a note I'd written on one of my calls with Gillian. I didn't remember it until now."

Erin stopped walking.

"It was one of those off-handed things. I'd written his name down. Then I did some more digging. I went back through a different file, sideline stuff."

"And?"

"And, he was one of her sources."

Jonah Lennox was one of mom's sources…, she thought.

"What was his connection?" she said.

"I don't know. He was a nobody. It was the only time she ever referenced him."

Erin thought about this. It wasn't much.

Then she realized, for the first time today, for the first time in years, she was smiling. Not the kind of smile that shows up on your face, but the kind that buoys you from deep inside.

"Erin? You still there?"

She picked up the phone, turned off the speaker, and put it to her ear.

"Yeah," she said, "I'm here."

"Sorry, it's not much."

"It's enough," she said. "Oh," she'd almost forgotten, "Carl just called me a minute ago. This is really weird…and I'm not sure I know what to think about it. But he's sending me to Ghana."

"Ghana?"

"Yeah. The loggers who were killed by the bacterium."

"Right, but… why? AP's already picked that one up."

She considered that for a moment.

And then she thought about the van and the warning Paul gave her.

"Well," she said finally, "there might be more to it."

"Okay," he said, "keep me posted."

Erin hung up and sat back on her couch. She began to feel the wave of adrenaline wearing off. She wanted to think through this more. To at least figure out Carl's angle. She opened her email again and looked at the message from Julia. It was an early flight, tomorrow morning.

She didn't have time to buy anything new. But she'd done these last-minute trips before. That in itself didn't bother her. But it was Carl… and that van, and… before she realized it, she was falling asleep. She walked upstairs while she still could, and fell into her bed, setting the alarm on her phone as she did.

14

THE MINISTRY OF DEFENSE

Lennox held out his arms. The security guard passed the wand down one side and up the other.

"All clear," the guard told him.

"Mr. Lennox," the tan-suited man stood waiting for him. "It's good to see you again. This way, please."

The two of them walked briskly down the hall, deeper into the Ghanaian Ministry of Defense.

"The Minister has briefed me on the nature of your visit," the tan-suit man said.

"Mm-hmm" Jonah said, without looking at him.

"Yes, and we are grateful for your contributions. Normally, something like this would be handled by the Ministry of Health, but as it has a...," he hesitated, "weaponized component, we are, of course, naturally taking the lead on it."

Lennox continued to not listen as they walked.

They approached another checkpoint. Tan-suit held up his badge. The guard looked long enough to verify it was, in fact, a badge of some sort and then waved them through. They walked into a large atrium, lined with portraits of past presidents. Busy workers moved about. They approached an elevator on the far wall. Tan-suit pulled out his badge and swiped the card reader. The light turned green, and the elevator opened. They walked in, and Tan-suit pushed the button for the fourth floor. The shiny brass mirrored interior reflected them in all directions as the two of them stood in silence. The elevator beeped and jiggled as it moved up.

With a ding, the doors slid open to two armed guards, permanently stationed on the fourth-floor landing.

Jonah exited, not waiting for Tan-suit, and began walking down the hall.

The other man walked a few steps at a time, to catch up with him. They entered an octagonal wood-paneled room, a kind of foyer for several key offices. On the opposite wall was a large, heavy wooden door with a brass plaque next to it that read, 'Defense Minister: Ebo Rumfa.'

The door was open slightly, and Tan-suit knocked on the door frame.

An older, thickset man sat at the far end of the office. In front of him was a large wooden desk, and behind him, large windows overlooking trees and a street not open to the public. The walls were lined with bookshelves and awards. In the middle of the room were a pair of couches situated around a coffee table.

At the sound of the knock, the man looked up from his paperwork.

"Mr. Lennox here, sir," Tan-suit said.

The Minister motioned with his hand.

Lennox walked in, and Tan-suit followed. The man stood awkwardly, apparently not sure if he were expected to stay or go.

Lennox turned and looked at his escort for the first time.

"That will be all, Isaac," the Minister said.

"Sir," he said with a slight bow.

"And," Rumfa added, "shut the door."

"Sir," he said again and walked out.

Rumfa stood from his desk as Lennox sat on one of his leather couches. The older man walked to the cabinet to his right, opened the glass door, and pulled out a crystal bottle of brandy.

"Imported from Tbilisi," he said, with a slight smile. He held out the container to Lennox. "Drink?"

"No."

"You're missing out," he said in a sing-song voice that didn't seem to match his appearance. "This is better than your *Kentucky* bourbon."

"*My* Kentucky?" Lennox said.

"Not European accent," Rumfa said as he poured his own glass. "Where else?"

"Ebo," he said slowly, not bothering to use his title or even his last name. "I didn't come here to talk genealogy."

"See, that's the problem with Americans," he said, sitting down on the couch opposite Jonah. "It's always go, go, go. And then, before you know it," he held up his hands, theatrically, "life is over."

Lennox stared at him as he talked. Not responding. Not doing anything.

Rumfa waited for him to respond, but he didn't.

"So you're here," Rumfa said, "about our little project then."

Lennox continued to look at him.

"Do you have it?" Rumfa said. His voice no longer had the playfulness from before.

"Soon. We know where it is. And we've," he paused to find the right euphemism, "cleared the decks, to make for a quiet extraction."

Rumfa stood and began pacing, drink in hand.

"And about the different…," Rumfa said, as if he were working through a mental checklist.

"Taken care of," Lennox said.

"And," he lowered his voice, though they were the only ones there, "what about the…other thing?"

"Your money," Lennox said, not bothering to lower his voice.

Rumfa winced slightly. "Our arrangement," he said.

Lennox pulled out his phone and pushed a single button. He held it to his ear, watching Rumfa he waited for the other end to answer.

"Transfer," he said to the phone. He waited. "A wire," he spoke again, "Jonah Lennox." And he raddled off his twenty-one digit account number. "Yes," he said, still to the phone. "Hold."

He leaned forward on the couch, holding the phone out for Rumfa.

"Your turn," Lennox said.

Rumfa set the glass down and took the phone.

"Hello," he said flatly. "Yes. One moment." He walked to this desk and slid a paper aside and began reading off his own twenty-one digit Swiss bank account number.

He handed the phone back to Lenox, who, without looking at it, put it back in his pocket.

Lennox stood and turning. He began walking to the door. As he reached for the handle, he heard Rumfa behind him.

"Wait."

Lennox paused, not turning back around.

"I want to *see* it," Rumfa said. The hunger in his voice was almost palpable. Lennox had built a business over the past quarter-century around people like this. People who wanted something so badly it had controlled them.

Lennox turned to face him.

"Ebo," he said in a soft voice that was anything but kind, "you know we can't do that."

Rumfa seemed to be deciding something.

Lennox didn't wait for him to finish talking. He opened the door and left.

15

RECON

PAUL SAT WATCHING THE DARK SUV, SITTING TWO houses down from Erin's, parked with its engine running.

"Here's good," Paul told his taxi driver. It was five houses away. From here, Paul had a clear view of the SUV but was still far enough to avoid being seen. "Kill the engine and the lights," he told the driver.

Paul sat, leaning against the inside of one of the back doors, watching the SUV out of the back window. Despite its tinted windows, Paul knew the SUV's driver was still in the car. Not only was the engine running, but the driver-side window was cracked. Every few seconds, a puff of cigarette smoke wisped out.

"You some kinda cop?" the taxi driver said, moving his rearview mirror to look at what Paul was looking at.

"No," Paul said, without taking his eyes off of the black SUV.

"Guess not…they usually have their own cars."

The black SUV's driver-side door opened. Its driver tossed a cigarette butt onto the ground.

"Um," the taxi driver said, "how long are you going to be doing this?"

That was a question Paul had been thinking himself. After the van, he decided to follow Erin. Just in case. He'd kept a low profile on the train. He'd never been to her house. But he had the address. He noticed the SUV on the walk. It made two passes. In a residential neighborhood. A few blocks before Erin's street, he called a twenty-four-hour taxi service. It was one of those taxis that was also a ridesharing service, so it only took him a minute to meet up with Paul. He got in and told the driver to drive slowly.

"What's your hourly rate?" Paul said.

"Just to sit here?" he said. Then, after a slight pause, "dollar a minute."

Paul was sure this was inflated, but he didn't care. Without taking his eyes off the black SUV down the street, Paul passed a small handful of twenties up to the driver.

"We'll be here a little bit longer," Paul said.

"Hey…uh," as if a thought had just occurred to him, "this isn't anything illegal, is it?"

The driver of the SUV got out, shut the door carefully, and began walking on the sidewalk toward Erin's house. Paul opened the door, reached up to the taxi ceiling, and flipped the switch so that the cabin light wouldn't come on when he opened the door. Then, looking at the taxi driver, "no," he said, "it's not illegal. And don't go anywhere. I'll be back in five minutes."

Paul shut the door quietly and crossed the street. He was following the man from the sidewalk. The man was dressed in dark pants and a dark long-sleeve fitted shirt. Best Paul could tell, he didn't have a gun. But that was only from catching glimpses of his figure in the streetlight. For tonight, he was operating as if he did.

The man walked past Erin's house, but he didn't look at it

as he passed it. Paul continued to follow him. Then, suddenly, the man ran across the street. In the streetlight, Paul caught a brief glance of him. Nothing to identify him by.

Now the man had doubled back and was walking back toward Erin's house, slower now.

Casing.

Paul stayed on the opposite side of the street, in the shadows, behind a large oak near the street. From this point, he could see both sides of Erin's house.

The man walked up to her house and then around the side, into the dark. For a moment Paul thought he'd lost him, as if he'd jumped the fence into the backyard or something. Then he was back again. This time he walked at a normal pace away from her house and back to his SUV. Paul stayed where he was, hidden. He had a clear view of the SUV.

The man got in the car, started the engine, and calmly drove away. Paul walked back to the taxi and climbed into the back seat. He considered following the SUV before deciding against it. He waited another twenty minutes or so, to see if the SUV would double back. It didn't. The street was silent. Asleep.

"We're done here," he told the driver. "Let's go to the airport."

The driver looked up from his phone, its blue light throwing a blue light on his face. "Reagan or Dulles?" he said.

"Dulles," said Paul.

It was late. The airport was deserted.

Without a bag, Paul walked through security effortlessly. He walked past vendors with their metal gates closed. He found a set of large pane windows, laid down facing them, and with his hand behind his head, went to sleep.

He awoke as the sun was just peaking over the horizon. A few yards on the other side of the floor-to-ceiling window was a parked plane being preparing for the day's flights. And one or two shops behind him were beginning to open. There were a few people in the terminal, but it was mostly still empty. He walked to the nearest vendor. The woman was counting the cash in the register. He ordered a large black coffee, paid in cash, and sat at a table. As he did, he pulled out his phone to check his email.

From Erin. *'Fw: Fw: Your flight confirmation from IAD to KIA'*

Paul took a sip, burning his mouth, swearing — he reflexively jerked, which sloshed a small black tidal wave onto his hand.

More swearing.

Dripping with coffee, he reached for a napkin. No napkins. He flung his hand down next to him, wiping the rest on his pants. With his dry hand, he tapped the email from Erin.

In it was a single line:

"Looks like Carl changed his mind. See you in Accra."

He put his phone away and rubbed his eyes.

This would complicate things, he thought.

He picked up his coffee, his hand still tingling from where he'd spilled it a minute before, and walked to his terminal to wait for his flight. There wasn't much he could do at this point. At the moment, he was glad he was about to get onto ten-or-so hour flight. It would give him time to think. And right now, that's what he needed most.

16

GHANA

Erin walked down the steps of the 737, feeling the Ghanaian heat hit her like a blanket. She stepped down onto the tarmac. The pilot said the temperature was 84. It must be at least in the mid-nineties, she thought. The sun was everywhere. As the people flooded out of the plane, a baggage handler piled luggage onto an airport cart.

She walked with the rest of the passengers to the nearby building, walking through an unlabeled open door. Down the hall, they reached a room that opened up into a large space with a line of different people and a large vinyl sign hanging from the ceiling: 'Entry Customs.' She stood in line, waiting. The line moved fast.

"Next," a man behind a window called.

Erin looked to see an empty spot at the far end. She walked, backpack on and passport in hand, to the far counter. The man sat behind heavy glass, talking through a small semicircle cut-out. Without taking his eyes off of his computer screen, he held out his hand. "Passport," he said.

She slid her passport with its folded yellow card through the semicircle in the glass. The man opened the passport, flipped through it, turned it sideways, and looked at it, then looked up at her.

"What is your business?" he asked in a bored, mechanical voice.

"I'm…," She said, then stopped.

In all of the rush to get here, she hadn't actually considered an answer to this question. Officially, she was doing public relations for her international client. In her experience, 'public relations' tends to raise more questions than it answers. The other answer — the unofficial one: she was here tracking down a lead that may tell her who killed her mother twenty-six years ago.

The man behind the counter stopped typing and looked at her. "Your business here in Ghana," he said.

"Journalist," she said, "I'm a journalist."

"Jour-na-list," he said, typing it into his computer.

Then, without any indication the transaction had ended, he called out, "next," as he slid her stamped passport back through the glass.

Erin grabbed her passport and walked to the exit. The next person was already at the counter waiting for her to move.

She walked down a curvy hall, seeing large cultural artwork screen prints on the walls, along with the floor to ceiling stenciled letters that said, 'Welcome to Ghana.' A mixture of modern and ancient. As she looked at the walls, she saw brief descriptions and timelines of Ghana's history, noting empires like the Ashanti, Akwamu, and Mankessim. A vintage-looking map showed a good portion of West Africa, segmented off as 'Ghana,' during one of the long-ago empires.

As she walked, a new thought occurred to her. She hadn't planned on how she'd contact Paul once she'd got here. She brought a sat phone with her, but she didn't have his number.

She'd only barely told him she was coming. Her face flushed slightly at the stupid mistake. She kept walking. She thought about finding wifi and sending him a message. Maybe she'd—

"Hey," a voice called to her as she walked by.

She glanced over her shoulder, and then she stopped. The tension she was holding in her shoulders faded.

"Paul."

He was standing against the wall, arms folded.

"I realized I hadn't—" she started.

"Come on," he smiled. "Any checked bags?"

"No, just this," she said.

"Good girl," he said. "My car's this way."

They walked through the airport. There were people shuffling everywhere. They passed a small window in a wall with a line of people at it. Above it, an electronic ticker showing currency prices. Cedi to USD, Cedi to EUR, Cedi to GPB. It looked like a pawn shop with its locked-down window. They kept walking. They approached two lines near a glass door that led outside. It was a second Customs inspection, for luggage.

"Don't make eye contact," Paul told her. "Just put your bag down, let them look at it, and pick it up. Don't hesitate, and don't talk."

The lines were flanked by men wearing camo gear, cradling black automatic weapons. Erin put her backpack down and waited in line. When it was her turn, the man in a tan airport uniform took it. He looked at it, then set it down. She glanced at Paul standing past the line with his arms folded, watching. Without making eye contact, she picked up her bag again and walked toward Paul. Her heart thumped as she walked past the soldiers. And it was all she could do to not look at them as she passed. Paul kept eye contact with her, motioning her to him with a nod of his head. As she caught up, they both walked through the double glass doors out into the sun.

The crowd outside was worse than inside. There was no order to any of it. Paul stood in the middle of the people. She was about to ask Paul what they were waiting for, when a black Land Rover pulled up, driving into the crowd.

For a moment, Erin thought the vehicle had lost control and was going to plow into the crowd in front of them.

But the people made room, and the Land Rover stopped just in front of Erin and Paul. It was dirty, Erin noticed. The door opened, and a black man in a bright shirt stepped out, leaving the driver door open as he did. Paul walked up to him and handed him a palm-full of paper money.

"All okay, Jacob?" Paul asked him.

"All good, my brother. Even washed it for you," he said, laughing, as he handed Paul the keys.

Paul looked at Erin, "This is us."

They got in, and Paul drove them out of the airport and into the heavy mid-day traffic. Motorcycles moved in between cars, and the taxis, marked with their yellow quarter-panels, filled the roads all on a crash course for one another. Accra, Ghana's capital city, was a busy place.

Paul exited the main road, leaving the congestion behind. "Taking a short cut," he said.

They followed the port, the road snaking as it followed the shoreline. Over the wall, Erin could see permanently mounted cranes used for lifting shipping containers off of vessels. The port wall went on for several miles.

Once out of the city, the road turned into a two-lane rural highway. The driving here was faster. And it was mostly paved, with trees on either side. The red dirt, Erin thought, looked almost at odds with the green bushes and trees growing out of it. The repetitious scenery, the hot afternoon sun, and the jet lag were a combination that Erin had a hard time fighting. She lay there, wedged between her seat and the door, drifting in and out of consciousness. A few times, she jerked awake as the Land Rover slowed for a small village, while the people and animals crossed the road. For almost three hours, they continued this way.

"This is us," Paul said, turning off the road onto an unmarked dirt road. "We're about a mile away. Our camp is a little bit outside of Bergora. That was the town we just passed."

"Our camp is small," Paul said. "It's a mobile unit, designed to go wherever we need it to. And there's only a few of us. So it works. Oh, and…uh," he hesitated, "just to warn you, comfort is relative out here. But if you think about tent-living, it's a few steps up from that."

Erin was tired, and she didn't have the energy to give that much thought. The Land Rover bounced under trees, following slightly worn track marks.

"Something else," Paul said as they pulled into a clearing. Up ahead, Erin could see a few heavy-duty trailers and an old yellow Land Rover and a truck. "The data we've collected," he continued, "seems to be getting out almost as fast as we can collect it. The problem is, we haven't actually been releasing it."

"I'm sorry…," she said, "it's been a long day."

He pulled into the camp and parked the Land Rover near one of the trailers, resting his arms on the steering wheel. He looked over at her. "I don't know anything for sure yet — it's all speculation. Just…keep an eye out for anything that doesn't look right."

She registered the change in his tone but hadn't yet put together what he was talking about. "What do you—"

"I think," he said, looking tired, "we might have a leak in our camp."

Erin looked out her window. A couple of men stood

waving at them. One was black and tall, with pink hair. And the other was a white guy who looked sorely out of place. Both of them had stupid grins on their faces.

She turned back to Paul, to ask him more about what he'd told her.

But he had already opened his door and was getting out. He ducked his head back into the truck before shutting his door. "Welcome to SERA," he said.

17

SERA BASECAMP

"Just smile," Ben told Gavin not looking at him.

"This *is* my smile."

Ben looked at Gavin as a cloud of dust entered the camp.

"And whatever you do, don't look at the Land Rover."

As he said this, out of the corner of his eye, he saw Gavin glancing at the truck.

"I said *don't* look at it."

"I…," Gavin started. "What if Paul—"

"He won't," Ben said.

"How do you know?" Gavin hissed back at him.

"It's taken care of," Ben said.

Paul parked his own, newer, Land Rover under a tree at the edge of camp.

"How did you get a replacement tank way out here, anyway?" Gavin asked.

"I've got a friend," Ben said casually. "Works with Keeler. They're funded, get whatever they want. And we…swap favors every now and then."

Gavin looked at him, but Ben's attention was on Paul's vehicle. Specifically, the passenger sitting next to him.

"Who's that?" Ben said.

"No idea," Gavin said, noticing her for the first time. "Maybe Paul found a girlfriend in D.C.?" he said with a grin.

"Yeah…that sounds like Paul. Ladies man."

Paul and the woman got out of the car and walked toward them.

"She's—" Gavin started.

"…pretty," Ben finished.

"I was going to say 'too young,'" Gavin said.

Jokes aside, Ben knew Paul well enough to know he wasn't the relationship-type. But as the pair walked over, he couldn't help but think — they did seem to match each other somehow. It certainly wasn't the clothing choice. Paul was in his standard ripstop-pants-and-camp-shirt uniform — the opposite of fashion by just about everyone's standard. 'Functional' was the euphemism. *She*, on the other hand, looked put together. She wore fitted khaki shorts and a plain v-neck t-shirt. Neither made her look like she belonged here. But, somehow, she was doing all right…

"Don't stare," said another voice, startling Ben.

Marisol walked up behind Ben without him noticing. She'd been with SERA for a few months, but it seemed like longer. Some days that was a good thing. Other days, it was…

"What?" Ben said. "I wa—" he caught himself, realizing how forced his surprised-voice was coming out.

"You were definitely staring," Gavin added.

Ben began to get annoyed with the two and started to respond.

Kwami, SERA's permanent guide came over. Kwami was a native Ghanaian. And he was old. Though no one was really sure how old. On different occasions, he'd given vastly different years for his birth, so it was just one of those things.

"What are you look—" Kwami started. "Oh," he seemed

to find his own answer. "Paul is back. And he has a pretty girl with him."

Marisol looked up at Ben, smiling about as broadly as her face could handle.

Paul walked up.

"It…looks like everyone is here," Paul said, seeing everyone lined up. "Well, then. Everyone, this is Erin," he said to the group. "She's here on loan from R4 Worldwide, one of our partners in D.C. Doing a story for one of our donors."

He held out a hand, motioning to Marisol, "This is Marisol," Paul said. "She does special projects, which basically means a lot of different things and whatever we need at the time."

Marisol smiled and held out a hand.

"It's good to have another girl here," Marisol said.

"Nice to meet you."

She smiled when she said it.

A nice smile, Ben thought.

And then stopped himself.

"*Ben*," Paul said.

"What?" Ben jerked his eyes to Paul.

"It's your name," Paul said slowly. "I'm introducing everyone, remember?"

"Yeah…I know that."

Paul paused for a moment and looked at him before continuing. "Ben," he said again, "mostly does my job when I'm gone. Which—" Ben heard the shift in tone. He knew Paul was about to say something sarcastic.

"Which—" Ben jumped in and finished for him, "is very challenging, but," he held up a finger, "rewarding."

Marisol looked at him sideways.

Ben reached out his hand to shake Erin's, using the rest of his energy to keep the appropriate sized smile on his face.

"Um, Hi," said Erin.

Ben noticed Erin's smile was notably smaller now. More of a cross between a smile and a question. He felt Marisol's eyes barreling into the side of his face. He pulled his hand back and diverted his eyes.

"Next," Paul said, still looking at Ben. "Kwami. One of my oldest friends in Ghana."

"And wisest," Kwami said, in his smooth voice.

"He's our local guide and our chef," Paul said. "He can do anything with anything."

He stepped forward and shook Erin's hand with both of his. "Very nice to meet you, Ms. Erin."

Erin shook his hand and smiled again. "Same to you."

Kwami put most people at ease. Right now, Ben felt sure he was doing the exact opposite.

"And this," Paul said finally, "is Gavin. He does all our data work."

Gavin jutted out his hand out to shake. "I am so glad you're here. We've heard a *lot* about you."

"You have?" Erin asked.

"Well…," for a moment, Ben thought Gavin was going to make a not-too-subtle joke. "No," Gavin said. "But, we are glad you're here."

That could have gone worse, Ben thought.

"Right, Ben?" Gavin added, sharing a knowing smile with Ben.

There it was.

Erin, and everyone else, looked at Ben.

"Of course," Ben said, smiling, giving his best this-is-what-Gavin-always-says-after-he-meets-someone-new answer, making a point to not meet Gavin's look.

Erin looked back at Gavin and then at Ben again.

"He…," Ben said, "doesn't get out much. We keep him mostly tied under the tent behind the computer."

"That's actually true," Gavin said.

"Okay," Paul said, shaking his head, motioning for Erin to move on. "That was the team — I'm sorry — and this is the camp. I'll give you the tour."

Gavin turned around and looked at them. "The tour?" he asked.

Ben looked at him hard.

"What?"

Marisol started to say something, then seemed to think better of it. Ben wasn't sure if she was using her better judgment, or if she just couldn't trust herself not to laugh. Either way, Ben was thankful.

"At least," Gavin said, "we didn't look at the truck."

18

MARISOL

The sun was lower now. It was breaking through the trees in the way that saturates everything with a heavy orange-red hue.

As Paul walked Erin through SERA's camp, she thought it was less of a camp and more of a stopping point. Its sum total consisted of three trailers parked in a u-shape. One of the trailers had a large awning that extended out. Under it was heavy plastic containers, the kind that kept expensive equipment from breaking on impact. Some of them were turned on their side, doubling as tables.

"This," Paul motioned under the overhang, "is where Gavin does most of his work." Erin saw a laptop with several cords running to it and several computer screens. Under it was a rack sprinkled with tiny lights, some flashing, along with more computer equipment. "You can find a space and set up if you need it. We have wifi, too."

"Wifi, really?"

"It's satellite," he said. He pointed to a small metal dish on top of the largest trailer. It had two cords running from it down the side of the trailer and into Gavin's work area. "It's small," Paul continued, "but it gets decent reception. Depending on what you're trying to do. The rest of us do mostly field work, so we don't use the space too much."

The main trailer was used mostly for storage — all of the equipment was put up each night, which explained why after months it still looked like they just arrived — and for cooking. Erin hadn't noticed until Paul pointed it out, but on the far end of the big trailer, there was another overhang with a large plate window. There were a few chairs set up outside. Paul took her inside the trailer. On one end she saw empty storage space where all the equipment was stored each night. On the other end was a fully stocked kitchen. "Kwami takes one of the trucks down to Accra about once a week to stock up on supplies," Paul told her. Erin was starting to see how they could live like this for months and months at a time.

As they walked back outside, Paul pointed upward. "All three trailers are retrofitted with extra solar panels on top. We also have generators, but this time of year, with our load, we usually don't need them. We have enough panels and batteries to work on solar power almost exclusively."

"These," he said, pointing to the other two trailers, "are for sleeping. Ben, Gavin, Kwami, and I have that one," he pointed to the far trailer. "Marisol — and now you — are in the other. You can put your stuff in there and shower. They have hot water. Sometimes. We'll probably be eating in the next hour."

Erin left him and opened the door to her trailer. She stepped up and walked in, looking around. She was surprised at how comfortable it looked. The outside looked military, with its large knobby tires and external metal bracing. But inside, it seemed to be built for comfort. To her right, it had a bathroom that took up the entire end. In the middle was a table, and on her left were beds. The door opened again behind her and Marisol walked in.

"We're lucky," she said.

"Lucky?"

"These things sleep four people," she pointed to a spot under the table. "That folds up and more beds come out. The guys have to use all four of them. Well, Paul's not here half of the time, but still. A lot of them all in one can. Just us in this one, so we've got more room. And when you get used to roughing it like this," she held up her hands, motioning to the trailer, "it's actually pretty nice. Especially since we have it to ourselves."

Erin was surprised at how much she was already agreeing with this girl. As she looked around, she had to admit, it really didn't feel cramped on the inside.

"Plus," Marisol went on, "the bathroom used to be a shower and kitchenette. Paul had them modified to make the bathroom much bigger. Gives you an extra layer of privacy. Or normalcy. Or whatever. Then, on the outside, there's a little washing machine. No dryer, though."

Marisol was talking a lot, and Erin wasn't sure she was catching it all.

"Anyway," Marisol said, as she laid down on her bed, "feel free to make yourself at home."

Marisol pulled out a set of earbuds and put them in, closing her eyes. "Kwami's going to make us food soon," she said, closing her eyes. "In a strange way," she kept talking, even with the earbuds, "if you can get past all the living-in-the-middle-of-nowhere parts, it's kind of better than normal living. People cooking for you, do what you want…"

Erin thought about that for a moment. Marisol might have been partially right. They weren't in tents. But this was a far cry from 'better than normal' living. Erin walked into the bathroom and shut the door behind her. She peeled off her clothes and turned on the shower. The water was mercifully hot. She stood in it for a moment, resting her head against the side of the shower. Letting the water and steam flow over her.

She was tired. She'd left home in D.C. several hours before it was light. *Was that this morning*, she wondered. Standing here, now, that seemed so long ago. She tried to calculate what time it was back home. What time was it here? Her plane landed mid-afternoon. It was a three-hour drive from the airport. Maybe six? Then, that would make it around midnight at home. She quit trying to calculate.

From the other side of the trailer, she heard Marisol still talking. She caught some of it. Marisol was from somewhere in Europe. She somehow got connected with Paul. Erin drifted in and out of listening as the steam built up.

As she stepped out of the shower, she sunk her face deep into her towel, holding it there for a moment. When she pulled it away, she felt different. Refreshed. Though, it was probably just a second, or third wind. But for the moment, she felt new, and better.

Erin pulled on a pair of jeans from her bag and a fresh shirt. She opened the door to rejoin Marisol, who, she realized, was still talking.

Erin towel-dried her hair.

"How long did you say you've been with SERA?" Erin said.

"Just a few months," she said, as Erin sat at the table, brushing her hair back.

"I had long hair when I got here," Marisol said. "But I cut it short. Well, Ben did. He's handy in a lot of unexpected ways."

"Really? He cut your hair?"

"Mm-hm. Like it?" She asked, turning to the side and immediately turning back.

"Yeah." And she did. Marisol had a round face. Her close-ish cropped dirty-blonde hair suited it. Erin's hair was longer, but not long.

"Do you ride?" Marisol asked, shifting the conversation again.

"Ride?" Erin asked.

"Yeah, motorcycles."

"Oh, uh, no. I mean — why?"

"No reason. SERA has three main vehicles. But there's a motorcycle on the back of the equipment trailer," she pointed a thumb over her shoulder. "It's strapped on with an electric motor, so you just push a button and it comes down. But we just keep it for emergencies."

"Okay," Erin said.

"Wow," Marisol said, pausing and looked at Erin.

"What?"

"I just realized I've talked to you more or less *constantly* for the last thirty minutes."

"Yeah," Erin said with a laugh, "that's okay."

"I've just been with all-guys for a while now. And, you know…it's not the same," she said. "It's nice to have a girl here, is all."

Erin smiled. She didn't really have any girl friends. At least not for the last few years. She's spent so much time in her work, the friends she did have were mostly colleagues. Sitting here, like this, reminded her of when she was younger. When she did have friends. When life was…simpler.

"I'm glad to be here, too," she told Marisol, even if she wasn't yet sure if it was true. "Just a little jet-lagged."

Erin hears a *tinging* noise outside. She looked to the sound, then heard it again. *Ting.*

"That's Kwami's dinner bell. It's an actual triangle he brought and hung up."

Erin hadn't realized how hungry she was. She hadn't eaten a real meal since D.C.

"Good," she said, "I'm starving."

19

LAKE VOLTA, GHANA

THE ONLY LIGHT IN THE ROOM CAME FROM A BANK OF monitors on the wall.

Bryan Milson from Nebraska sat in the operator's chair, in the middle of nowhere in West Africa, carefully guiding an underwater machine. He was moving the joystick with one hand, while keeping his other on the toggle, constantly adjusting the amount of green phosphorus that showed up on the screen. His eyes were trained on the center monitor, hardly blinking.

He'd done security for the last five years. Mostly low-level stuff. So when a job paying three times the going rate (and including all room and board) came up, he jumped on it. He'd never heard of ROM Defense, and the job was somewhere in Africa. He'd also never been to Africa. Or out of the country, for that matter. But it was only a six-month contract.

Not to mention, this would get Marie off his back. For Bryan, life was generally pretty good. For Marie, his girlfriend, life was missing one critical thing. Marriage. Bryan liked Marie. And he didn't mind the idea of marrying her.

What he did mind was the cost. When Marie told him the average wedding in Nebraska was around twenty grand, he didn't care. When she told him it was really more of a minimum, he started having what his doctor was calling 'mild panic attacks.'

That's when this job from ROM Defense showed up, out of the blue.

There weren't many specifics, but ROM had already run a background check on him. Checks were standard. Doing them before you applied wasn't. That was the first of many slightly-off things he began to notice. They hired him through email, no interview. But, he told himself, the money was good. Really good. A week after that, a plain white envelope showed up. It was a ticket to Africa. Leaving in two weeks.

Doing security wasn't like in the movies. In real life, you prepare and train…and then it's a whole lot of nothing. There's almost never any real action. And that's how this job started, too. His boss, an ex-military guy called Keeler, seemed like a bit of a loose cannon. But those types were pretty common in this field. Ex-military or ex-cops, getting paid to carry around guns without the public scrutiny of working for the government. That was all pretty standard.

What wasn't standard is what happened a few days ago.

They'd been at this particular site for a couple months. Hired regular locals to do the grunt work, like always. Some stayed on. Some would come and go. But honestly, he wasn't even sure why he was there. They had big, expensive machinery. But it was all way out in the middle of nowhere.

And none of the locals ever got rowdy. He made friends with a British guy working for a charity or something. The nightlife out here was pretty low key. On the whole, it was all pretty uneventful.

Or, at least, it was.

While walking down a standard perimeter check the other day, his radio crackled. It was his boss, Keeler. "Report to the conference room, ASAP."

When he arrived a few minutes later, he walked up to the second-floor and opened the conference room door. What he saw actually took him a few seconds to process.

It was a blood bath.

If he didn't know where they were, he'd have thought it was a scene from a movie.

There were bodies…scattered everywhere…laying on top of each other. Blood was everywhere.

As he entered, he just looked. No reaction, just shock.

Keeler was standing on the other side of the room.

His mind still didn't believe his eyes until one of them started to move. One of the men on the floor actually started to move.

It had to be some kind of trick, or show, or…there had to be some explanation to what he was seeing.

KACK.

The sound shook him. It was from Keeler, who was resting his boot on the man, pointing his rifle at him. Bryan saw the body under Keeler's boot shake with the sound. And then the man didn't move anymore.

Keeler, for his part, stood calmly, like a vampire, before speaking.

"Clean it up," he said. "One out there, too," he motioned to the second-floor balcony outside behind him.

Bryan spent all afternoon and well into the night digging, having to pull out portable lights just to finish. There were fourteen of them. Twelve bodies. He buried all of them. He'd recognized almost all the faces. Some he'd talked too. Bryan didn't normally get into politics. What his employers wanted to do was their business. He was there for the paycheck. But this was over the line. *Way* over the line.

This was how Bryan found himself operating this unmanned underwater machine in the middle of the night. The last guy who did this was in a hole in the ground outside.

He closed his eyes tight, breathing in slowly, making himself focus.

Two men stood over his shoulder — neither of which he trusted. And they were watching each move he made.

One was Keeler, his boss.

The other guy, the blonde mane, he was different. If Keeler and his extra-itchy trigger finger stood out in a place like this, this other guy stood out even more. He looked like a model or something. Though…it wasn't because handsome, he wasn't. Maybe it was just because he felt so…dangerous. Keeler had a kind of evil that was obvious. But this other man, he was more subtle. Like an animal that would catch you before you even knew it was hunting you.

"Is this it?" the blonde man said.

"Yes, sir," Bryan said,

"What's that?" the blond man pointed to the screen.

Bryan moved the controls, adjusting the view.

"This is the target area we've isolated," Bryan said.

We…, he thought.

There was no 'we.' After Keeler unloaded a backpack full of ammo on the staff, and after Bryan had finished 'cleaning up,' Keeler shoved a stack of files in his hand telling him, "Promotion. Learn this." Bryan began reading through the paperwork. It was mostly status reports about the underwater exploration. Stuff he'd only vaguely guessed at before…and a lot more. It was the work a few of the hired men had been doing. As he looked through the reports, Bryan began to understand why they were so concerned with security. The whole logging operation was a cover. A cover to find something. An object, or artifact, that had been buried. It was seriously like Indiana Jones stuff. Except, he'd just realized, he was working for the Nazis.

But, at this point, what choice did he have if he wanted to stay alive? So here he sat, learning on the go how to operate this underwater machine.

"How sure are you?" the blonde man said.

"They — *we*," Bryan corrected, "used a combination of sonar and ground-penetrating radar." He was pretty sure he'd read that in one of the reports.

"I know that," snapped the blonde-haired man. "How far *in* have you gone?"

"In, sir?"

"Yes, how do you know *it*" — he stressed that word — "is really in there? Have you had a direct visual on it?"

Bryan's mind was racing. He hadn't seen anything in the reports that actually confirmed the thing they were searching for, whatever it was, was actually in there.

"Sir," Brian said, "everything in the reports indicates this is the spot we've been looking for." He was doing his best to make his voice level. And confident. Like this was all normal. And like he was competent. Competent enough to live.

Keeler spoke for the first time.

"How far is it beyond this point?"

"It's close," Bryan said. "We believe there's a small hill and then, based on the soundings, it's about four yards after that." Bryan surprised himself, saying that. He knew it was true. He'd read the description in one of the reports Keeler handed him. He just had a sinking feeling his performance was beginning to falter. He reached up and wiped a line of sweat off his forehead.

"Is it completely submerged?" the blonde man said.

"Yes, we believe so." This was a complete guess. He felt a slight bolster of confidence from the success of his last answer. Underwater, after all, is usually submerged. He felt pretty good about that one.

"Move in," the blonde man said.

Bryan tilted the joystick forward, and the screen changed. The robot was moving. He toggled the dial to get a better contrast on the screen. Most of what he was looking at was a smattering of green and black lines, because there was no natural light in the cave at the bottom of the lake. He kept an eye on the progress data, telling him how far forward and up and down the machine had moved. That was more helpful than the video feed. The underwater robot crept forward, passed the small hill and entered the underwater cave.

"Stop," the blonde man said in a tight, controlled voice. He leaned in, putting a firm hand on Bryan's shoulder. He could smell the faintest whiff of cologne. A smell that might be pleasant in any other circumstance.

"Do you see that?" he said, to no one in particular.

Bryan saw more squiggly lines. Something curved, maybe. It *could* be something. Or it could be more rocks.

"Backup. Move lateral. Approach it from the side."

Bryan shifted as the pressure on his shoulder changed. It's like the hand on his shoulder had turned him into a joystick.

"Stop," the blonde man said abruptly.

He removed his hand from Bryan's shoulder, stepping back. Bryan could feel the shift in the room. It wasn't any less tense. If anything, it was now tenser. But it was a different kind of tension.

Bryan didn't turn his head. "Should I—" he started

"Shh," the blonde hair hissed.

Bryan stayed still.

In the reflection of the monitor, he could see Keeler and the blonde man, staring at the screen. Then Keeler looked at the blonde man. The man returned the look. But neither of them spoke. It was too dark for Bryan to read their faces.

"Leave," the blonde man said, finally.

Bryan didn't hesitate. He stood up and left the small control room, making no eye contact as he did. Walking out of the room, he heard the blonde man tell Keeler, "Get your team ready."

20

THE ASHANTI LEGEND

Erin sat near the fire, watching as the light made strange shadows on the new faces of the SERA team sitting around the fire.

Ben dragged a case of cold beers and set it next to the circle, sitting down next to Erin. He pulled open the container and handed her one.

"See, we have standards," he said.

"Thanks," she smiled.

Paul sat a few yards outside the circle, his feet propped on an empty plastic equipment shell, pointing away from the fire. Kwami, Marisol, and Gavin sat lazily around the fire.

Kwami opened his bottle and kicked a log into the fire. "Have you heard," he said, to the group, "they've found the lost Ashanti treasure?"

Paul huffed out a laugh, not turning around.

Kwami didn't seem to hear him.

"Ashanti…" Gavin said, "as in, one of the local tribes?"

"Not just 'a local tribe,'" Kwami said, leaning forward in his chair. "The Ashanti once ruled Ghana." He spread his arms as he said this, spilling a little bit of his beer in the process.

"There you go…," Paul said.

"Once they were one of the most powerful empires in all of Africa," Kwami said. "This was before Ghana was the Ghana we know today. Back then, the Ashanti Empire extended throughout most of West Africa."

"What happened?" Erin asked.

"What happened to most of Africa," Kwami said, leaning back in his chair. "Europeans," nodding his beer-hand toward Ben.

Ben seemed to want to contest that, but Kwami kept talking.

"In the late eighteen-hundreds," Kwami said, "the British and Ashanti had an agreement. The Ashanti allowed the British to work and trade inside their kingdom. In return, the British stayed out of Ashanti affairs. And that went well until the British decided they wanted more. They didn't want to exist with the Ashanti; they wanted to rule over them.

"The Ashanti had great wealth," he said, "But many empires had wealth. The Ashanti, however, had something more, something sacred the others didn't. And it was what eventually caused a war between the British and the Ashanti…"

Kwami sat back and sipped his beer. He looked off into the jungle, at nothing in particular, sitting silently.

Erin looked at Ben and then back at Kwami.

"Well," Marisol said, "what was it?"

Kwami didn't acknowledge her question for a moment. Still staring off. And then, "what was…what?" he said, looking back at the group.

"What was the sacred Ashanti thing?" Marisol said.

"The seat of the gods, of course," Kwami said.

"The what?" Gavin said.

"It is said," Kwami said, "that the seat — the golden chair — never touched the ground. That it had the ability to float"—he gestured again, spilling more beer again—"and that it appeared and disappeared whenever the great Ashanti leader needed it."

"Come on…," Gavin said.

"Come on, what?"

"That stuff," Gavin said. "It's not real…I mean, you don't believe that, do you?"

"I warned you," Paul said, from his seat outside the circle.

"It is you," he pointed to Gavin, "who do not believe. How do you know it is not true? How do you know if anything, for that matter, is true or not?"

"Yeah," Marisol chirped, "how do you know, Gavin?"

Gavin opened his mouth and then shut it again.

"Okay," Ben said. "So there's this sacred object, a chair or whatever, and it belongs to the Ashanti tribe, right? What does a magical chair have to do with this lost treasure you were talking about?"

"One day," Kwami said, "some fool, a representative of the Queen of England, demanded, that his own queen be allowed to sit on the holy Ashanti chair. To the Ashanti, this was, understandably, a great insult. Soon, tens of thousands of Ashanti warriors had gathered, and they drove the British out of their land. Ending their agreement. And, for the British, it was a massacre."

"Of course," Kwami continued, "a few years later, the British came back and conquered the Ashanti and all of their empire. But…they never found the golden chair."

"So what happened to it?" Marisol asked.

"There were many rumors," Kwami said. "Some said it went back to heaven, where it came from. Others said that the British found it but hid it. Some later said the Nazis found it when they went all over the world looking for artifacts. But, these are all rumors. The chair was not a treasure to be found and owned. It was holy. The Ashanti protected it."

"I'm confused," Gavin said. "So the Ashanti had the golden chair thing the whole time?"

"May-be," he said slowly. "The Ashanti had a holy room, where the chair appeared. The British knew about this room. But they did not know where it was. And they searched more or less until the mid-teens, when they had to stop because of the First World War. And not too long after that war came the second. The Nazis too, they searched for it. Part of what they called their cultural collection initiative. Where they went around collecting sacred objects from many different cultures."

"Okay, so…," Marisol said.

"Do you know why the Akosombo Dam was created?" Kwami asked.

"Uh, no," Marisol said.

"About fifty years ago," Ben said, "the dam was built, and once the Volta basin was flooded, it created Lake Volta. The same 'Lake Volta' very close to where we are now."

Kwami looked at Ben, apparently impressed, "that's right," he said, "the largest manmade lake in the world. Right here in Ghana. And, do you know why it was created?"

"I imagine, the same reason all dams are created," Ben said. "To create electricity."

"That was the official reason. But not the real one," Kwami said. "The dam was created in the early 1960s by Kwame Nkrumah, Ghana's first Ghanaian president. Ghana had just won its independence from the British. The Cold War was just beginning to heat up — especially in non-western places like Latin America and Africa — and Nkrumah believed—

"Wait," Marisol said. "How do you know all this... random stuff?"

"Don't you know about your country?" he said.

"I...," she started and looked away.

"As I was saying, many Ghanaians believe that the holy site for the golden chair was where the city of Akosombo was. That," he said, "is why they picked *that* location for the dam."

"So you're saying that it was just, what...a conspiracy?" Ben said.

"I'm saying," Kwami said, "that the timing was right. In the mid-sixties, Ghana was still a new country. And world powers like Russia and the United States were increasingly vying for control of the free world. And so the United States and Britain helped finance the dam that would create Lake Volta. Their interest was diplomatic and trade. Our interest was—"

"The golden chair," Marisol said.

"Right," Kwami smiled.

"Okay," Ben said, "even if this is all true...wouldn't flooding the whole area have destroyed the holy room and the chair and whatever else?"

Kwami looked at him for a moment before answering. "You," he pointed to him, "come from a country of wealth. You do not understand what it's like."

"Okay, but still—" Ben said.

"Sometimes," Kwami continued, "it's better some things go undiscovered."

"But," Marisol said, "you said the golden chair *was* discovered, right?"

"Yes," Kwami said, going quiet again. "Yes, it seems that...it might have been."

The rest of the group became silent.

Erin took another sip of her beer and realized that the

bottle was empty. She'd been listening to Kwami's story; she hadn't even noticed she'd finished it. And for a moment, she'd forgotten where she was. She'd forgotten that she was halfway around the world with people she'd just met, and camping in the middle of nowhere.

And yet, despite all that, she didn't feel alone or isolated. She listened, and laughed, and drank, feeling already like she belonged with these people. At least, for tonight she did.

Or, then again, maybe that was just the jetlag talking.

✶

Erin lay in bed. Awake. Listening to the sounds out in the jungle. In her mind, she kept jumping from thought to thought. The only thing her brain wasn't doing now was sleeping.

She kept turning over what Kwami said. About the rumors of some mythical chair being found…could such a thing even be true, she wondered.

Then, soon, other thoughts flooded her mind. Like about Carl and why he changed his mind…and what his relationship to Jonah Lennox was…and what did mom know about Lennox…and why did she trust him…and why he would have betrayed her…

Maybe McGillis was right. Maybe the only connection between her mother and all of this was the connection in her imagination. Involuntarily, her mind flashed back to the time in Trinidad. Hunting down a lead, chasing it into a dead end. *A dead end*…she thought. She'd almost died the last time she tried to chase down the truth about her mother…

She turned her head to the side, looking around their trailer. Her eyes had long adjusted to the dark. The shadows, she thought, made really weird shapes on the ceiling.

Marisol, in the other bed, was still. Sleeping. Erin wished she was sleeping.

Outside she could hear a rhythmic, mechanical chirping. It was sometime before she realized these were the sounds the bats were making as they hunted their prey. She wondered, vaguely, as she began to drift to sleep, what it would feel like if some giant bat was methodically watching her…chasing her…hunting her…*beep*…*beep*…maybe that's what happened to her mother…*beep*…maybe a bat got her…

21

DOUBLETAP

Erin woke up with a headache. Light poured in from the shades she didn't draw last night. She could feel it, even before she opened her eyes. She turned her head to the side and looked at Marisol's bed. It was empty.

Outside, birds were making loud, obnoxious noises.

Or…were those voices?

She rolled out of her bed, pulled her hair back, and slipped her boots on. She opened the door and looked out. If it were possible, the sunlight outside was even louder. Her head throbbed.

She raised her arm and covered her eyes. As she did, she saw Ben lobbing one of last night's bottles into the cloud of dust. It was a truck, speeding out of camp. There was a lot of swearing.

"Ben," she heard Paul say. "Now is not the time."

Ben didn't respond.

As Erin looked around, she noticed everyone else was standing by, looking at where the truck was. She walked over to Marisol. "What's going on?" she asked.

"Keeler," Marisol said, not taking her eyes off of the cloud of dust.

"Who is Keeler?" Erin asked, still squinting, everywhere was bright.

Marisol didn't answer at first.

Erin looked at her and saw her slide something under her shirt into the small of her back. It looked a bit like an external hard drive.

"Trouble."

"What do you mean? What did he want?"

"He works for Lennox."

"Lennox? What was he doing here?" Erin said.

"Yeah," Marisol said, looking at Erin for the first time. "Delivers data every few days. Reports, stuff like that. The lab where they process isn't far from here."

"Okay…What does th—"

"Gavin started running some tests recently," Marisol said. "Stuff wasn't lining up. So we started collecting some of our own data. Turns out, they've been fabricating what they send to us."

"Why?"

Marisol was quiet, as if she didn't hear the question. "He drives in our camp," she said, "slings an automatic rifle over his shoulder, finger on the trigger, and walks around like he owns the place. It's a message," Marisol looking at Erin again. "A power play. He's saying he doesn't care what we know, and if we say anything…"

Marisol turned to walk back to the trailer. Erin walked back with her. As they stepped inside, Erin was beginning to wake up, and her mind was filling up with new questions.

Marisol sat down on the bed, reached under the back of her shirt and pulled out the hard drive Erin had seen earlier. Except, it wasn't a hard drive. She tossed it on the bed next to her. It was a tiny gun.

"Is that a…gun?" Erin said.

Marisol picked it up again, and it fit inside the palm of her hand. It made a clicking sound as she flicked it open. She looked into the small barrels, closed it again, and dropped it on the bed beside her. All like she'd done it a thousand times.

"It's called a Doubletap," she said.

She looked tired, Erin noticed.

"No magazine, no revolver. Just two bullets, one in each barrel. It's small enough to fit into the palm of my hand, or easily hide under clothes. Wanna hold it?" she said looking up at Erin.

"Oh," Erin said, not reaching for it. "No…I'm not really much of a gun person."

Marisol shrugged.

"Do you think you really *need* something like that?" Erin said.

Marisol was quiet.

"I grew up in Catania, in Sicily," she said. "A place where…" she glanced at the gun on the bed, "where there's been a lot of crime for a long time. And unless you're at the top, or well-connected to the top — of which we were neither — then it's not a good place."

She was quiet before continuing. "So as soon as I could, I left. Sixteen. And, it turns out, when you learn to survive in a place like that," she nodded to the gun on the bed as she said it, "the rest of the world isn't so hard."

"I didn't know you were Italian," Erin said.

"Another thing I've learned," she half-smiled. "No matter what people say about Americans, most people still like them. Or at least, most people want to be one. So, that's what I did. I became what others wanted, and I made friends with the people who…," she didn't finish the rest of her sentence.

Erin wanted to say something else.

"But then," Marisol said, "I met Paul." Her face brightened a little as she said it. "It's strange," she said, looking out the window. "It's almost like, with Paul, you don't have to worry about some things, ya know…"

Erin nodded.

But the truth was, she wasn't so sure she did know what she meant. It seemed like everyone else knew Paul better than she did. That was just one more question she added to her already mounting pile. The biggest of which was *why*…

SERA did humanitarian aid work. Their whole mission was to help developing governments plan strategically for environmental issues. She could understand them being kept in the dark on some things. For confidentiality, perhaps. But giving them *wrong* information…that was something else.

Why was Lennox changing the data…and why was Paul going along with it…or…was he? Maybe he didn't know, she thought.

"Anyway," Marisol said, her tone more like herself again. "I'm hungry."

She picked up the little gun, put it in the small of her back, pulling her shirt at the edges, and moved toward the door to leave.

Before she left, Erin called to her. "Marisol?" she said.

"Yeah," she paused at the door.

"Does anyone else know you carry that?"

"No," her eyes darted down as she said it. "I'm…not trying to keep secrets," Marisol said. "I just find it easier this way."

She didn't have to explain anymore. In a strange way, Erin understood what she meant.

Marisol walked outside to get breakfast.

Erin stayed inside, sitting on her bed, thinking. She pulled out her laptop to see if she could get on SERA's wifi.

22

NKONYA MARKET

Mofi sat in the back of another truck; his head rocked to the side as the truck went over a bump.

He'd spent most of the last few days in the rural Jasikan district, walking and hitching rides. There were no *tro-tros* out here — the over-crowded buses that filled the metropolis of Accra, that he'd come to rely on. And so travel in the bush was harder, slower.

Sitting under the morning sun, already high and hot, Mofi thought again about Tano. About where he was. About what might have happened to him. Wondering if he made it away before the big man found him — the same big man who'd shot at Mofi as he ran.

The driver of the truck reached a hand out of his window and banged his palm on the side of the door. "Nkonya," he called, as the truck slowed. Mofi sat up and looked out. He saw a small market he'd last seen many years before. He hopped over the side as the truck picked up speed again and drove off.

Nkonya was Mofi's lead.

His only lead.

When he'd last seen Paul, he was working in this area. Years ago, Tano was working for him, as a guide and translator. Mofi walked past an old shipping container that had been converted into a business front, a large pile of black tires lying next to it. He turned off the main paved road and walked into the market.

He stopped and talked briefly to shop owners, asking them if they remembered the white man who worked with Tano. Africans have good memories. And when a white man shows up in a rural area like this, he stands out. People still remember it years later. And most he talked to did remember Paul. But none of them had seen him in a long time.

Mofi kept walking.

And that was when he noticed the other man.

Ghana has been a peaceful and prosperous country for many years. As a result, a lot of tribes have come to live here. To Westerners, they often look indistinguishable. But to the locals, they were anything but. One of the key distinctions between different tribes who live near each other is their markings. The scars on their face, carved when they were young boys and girls. To some, such a practice sounds barbaric. But it's not here. It's a sign of honor and heritage. And it was how tribes could immediately identify their other members. It's how people knew and trusted one another. And it was one of the ways Mofi knew the man following him now didn't belong.

Mofi had never been followed before. And before a few days ago, he'd never been *shot* at either.

The man wore a white and red checked shirt. And he knew he was following him, because he'd seen the same white and red checked shirt yesterday. Far from the Nkonya market where he now was. The chances of that were pretty small.

Mofi looked over his shoulder again, but the man had turned. He couldn't see his face. Mofi kept moving. Faster now. He risked another look. But…the man had disappeared.

Mofi stopped walking. He doubled back, taking another way around.

Through the crowd, he thought he saw the red and white pattern. He stared longer. But…nothing.

Since arriving, the best lead he'd found — which wasn't a very good lead — was some white people over at the coast. Mofi was now on the other side of Lake Volta. And he was keenly aware he was moving in a circle since he left a few days ago.

The more he dwelled on it, the more he developed a bad feeling about the man with the white and red checked shirt.

Finding Paul was important. Tano had told him that. But getting out of here right now felt more important.

He hurried back to the paved road, watching over his shoulder as he did. He flagged down an approaching pickup, hopped into the back without it stopping. It sped off. Mofi looked behind him. He didn't see any sign of the man in the white and red shirt.

23

A FEW MORE THINGS

Paul stood at the tailgate of his Land Rover, parked on the edge of the SERA campsite. He held up the small laminated badge he'd just created, examining it from different angles.

Normally, he was pretty good at forging documents. Not the new kind — the ones with holograms — but the older kind, the kind they could often get away with in places like this. Ghana was a modern country, but they still had a long way to go before his skills would be obsolete.

SERA, though, was completely above board. All legal and sanctioned. But that didn't mean, from time to time, a few supplementary tools didn't come in handy. It was a standard practice. He'd created a few different sets for all of his team. Some were press badges. Others looked vaguely similar to the diplomatic passes Americans in uniforms were not unlikely to be carrying. And if anyone looked closely, they just said something about being a nonprofit doing official work for the government. Good words that didn't really mean much.

As he looked closely at the seams, he could see where the original stopped and his new creation started, but it would work. His chop-shop was light, a small scanner, a portable printer, and a laminator, small enough to fit in a duffel bag and run off his truck's DC power.

Erin walked toward him. "Hey," she said.

"Morning," he said, tossing the badge into the duffel. "How'd you sleep on your first night?"

"Er…not that great. The accommodations were fine," she added, "just…"

"The jetlag," he said, starting to work on another badge, "and too much booze," he smiled. "Spend another couple years doing this, and you'll be used to it in no time."

She leaned against the side of the truck, crossing her arms, and watched him work.

"What's the story with Keeler?"

"How do you mean?" he asked, not looking up.

"As in, the fake data he's giving SERA," she said. "Why go along with that?"

Paul looked up at her.

"Marisol told me," she said.

He glanced over at Marisol's trailer, then looked back at Erin and put down his work-in-progress.

"There's something you need to understand about all of this. First," he said, "we're collecting our own data. We don't even know *how* much they're tampering with it, much less why."

"This is the same data that's going into outbreak reports, right?"

"Right," he said.

"So why didn't you mention anything when you were in D.C.? To Carl. Or to the board. At least let them know—"

"And second," he continued on, gently. "If you rush these things, you get yourself into trouble."

"What do you mean, 'trouble'?"

"Either all your leads disappear, or…," he trailed off.

She seemed to consider that.

"Paul," Erin said, "are they dangerous?"

"Who, Keeler?"

"Yeah,"

He looked at her for a moment before responding.

"Everyone's dangerous in the right situation."

She looked back over her shoulder. Kwame and Ben were eating breakfast. Marisol was walking back to her trailer.

Paul held up his new ID card.

"What are you working on?" she said.

He handed them both to her, and she took them, looking at them.

"It's…me," she said. "What are these? It says I'm a—"

"Don't worry about what they say," he told her, "just keep them close, in case you ever need them."

She handed them back to him, but he didn't take them.

"Think of them as insurance," he said. "I hope you never need them. But sometimes the channels that should work don't. And sometimes….you just need a little extra help. Besides, they're standard issue. I make sure everyone's got a pair."

She looked at them again and then slid them into her back pocket.

"Paul," she said, "can I ask — I mean…," she hesitated and looked down.

"What is it?" he said.

"I'm not sure I can…I just…maybe I shouldn't have come here. Maybe this was all a mistake."

He sat down on his tailgate, sliding his bag out of the way.

"Look at me," he said. "Back in D.C., I told you to stay away from this—no," he said, seeing her response forming, "it's not because you couldn't handle it. It was because I didn't know what *it* was yet. And…to be honest with you, I still don't. But," he let out a deep breath, "you're more like your mother than I sometimes want to admit."

"But she…," Erin started.

"Gillian," he cut her off, knowing where she was going, "could handle herself. And so can you."

He thought about the words as they were coming out. Paul was never very good at pep talks. He always felt like more of a doer than a talker. And he wasn't lying. Gillian could handle herself. But he couldn't help thinking, she was 'handling herself' on her last assignment…

She looked at him.

"I'm not so sure," she said, looking away from him.

"I'm not worried about you," he said.

Neither of them said anything for a long moment. Erin watched the rest of the camp doing its morning routine.

"Oh," Paul said, "and there's something else I have for you."

He turned and dug through his duffle. Not finding what he was looking for, he felt his pockets, "here it is," he said, pulling out a folded card out of his shirt pocket.

He handed it to her.

"What's this," she said.

"Just a precaution," he said. "You'll probably never need it. But, just in case, if you get into trouble and can't get ahold of me, call this number."

She took the small folded card and looked at it.

"Whose number is it? And why wouldn't I be able to—"

"Just a friend," he said. "And, again, you'll probably never need it," he smiled.

She folded it back and slid it into the pocket of her shorts.

24

DATA

Ben sat in the shade, preparing paperwork for an upcoming SERA project.

In the last year, Paul had come to rely on Ben to run the administrative side of SERA. That mostly meant getting documents in order for the grants and working through any local permitting issues. But Paul still talked to the donors directly and did all of the fundraising. But Ben did a lot of the prep work. Ben's 'office' was outside, under the supply trailer's canopy. It was a makeshift table he shared with Gavin and his computers.

Normally, on the days Ben had to do 'office work,' it would be complete by mid-morning, at the latest. Which is to say, as soon as possible.

Except today.

Today, now nearly noon, and he's been carefully spell-checking all of his forms, and re-reading for the third time what he'd recently written.

"Show me that again," Erin said, as she leaned closer to Gavin, pointing to his screen. "How do you know that's an anomaly?" she said.

"Because of this," Gavin said, typing on his keyboard. "This," he pointed to the screen, "functions like a baseline. It's the data we've been collecting directly. When you consider how an outbreak normally spreads, there's a pretty normal distribution curve. The WHO — the World Health Organization — has given us access to a lot of their data for modeling purposes."

"So when we run the data we've collected against their data sets," he said, "we see a pattern that looks like this," he pointed. "Namely, it's not an outbreak. In fact, that data we've collected isn't *anything*. It's a complete false alarm."

"This is your data?" Erin said, pointing to the screen.

"Yes. And when I first compared it, I thought I'd set the parameters wrong."

"What do you mean?"

"WHO gave us a lot of data, and it would take a long time, not to mention, more computer-power than I've got here, to compare ours against all of theirs. So when the results showed nothing, I just assumed I'd made a mistake. Then I ran it several more times, and I kept getting the same results. Nothing."

"How does the data from Jonah Lennox compare?"

"That," he said, typing a few quick commands, "looks like this." His screen flashed a new set of numbers. He typed another command, and a colorful line-graph appeared on his screen.

"Now watch when I overlay what Lennox has been giving us with the data we've been collecting directly." He typed a few more strokes.

"Here," he angled the monitor toward her. "Ours is the green line. His is the red. See that?"

Ben leaned in, having now given up the pretense of paperwork. Of course, none of this was new to him. He'd been the one that collected many of the initial soil and water samples. That was the basis for the data Gavin was now discussing.

In fact, it was Ben's suspicions in the first place that set off their hunt. As soon as there was talk of the outbreak, Ben began visiting local populations, the places where an outbreak was most likely to start showing up. This was all standard operating procedures. SERA worked out in the bush for this very reason. But there was no sign of any outbreak. If there was something going on, it certainly didn't look like a deadly outbreak.

"The two aren't even close," Erin said.

"Right," Gavin said.

"Exactly," Ben said.

Erin and Gavin both looked up at him.

He sat there for a moment, wishing he had something else to add. "I...," Ben started and then trailed off. He sat back and picked up his paperwork, feigning a fourth proofread.

"Good point, Ben," Gavin smiled.

Ben didn't look back up.

"Any-way," Gavin said, "that's the problem in a nutshell."

"So...," Erin said, "what do you do with the data Keeler brings?"

"Well, I'm still analyzing it," Gavin said. "If you notice here," he pulled the comparison graph back up. "It's not *all* wrong. This area here," he pointed, "actually lines up quite nicely with what we've found on our own. And, in fact, most of the discrepancy on our end comes from when you compare it to the projections only."

"I'm not following," Erin said.

"Epidemics have a pretty standard bell curve. They're logarithmic through here," he said, pointing. "But this," he motioned to a different area, "is all hypothetical. It hasn't happened yet. But because it's been studied so extensively, we know pretty confidently if certain markers happen, then this will happen. In other words, it's what we expect to happen, based on what's happened a lot of times in the past."

"So then how do you know the data *you've* collected is right?"

"Because, again, if you look again at the WHO data," Gavin said, "the timeline of Lennox's data is all wrong. If there was any kind of outbreak, it would have leading indicators or markers. These are what we use to spot tipping points."

"What kind of indicators?"

"The workers who were exposed, the ones who died, they'd have at least transmitted it to their families or to nearby village markets or something like that, right? But first, no virus or bacterium travels so fast that it kills people within a day or two. In fact, that's often what makes some of these outbreaks so dangerous, there's a latency that allows people to spread it around."

Erin leaned back in her chair. "So, you're saying, Lennox's data is consistent with the typical epidemic projections, but it doesn't line up with the data you've collected yourself."

"Right."

"And if an epidemic *was* about to happen, then we'd see warning signs, like others getting sick. But so far…nothing."

"Exactly."

She was quiet for a moment. "How sure are you about all this?"

"Quite. We have some more tests to do, and it would be good to have a larger data set, but…it's pretty hard to see how it could be anything else."

"Can you print me copies of this?"

"Sure, what do you want?"

"All of it," she said, standing up.

"All of it…?" Gavin said, "okay."

The printer under their makeshift workstation started to hum, and paper with black and white graphs and columns of numbers filled the tray. Erin reached down and picked up a few pages and then walked back to her trailer.

"What are you going to do?" Ben said.

"I need to make a call," she said.

"Do you…need any help with that?" Ben asked.

She turned to him. "You mean with making a call?"

"Yeah, just…satellite stuff…it's…and…," he trailed off lamely.

"I think I've got it under control," she said.

"Right…," he said, "under control…good."

Her trailer door shut behind her.

"What was that?" Gavin said.

Ben held up a finger, about to make a point, and then, thinking better of it, pulled it back, and looked down again at his paperwork.

PLAN A

Carl Ibsen's phone vibrated on his polished mahogany desk.

He looked down at the screen. The D.C. morning sun was still low, raking across his desk, throwing long shadows.

Erin.

For a brief moment, he considered not answering.

He picked it up and answered.

"Hey, Erin," he said, "how's it going?"

"Good," her voice was a little distorted. Satellite connection. "I think I might have something," she said.

"Already…"

"But, I'm not sure you're going to like it."

"What," he said, not a question.

"I don't have anything solid yet. But someone is messing with the outbreak-data."

Ibsen closed his eyes and rubbed one of his temples. He leaned back in his chair, opened his eyes and looked out of his window.

"You still there?" she said.

"Yeah, I'm here," he said. "What do you know for *sure*?"

"Nothing for sure, yet."

"Tell me your guess."

"Lennox."

"Lennox *what*?"

"Lennox," she said, "is messing with the data."

"Why do you say that?"

"I…can't say yet."

"Can't?"

"It's all just speculative still," Erin said. "And I don't have any hard proof to fall back on yet."

"Apparently solid enough to name Lennox, though," he said.

There was silence on the other end, and a brush of static.

"Are you defending him?" she said.

"Look," Ibsen said. "This makes things…," he paused to choose his next word carefully, "*complicated*."

"No kidding," she said.

Erin was good. Always good. And reliable. But she was an idealist. Not practical. These days, R4 needed friends. *Ibsen* needed friends. High-place friends. Business was, of course, good, but it was only that way because of the relationships he'd cultivated over the last few years. Powerful relationships. And if he'd learned anything since starting this company, survival wasn't about skill or quality or any of the other business-school virtues.

It was all about alliances.

And right now, he was straddling an important one. Status quo wasn't good enough anymore. If they — if *he* — were going to survive, he had to play this one right.

"Plan A," he said.

"What?"

"Still the same. ITG needs a good report. That's what you're there for. Find that. Do what you need to do to get it. Ignore the rest."

"What about Lennox?" she said.

Ibsen thought about that for a moment. Erin was now in the middle of something…something difficult. To Ibsen, there were no gray areas. Only objectives and finish lines. Everything in-between was either a help…or an obstacle.

But Erin was different. And it's what made them a good team.

Now, however, he was concerned that their time might be coming to an end. Erin wasn't a shark like he was. She didn't have the stomach for what it sometimes took to make things happen. No, she was more like a bulldog. When she found something, she didn't let it go.

And the question Ibsen was now wrestling with was, could R4 afford to have a bulldog? Was there still a way forward, like there had been in the past?

"Carl?" she said. "Are you still there?"

"No…," he said, "I mean, yes. Erin, stay away from Lennox. Get what we need — get the story for ITG — and come back. And Erin…"

"Yeah?"

"The sooner, the better."

"Okay."

"Oh, and one more thing… Have you talked to Paul about this yet?"

The line was silent again for a moment.

"No," she said.

"Good…good," he said. "Keep it that way. Just, get the story and come back."

Ibsen ended the call and put the phone down on his desk. He picked up a pair of metal Baoding balls and rolled them over each other in the palm of his hand…thinking.

Erin tossed the sat phone onto her bed.

She'd had the charts from Gavin in her hand the whole time she was talking to Carl. Why didn't she tell him about those…this was hard evidence. The only thing better than this would be an on-the-record confession directly from Jonah Lennox himself. But…something about the way Carl was handling this made her think it wasn't *evidence* he was after. Something else was going on. And while Carl had never exactly been a straight shooter, he'd always been honest with her. But now, however, she wasn't so sure.

The other question nagging at her was the one that had been with her since she talked to McGillis back in D.C. The connection between Lennox and her mother's death. It was thin… So thin there wasn't actually anything there… Except for the one thing: Lennox was in Mogadishu when her mother died. That, and her mother named him in her notes.

She looked again at the graphs in her hand. Paul was right. If there's a play here, it needs to be made…carefully.

The next few days would be critical, she decided. Right now, she wasn't on anyone's radar. Carl, despite whatever he was doing, had given her some latitude. And Lennox didn't know she was here. If she was going to find something, she needed to do it fast, while she still had the upper hand.

26

THE MOH

Erin paced back and forth in the trailer that was too small for pacing.

The door opened, and sunlight blanketed the inside. Marisol walked in.

Erin sat but didn't look at her.

"Am I…interrupting something?" Marisol said.

Erin held up a finger. "What are you doing right now?" she said.

"Uh…nothing," Marisol said. "What's up?"

"If we borrow one of the trucks, do you know the way back to Accra?"

"Yeah, but why?" Marisol said.

"I have something I need to…," Erin said, still in thinking-mode, "Something I need to do. Can you take me?"

"Sure, when do you want to go?"

"Now," Erin said, looking up at her again. She picked up the printouts from Gavin and stuffed them in a small bag she slung over her shoulder. The two of them walked out of the trailer.

Outside, Paul was still sitting behind his Land Rover

parked under a large tree. His chair was leaned back and his feet were propped on the tailgate. He was looking through a set of papers, pen in hand.

Erin started to walk to the older Land Rover. But Marisol stopped her, "No way we're taking that one," she said, "no air condition." Marisol walked up to Paul.

"Paul," she said, "need to take your truck down to Accra."

He looked at them both and started to respond.

"Girl stuff," she said, "you know." And without waiting for a response, she held her hand out, palm up. "Keys, please," she smiled.

Erin thought Paul might say something, but he didn't. He just reached into his pocket, trying to pull his keys out without standing up. "When are you coming back?" he said.

"Oh…," Marisol said, "we'll, um, definitely be back by…" She cut her eyes toward Erin.

"Tonight," Erin said.

"Tonight," Marisol finished, nodding her head, still holding out her hand.

Paul dropped the keys in her hand.

He opened his mouth to say something, but Marisol had already turned and started walking toward the truck. She got in and started the engine.

Erin climbed into the passenger side. And as she was pulling her door closed, Marisol had already started driving. Marisol pushed a button, and the sunroof slid open.

The ride down to Accra was uneventful. The road was flanked by the same red dirt and endless green trees she'd seen on the way up. The only changes to the scenery were the small towns they'd occasionally pass through.

Marisol spent most of the ride, to Erin's relief, doing the talking. Erin, for her part, spent the ride looking out the window and making occasional 'mm-hmm' sounds.

As they drove into the city limits for Accra, Marisol turned to Erin.

"What's the plan? Where to?" Marisol said.

"Ministry of Health. Do you know where it is?"

"Yep," Marisol said, nearly clipping a motorcycle that had buzzed through their lane. "We have to file paperwork with them every few months. Have to get their stamp. So we have to drive in and do it in person."

Marisol turned off a larger road, nearly missing a completely different motorcycle, and pulled onto a smaller tree-lined road. It was a strange dynamic, Erin thought. Neither the motorcycles nor Marisol seemed to notice how close they kept coming to one of them ending up under the wheels of the other.

"This is where a lot of government buildings are," Marisol said.

Even though they were still in the middle of the city, it immediately felt quieter. There weren't as many people walking around in this area.

"The MOH — the Ministry of Health — is here," Marisol said. "Along with the trade office. And the Port Authority has a central office here, too."

They passed through a checkpoint. A soldier in dark green fatigues, rifle slung over his shoulder, stood next to it. Marisol rolled down her window and held out a badge. She slowed the Land Rover but didn't stop. The guard took a short step forward to look and then motioned her through without reading any of it.

They drove on through the tree-lined street. Erin saw larger, non-descript buildings. Marisol parked in a small parking lot near one.

"This is it," Marisol said.

Erin looked up at it.

"If what Gavin showed me is correct," she said, "then all

we need to do is prove it. We can't put SERA in the middle of it. That would risk…other things."

"Such as?" Marisol said.

"Well, SERA is one of the NGOs my client, ITG, works with. And like most big organizations, they don't like controversy. They'd just as soon cut ties than investigate the 'right' or 'wrong' of the matter. Besides," Erin continued, "if Paul had wanted to bring SERA into it, he'd have done something already."

"So…"

"So what I really need is for the Ministry of Health to agree to back me on my investigation. I'm not bringing them an official problem yet. But when I do bring a case to them, I want them to be ready for it. Plus, I want to *quietly* start looking into Lennox. I don't want to raise any alarms."

"But, won't that still spook your client?" Marisol said. "I mean, if you find something, that'll create controversy, right?"

"Not necessarily," she said, "not if we do it right…"

"How do you mean?"

"I need to talk to the Minister of Health first."

They got out of the Land Rover and walked through the glass doors into the building. As they waited, Erin reached into her bag and pulled out her Washington Post lanyard, hanging it around her neck.

She was surprised to see almost no security inside the building. It felt more like an office park than a government building. They walked up to the circular reception desk.

"We're here to see Minister Djan," Marisol said.

"Do you have an appointment?" the woman behind the desk asked.

"No, but my name is Erin Reed," she said, holding up the ID badge hanging around her neck. "I'm here with *The Washington Post.*"

The receptionist looked at it and picked up the phone. She pushed a button, holding the receiver to her ear, and waited. "There is a reporter here, for Minister Djan," she said.

Erin and Marisol stood by, hearing only the downstairs-end of the conversation which was mostly a series of yes's and no's. The receptionist put down the phone and said, "I'm sorry, Minister Djan is not available right now. But one of his aides will be down shortly to talk with you."

"Thanks," Erin said. They walked across the room and sat on a couch.

A moment later, the elevator door dinged and opened. A younger man with a shaved head and a bright orange tie appeared. He glanced at the receptionist who gave a slight nod, and then he looked to Erin and Marisol.

"Good morning," he said. "My name is Akwasi Bamfok-wakye," holding out his hand to shake. "You can call me Waz."

Erin and Marisol shook his hand. "Hi Waz, I'm Erin Reed, from *The Washington Post*."

"My pleasure," Waz said. "I'm afraid Minister Djan is not available at this moment. But I can talk with you on his behalf. Please, follow me."

Waz led them to a nondescript conference room, which apparently doubled as the break room, as employees would regularly walk in to refill their coffees.

She told him she was writing an article about NGO corruption.

"Miss Reed," Waz said, "it is our policy to promote the good things in our country."

But, she assured him, she was also here representing her client, InTrans Global (ITG), a large conglomerate who regularly docks cargo vessels here in Accra's port. They too have "sensitive requirements," she said carefully. They talked a bit longer. Most of it, she figured, was him coming to trust her and her intentions. And that she wouldn't do anything to hurt the Ministry of Health in the process.

"What do you get out of this?" he said finally.

What she didn't tell him, is that this kind of alliance would give her the support she needed to push Lennox to show his cards. Carl knew something he didn't want to tell her. But there were too many coincidences. Something wasn't right.

"My client," she said, "has a strong"—she paused on that last word—"interest in keeping a good profile in the media. The last thing they want is controversy. But," she continued, "they also have a business to run. And that means they need things to run smoothly."

Waz considered all of this.

"I will share this with the Minister," he said, "and, we will be in touch with you."

With that, he showed them out.

Outside, Marisol looked at Erin. "You really think that's going to work?"

"No idea," she said, "but it's worth a shot. Besides," she continued, "it's like what you said earlier. People like Lennox and Keeler work on intimidation. They've made their deals, and so they think they can get away with whatever they want. But that's what makes them weak. They get sloppy. We're just going to push them to get a little bit sloppier."

The truth was, the words Erin heard coming out of her mouth sounded more confident than she felt. There were more than a few moving parts in all of this…

They got in the truck and drove back out onto the main road. Around the corner, Marisol pulled up to a public parking area and parked the Land Rover again.

"I need to do a quick errand," Marisol said. "While we're here," she added, stepping out.

"Um," Erin said.

"Won't take long," Marisol said, poking her head back in before shutting the door. "I'll be back in about thirty minutes. That, over there," she pointed, "is the Makola market. It's fun, if you want the whole 'Africa' experience, carved zebras and stuff like that."

Marisol shut the door and walked in the opposite direction, disappearing into the crowd.

Erin looked and saw a swarm of people flanked by buildings and bright colors. The truck, she could feel, was already getting warm. Marisol took the keys with her. Erin looked at her watch, thirty minutes… She got out and walked toward the mass of people.

27

SECURE LINE

THE SAT PHONE BEEPED IN HIS EAR. THAT MEANT THE connection was secure.

"All is in place, heading your way. Three days," came the scrambled voice on the other end. The scrambled voice… another precaution.

"Okay," Lennox thought for a moment. "That'll work."

"Will you be ready?"

"When the time comes, yes."

"Do you have the target?" the scrambled voice asked.

"We're close."

"And what about the girl?"

"I'm going to let it play out."

The voice didn't respond. The phone beeped again, still secure.

"From one to ten, what's our level of risk?"

"Two," he said, without delay.

The voice was quiet again.

"That's too high."

Lennox's voice remained neutral. "We might need her for leverage," he said.

"What about Paul Dannon? Is he going to be a problem?"

"Not," Lennox said, speaking slowly, "if I have leverage."

There was another pause.

"Keep me posted."

The click stopped, and the line went dead.

28

IT'S A GO

Erin was standing by the still-locked Land Rover when Marisol came back.

"Sorry I'm late," she said.

"It's okay, I bought a carved zebra," Erin said, holding it up.

They got in, Marisol backed the truck into Accra traffic, and they began making their way north, out of the city. Shortly after, they were on the N6, heading back to SERA's camp.

Erin's bag on the floor next to her feet beeped. It was her sat phone. She reached down and pulled it out, answering.

"Hello, Miss Reed," came the voice. "This is A—"

Static washed over the line.

"Can you say that again," Erin said, "I couldn't hear you." They were already out of the city now, and reception was less stable.

"It's Waz," she heard. "From the" — more static — "of Health."

"Oh, Waz, hi," Erin said, "I didn't expect you to call so soon."

Another wave of static disappeared. Waz was in the middle of another sentence: "…is very happy with what you proposed."

"The Minister?" Erin asked.

"Yes, the Minister. I just talked to him."

"That's great news," she said.

"But…there is something else," Waz said, almost apologetically, "and, I'm afraid, he was very firm on this point."

"Okay…," Erin said.

"He does not want any bad relations from this. Minister Djan does not want this to look like the Ministry is working *against* Mr. Lennox."

"I understand," said Erin.

"Or his partners," he added.

'His partners?' Erin thought. She briefly considered asking him about that, but then decided against it.

"We're on the same page, Waz. I will keep your office updated," she said.

"Thank you, Miss Reed."

Erin hung up the phone. They were on the long highway back to SERA now. She looked at Marisol.

"Well," Erin said, "it looks like we're a go."

"Good," Marisol said. "So…what does that mean?"

Erin had been thinking about that, too.

"It means," she said, "we're going to have to — carefully — find something solid on Lennox. Something that clearly shows he's purposefully endangering the health of Ghanaians."

Marisol nodded but didn't say anything.

"I'm going to have to do this under the radar, too, Marisol," Erin said. "I don't think I'm ready to bring Paul in yet. Or anyone else at SERA."

"We," Marisol said.

Erin looked at her.

"*We* are going to have to do this under the radar," Marisol said.

"Okay."

"Good. Because I know exactly where to start."

"You do?" Erin said.

"Yep," Marisol said. "The lab."

29

THE PLAN

THE SUN HAD SET, AND LARGE DROPS WERE BEGINNING to splatter their windshield. Erin reached up and closed the sunroof.

"All the data we get from Lennox and Keeler comes from their lab. It's close to us. Well, actually, *we're* close to *it*," Marisol said. "It's one of the main reasons we picked that location."

"What do they do there?"

"The best way to think of it is like a chain. Both us — SERA — and Lennox can collect raw material, like soil or water samples. But our ability to process them at the raw-material level is pretty limited. We can do some basic comparative tests. But when we need to do anything else, which is most of what we do, we don't have the tools, and so we have to go through them.

"They help us," Marisol continued, "by turning raw material into data that can be analyzed. Once it's ones and zeros, we can do our work."

"Which include projections and reports," Erin said.

"Right. Once we've got the data, Gavin can compare it to

the datasets we get from the WHO and the CDC. They give us access to databases for that reason. Then we make models and predictions, and Paul and Ben work with local governments to help them to help curb outbreaks and health issues."

"So…does Lennox run this lab?"

"Yeah, as far as I know he does. That guy, Keeler, works with him. But he's more like hired muscle. Not really the 'science' type."

"How long has SERA worked with Lennox?"

"For as long as I've been here. SERA hasn't been in this location for too long. SERA has other units and offices in other parts of West Africa, too. In fact, there's a regional office in Accra, which is one of the reasons our field team is so light."

Erin thought about this for a while.

It was dark outside now. The two had stopped talking, and the rain outside was falling steadily now.

"Marisol," Erin said, "how did you ever get connected with Paul?"

"That," she said with a smile, "is a long story. But I think we've got other, more pressing things to talk about. Like how we're going to actually get something we can use from Lennox's lab…"

That question had also been rattling around in Erin's mind, too. Anything illegal would be, well, *illegal*. And considering the stakes, that wasn't an option. No, it would have to be some—

"I've got an idea," Marisol said.

"Yeah?"

"We're going to need a camera. And…" Marisol looked at her, "how good are you at climbing?"

30

LEE JUN

Lee Jun sat at his desk, reviewing a series of charts that had just come over the fax. He was presently trying to fill in the gap where the transmission had left a gap.

Why are we still using faxes…

Jun was the regional director for SERA, and his office, which was comprised of *just* his office, was located in Accra.

The phone on his desk rang. It was one of those older styles that had an actual bell in it and a curly cord attached to the receiver. The color was "aqua mist," a green color the rest of the world hadn't seen since the seventies. He'd worked all over the world, and wherever he went, he brought it with him. *It was the little things…*, he thought.

He picked up the receiver.

"Jun," he said, still trying to make sense of the wavy fax report in front of him.

"Lee," the other end said, "it's Paul."

Paul Dannon, SERA's country director. Paul and Jun went way back. They were in the service together when they were young. And after that, they managed to stay in touch over the years. In fact, it was Jun that recruited Paul, after he'd sold his medical procurement business. Jun convinced him to come work for SERA.

"Listen…," Paul said, "there's been a development over here, and—"

"Everything okay?" Jun asked.

"Yeah, yeah," Paul said, "nothing urgent."

"But?"

"But," he seemed to be hesitating. "Lee," he said, "I don't like the direction this thing is going."

"You're talking about the loggers who died?"

"Just some things about it not adding up."

"You're thinking there's going to be an outbreak after all?"

Paul was not the kind of man to think out loud. Jun looked out the window, it was dark, and all he could see was his own reflection. He looked down at his watch. This wasn't what he'd—

"I'm going to be in Accra tomorrow," Paul said, "in the morning."

"You're…what?" Jun said.

"Best we talk in person. Not over the phone."

"Okay…right," Jun said, "tomorrow…I can…"

"Lee, everything all right?"

Is everything all right… Everything hadn't been alright for a long time, he thought. And he was afraid Paul was now… wanting to come in and talk. He'd need to find out what he knew. And, he continued to think through the situation, maybe he could just get him out of the way for a while. Let this whole thing blow. That might work…

"…you at ten, then," Paul was saying.

"Uh, yeah…," Jun said, "tomorrow, you said? Yes… that'll…that works."

Jun put the receiver back on its cradle. His elbows were

on his desk. His fingers massaged his temples. "Paul…Paul," he said, letting out a long sigh, "you're forcing my hand, my friend. I hope you can see that…"

31

WISE MEN SAY

THE RAIN FROM LAST NIGHT WAS GONE NOW. BUT THE ground still squished under Ben's boots as he made his rounds — a ritual he'd had for longer than he could remember.

There was nothing in particular to check on. He walked well outside the bounds of the camp, up and down the faint path the trucks drove out to the road. For Ben, walking was a way to start his day fresh.

He felt drops as he walked under the branch of a tree. He could hear small mammals moving somewhere above him, causing some of last night's rain to sprinkle down on him. The birds, Ben noticed, were especially loud the morning after a heavy rain.

Ben grew up all over Britain. His parents moved to the Welch countryside when he was a teenager. But before that they'd lived in Bath, then Salisbury, and, when he was still too small to remember, a flat in London. He discovered running as a solitary discipline that he could do no matter where he lived. But over time the running turned into walking. Which is where he found himself as he saw Paul's Land Rover driving out of camp.

As he made his way back down the dirt road to the camp, he watched the truck dip slowly down and then up again, following the lumps in the path that led out to the road. Paul slid his window down as he pulled up next to Ben. He slowed. "Heading down to Accra for the day," he said, without stopping. "Be back tonight."

Ben raised his coffee in response, making his way back to camp.

Once back, it was still quiet. The sun was just starting to tip above the girls' sleeping trailer now as the door opened. Marisol walked out.

"Morning Ben," she said, he noticed, with a bit more energy than usual.

He raised his coffee again, without words.

She walked to the supply trailer, then back into her own.

Ben sat in one of the fold-up chairs, finishing his coffee.

Next, Erin walked out.

He tried to catch her eye, to say good morning…but she didn't slow down. She, too, went straight to the supply trailer.

Ben stood up, then sat back down.

She walked back by and back to her trailer.

Ben got up and poured himself another cup of coffee. He propped his feet up on the portable table they left outside each night.

Erin came out of the trailer and walked up to him.

He pulled his feet down, looking at her directly now. "Um, hey, good morning," he said.

She looked at him, for the first time, he realized. She had actually walked to the coffee maker *next* to him.

"Morning," she said, in a disappointingly neutral voice, as she filled a tall insulated mug.

"So...," Ben said.

But she had already turned and was heading back to her trailer.

"Sorry?" she said, turning back to him.

"Oh," he said. "Nothing...I mean..."

She looked at him for a moment longer.

"...how's it going?" He said, lamely.

"Good...it's going good," she said with an amused smirk. "I'm going to...," she said, motioning back to her trailer, where she'd been heading before he'd stopped her.

"Yep, right," he said, "very good."

She continued to smile at him before turning to leave.

'Very good'...?

He closed his eyes, trying to think about ways it could have possibly gone just a little bit worse. A sadistic kind of comfor—

"Oh, Ben," she said, turning back to him again.

"Uh, yes," he said, opening his eyes, almost standing as he said it. "Um," he cleared his throat, "Yes," he said again.

She scrunched her brows as she looked at him. "Do you have a camera? One I can borrow."

"Uh, of course, what do you need? I mean, I've got all of my gear here."

"Just, something small," she said.

"Small? What are you planning to shoot?"

"Um...," she hesitated, glancing away as she said it, "I just need something I can fit in my pocket."

Kwami walked out of his trailer. He walked over to the coffee maker. He sat down, drinking his coffee. "Good morning," he smiled.

"Good morning," Erin smiled back at him.

A flash of jealousy washed over him, and he immediately pushed it away. It was not *that* kind of jealousy, as if she was interested in Kwami. Just...he wished she would...

Marisol walked out of her trailer again.

"Okay," Ben said to Erin. "I've got something you can use."

Marisol sat behind Ben, taking his chair and leaned over to tie her boots.

"Hang on a second," he said and walked back to his trailer. Inside, Gavin was still sleeping. Ben glanced at him as he slipped over to his side and started slowly looking into one of his bags. "Where…is…it…," he said under his breath as he moved things in Gavin's bag aside.

Gavin turned over, and Ben froze, his hands still in Gavin's bag.

He looked at Gavin, still asleep, and continued to search. And then, on the counter behind a pair of pants, he saw it. Gavin's small black point and shoot. "One for the team, mate," he whispered as he grabbed it and walked back outside.

As he walked to Erin, Marisol came up to him.

"Ben," she said.

"Yeah?"

"We're going to need the Land Rover."

He glanced to his old yellow truck. He didn't actually need it today. And he could use Kwami's pickup if he needed to go somewhere. But…

"You know, I could go with—" Ben started, pulling the keys out of his pocket.

"Nope," Marisol said, "we're good," taking the keys from him.

"Are you…"

"Yep," she said, walking over to it, with a daypack slung over her shoulder.

Erin walked up to him, and he remembered the camera.

"Oh," he said, "here you go," and handed it to her.

"Thanks, Ben," she said.

"Oh, uh, yeah," he said, "no problem."

Marisol was glaring at him from his truck. "Bye, Ben," she said a bit louder than she needed to.

Erin turned and walked to the Land Rover to get in.

"I could…," Ben called out after them, "drive you, or something, if you need…directions."

The two were already in the truck, starting up the engine.

"A wise man," Kwami said next to him, propping his boots up on the fold-up table, "once said, some things… cannot be forced."

Ben looked at Kwami.

"A wise man?" he said, watching the Land Rover drive away. "What wise man?"

"Me," Kwami smiled, lifting his coffee cup to him.

BERGORA

MARISOL TURNED OUT ONTO THE MAIN ROAD, followed it north before turning off onto a smaller highway. They traveled for a while, seeing nothing but red dirt and jungle on either side and a long stretch of winding road ahead. After about thirty minutes on this road, they began to see low mountains on the horizon. A minute later, they saw the signs of a city.

"This is Bergora," Marisol said. "This is where we need to start.

Bergora was a regional hub for the western Lake Volta region. It wasn't as influential as a place like Accra was, a port city with an international airport. Bergora wasn't even a regional capital. That was Kumasi, farther north.

But Bergora was full of local connections. The kind who knew things about the goings-on that needed to fly under the radar. In other words, it had people like Mandrell, the owner of the popular bar and grill by the same name. If someone in the area needed something extra, a special kind of help, they went to Mandrell's. And, for a price, Mandrell found a way to make it happen.

Marisol pulled the Land Rover into the bar and grill. She clicked her seatbelt but didn't open her door.

"There's a rumor I heard when I first got here," she said to Erin. "About Jonah Lennox's lab—which isn't too far from here. People would say locals went there to work, or went there for some other reason — it was always a little different, depending on who was telling the story. They'd go in…but they wouldn't come out."

She looked over at Erin. "It was all boogie-man stuff. And Paul never seemed to pay it much mind. But…," she shrugged.

"But," Erin said, "that might work. If we can at least give the Ministry of Health a reason to pump the breaks, it might be enough to stall things while we gather something more substantial."

"This place," Marisol pointed through the windshield, "is basically like the town's hub for gossip. If something's happening, Mandrell will know about it."

They got out and went inside.

Stepping inside was a bizarre mixture of classic Americana and tribal Ghana. Large colored tapestries and rugs hung on the walls, proudly showing Africa's red, yellow, and green. They were mixed with various black and white pictures of people like Humphrey Bogart and Ava Gardner.

"Marisol," called a booming, kind voice from behind the counter in the middle of the large room.

"That's Mandrell," Marisol said to Erin.

"It's been too long," he said to her.

The two of them walked over to the bar.

"Mandrell, this is my friend, Erin."

"Erin," he said, "it is a pleasure to meet you. But," he looked back to Marisol, "I'm afraid you've caught us a bit early. We're just opening."

"Oh, we're not here to eat," Marisol said. "We just need some information."

To the point. Mandrell acted like many other Ghanaians on the surface, but underneath, Marisol knew he was much more straightforward. She was good at sizing people up, finding out why they wanted what they wanted. And Mandrell wanted to be in the know more than he cared about what was right and wrong socially.

They stood at the bar. He leaned in from the other side.

"What are you looking for?"

"The lab," she said.

"Rumors…," he said, motioning with his hand and turning away.

"I've heard the rumors, too," she said quickly. "But I've also heard…," she trailed off, purposely, not taking her eyes off his.

"You've heard, what?" he said, feigning non-interest. "And from who?" he said.

"I've…got my sources," she said.

Mandrell looked from Marisol to Erin, and then back to Marisol again.

"Some things," he said, "are better left alone."

"What do you mean?"

"You are not from here."

"People are disappearing…"

"People always disappear. Besides, what do you care?" he said, his voice beginning to betray hints of anger at her questioning.

Marisol felt his anger was a sign she was getting somewhere. She didn't respond, letting his last comment linger.

"Listen," he said, his tone softer now. "You're right…"

She looked at him.

He looked over his shoulder, back to the kitchen behind him. "Give me a minute," he said.

He walked to the back, through a door into the kitchen.
Marisol turned smiling and looked at Erin.
"That was good?" Erin said.
"Good indeed. Watch."

●33

MANDRELL

MANDRELL SHUT THE DOOR OF THE SUPPLY ROOM behind him and pulled out a pay-as-you-go phone. He pushed the button for his contacts and selected the only one there. He held it to his ear as it rang.

"Go," came the answer on the other side.

"It's Mandrell."

"I know. What do you have for me?"

"Some of…" He looked over his shoulder at the closed door behind him. "Some of the ones you told me are here."

"Who," he said, not a question.

"Two women. The Americans who are doing the research. One I recognize. Her name is Marisol. But I've never seen the other one before."

There was silence on the other end.

"What do you want me to do?"

"Keep them there."

"For how long?" Mandrell said, starting to walk back and forth in the small room.

"Until I get there."

"I…don't know how long I can…," Mandrell said.

The voice on the phone was silent. Mandrell stopped walking and listened. "How long do—" he started.

"No…" said the man, interrupting him. "On second thought, don't delay them," he said. "Send them on to the lab."

"The lab?" Mandrell repeated. "You want me to send them *to* the lab?"

"Yes. And give them a good reason. A reason they can't resist."

"You mean…"

"That's right. Tell them what we're doing there."

"Are you telling me to tell them the lab has taken people," Mandrell said, "that the rumors people are circulating are true?"

"Exactly."

"But what if…"

"It won't," he said sharply. "They won't."

Mandrell thought about those words as they lingered.

"I'm on my way now. And I'll handle them. But I want them to go to the lab as soon as possible. Understood?"

"I…"

"You'll be paid," the man said.

"Well…," Mandrell said, trying to navigate the important bits carefully.

"And," continued the man, "our arrangement will stay in place."

Now it was Mandrell's time to be silent. He was pacing the small storage room again.

The arrangement. That was what they called the process of Mandrell being the lab's pipeline for sending people their way. And in return, the lab protected him. Kept suspicions away. Law enforcement away. Up until now, though, there hadn't been anyone high-profile. It had all been locals the lab had used for testing and experiments. People other people wouldn't miss.

"Are we clear?" the man said. "And Mandrell… don't get greedy. That *won't* pay."

It was the thinnest of threats, and Mandrell knew it.

"Okay," Mandrell said. He wiped his hand over his face. Breathed in deeply. "Okay, I will do it," he said.

"Good," said the man, and the line went dead.

34

THE TRUCK

Erin watched a moment later as Mandrell walked back out.

"What was that about?" Erin said to Marisol under her breath.

"Not sure," Marisol said, keeping her eyes on Mandrell.

Mandrell kept his distance but motioned for them to meet him at the far end of the room. As they began walking, he stopped. "Just you," he said, pointing to Marisol.

She looked at Erin. "I'll be back."

Erin stayed at the bar but made no effort to hide the fact that she was watching them. From her distance, she couldn't hear what they were talking about. Marisol's back was to her. But once or twice she saw Mandrell's eyes dart in her direction.

Whatever he did when he left, Erin thought, he seemed different now. Edgier… She couldn't place it, but something seemed off.

After a moment more, Marisol turned and motioned her over.

Mandrell went to sit in a booth in a far corner of the

room.

Erin walked up to Marisol. "He wanted to make sure you were okay," she told her.

Erin and Marisol walked over to the booth Mandrell was sitting in and sat across from him.

Mandrell looked at them but didn't say anything.

"Okay, Mandrell," Marisol said, leaning in. "What do you have?"

He looked down at his hands and then back up at the two of them.

"The stories," he said, "aren't *all* rumors."

"Which stories," Erin said.

"About people, locals, going to the lab and then disappearing," he said, twirling his hand. "The lab is new and expensive looking. People around here have never seen anything like that. And so…the stories started."

"And," he continued, "I didn't believe any of them myself. Just local gossip. But then, I heard a few more stories…stories that sounded more credible."

He paused for a moment, and looked through the corner of the curtain covering the window next to their booth.

"And then, something else happened. Keeler," he said, looking up at Marisol.

"Keeler," she said.

"Yes, he…," Mandrell was rubbing one hand over the other like he was washing them, but without water. "He approached me," he said.

"For what?" Erin said.

Mandrell let out a sigh.

"They have a truck," he said. "It goes around and picks up people who don't have work. They tell them they need good workers for some-such-thing at the lab. Work. Everyone wants work. So it's not hard to sell. The truck mostly stays out of sight. And it's not always the same truck, so…," he trailed off. "But they use it to pick up workers. And then they take them to the lab."

"And…?" Marisol said.

"And they do what they do with them there. I…honestly don't know what happens," he said. "But I know almost none of them leave."

"So what, they kill them?" Marisol said.

"I…I, don't know," he said.

He looked out the crack in the window shade again. Using his finger to pull it slightly.

"So," Erin said, "how are *you* involved in this? What did Keeler want you to do for him?"

He looked up at her, as if the answer was obvious.

"I'm the person people come to…," he said. "When people want to know the truth, they come to me. That's why you're here. People come to me, and I tell them, 'the lab's good, those are rumors,' or 'they gave that person another job down in Accra, he's making more money there.' That kind of stuff."

As Mandrell was talking, Erin was watching him carefully. What he was saying now would explain the change in behavior. He was essentially confessing to human trafficking. But…something else was gnawing at her, something else she was still missing…

"So you're saying, the lab has this truck — or several trucks — that go around picking up people who need a job. They take them to the lab and do…whatever they do to them…and nobody ever sees them again."

"For most, yes," he said, nodding.

"How often does the truck go around looking for people?" Erin said.

Mandrell looked up, thinking. "Few times a week, maybe a few times a day. Hard to tell."

"Thanks, Mandrell," Erin said, "for doing this, for telling

us this."

He didn't respond, or look at them.

Erin and Marisol walked outside and got into the Land Rover. Marisol turned it on. The hot morning air inside was stuffy, and they rolled down their windows.

"Why do you think he told us all that stuff?" Erin said.

"Guilt," Marisol said.

"You don't think guilt would have gotten to him before now?"

"The thing with Mandrell is that there's always an angle. It's not simple. This is his way of doing something about it," she said.

"Maybe…," Erin said.

"Either way, we've got a pretty good lead," Marisol said. "The lab's not far from here. We can go there, hide, wait for one of these trucks to show up, and then if we get pictures of them, we catch them in the act."

"But that doesn't prove they're doing anything wrong," Erin said.

"But it will prove the story about the truck is true."

"And…," Erin said, finishing the thought, "that could be the basis for testimonies…plus, if those same people never show up again, we can—"

"Right," Marisol said.

Marisol backed the Land Rover out, and they left Mandrell's. She parked it behind a building in a lot on the edge of Bergora.

"The lab's not far, but we should probably walk," Marisol said, "there won't be anywhere to hide it once we get there."

The two got out, leaving the truck, and began walking toward the lab.

35

SETUP

Paul had been sitting in his Land Rover for about two hours. He was currently — he looked down at his watch — an hour and thirty minutes late for his morning appointment.

You spend enough time in places like this, and you get used to people showing up late. Or early. What a lot of Westerners don't realize is that these things are just cultural. Some places, like America, ten o'clock means ten o'clock. But in other places, ten o'clock means more like mid-morning. And this was one of those places. But Paul and Lee Jun were both Westerners. And that meant something. Paul was actually a little surprised he hadn't received a call from him yet.

From where he was parked, a couple hundred yards down the road, he had a clear view of the front door of Jun's office. He also had a view of the alley out back, where the building's rear door emptied. If someone came in or went out, he'd be able to see them.

And, a few minutes later, he saw what he was waiting for. Two men, both in fatigues, walked up to the building and entered the front door. One had a rifle slung over his shoulder. The other, a handgun, holstered. Police.

A moment later, he saw them both walk out the back. That was it.

He pulled out his phone, not taking his eyes off of the building, and dialed a number.

"Hey, boss," came the answer.

"I'm going to need you down here."

"You in Accra?"

"Yeah. How soon can you get here?"

"Er," the man on the other end made a few noises, "couple hours," he said.

"Good."

"Everything…alright?" the man said.

"Get here as soon as you can."

"Got it," the man said. "Oh…and…," he added.

"Yeah?"

"Need me to bring anything, or…anyone?" he said.

Paul thought for a moment.

"No, not yet, just get here as soon as you can."

Paul hung up the phone and continued to watch. The police were gone. But they'd be back.

For him.

36

STAKEOUT

"There it is," Marisol said to Erin, handing her a small pair of binoculars. "That's the main entrance," she pointed.

Erin and Marisol sat on a branch, easily six feet wide, in a massive cotton silk tree. The tree's roots snaked out from the ground, as if some giant had started pulling it out and stopped halfway through. The tree was larger than any rooted thing Erin had ever seen. But climbing it had been easy, thanks to its network of roots and large spidering limbs so close to the ground. From a distance, it looked more like an explosion of branches than a tree. Erin and Marisol were just two dots hidden, high up.

They were now watching Jonah Lennox's lab. The front door Marisol had pointed out was a small nondescript door on a mostly nondescript white building. And if the building wasn't currently sitting in the middle of the jungle, there would be nothing unusual about it at all.

Erin pulled out the camera she'd borrowed from Ben, zoomed the lens and took a picture of the front door.

Marisol reached into the bag she'd brought, handed Erin a water, and pulled out a gray pouch.

"I'm *so* hungry," Marisol said.

"What's that?" Erin said, looking at the gray pouch.

"MRE. It's kind of like Jetsons' food. Just add water and it turns into stuff you can eat. Ever had one?"

"Uh, no. What's in it?" Erin said.

"It's," she dumped the bag's contents into her lap, "mostly…er…I'm not sure. But," she said, "they're filling. And they last four or five years, so we tend to keep them around for when we're out in the field," she said. "Want one?"

Erin began to notice how hungry she was.

"Sure," she said. Erin took one and opened it. She looked at the instructions on the bag and added the water. The bag started to hiss.

"Is that normal?" she said.

"Yeah, and it gets hot, too," Marisol said. "Chemical reaction. Warms it up for you."

After the bag cooled down, Erin used the plastic utensils that came with it and started eating.

"So…," Marisol said, still eating her MRE, "what's up with you and Ben?"

"Ben?" Erin said. "There's nothing going—"

"Come on," Marisol said, putting her plastic fork down. "Don't tell me you haven't noticed?"

"Well…I did…," Erin said, looking away.

That does explain some things, she thought. Like how awkward most of their conversations had been. She'd had so many other things on her mind, so many *big* things, that she hadn't stopped to even process the weird signals she'd been getting from Ben. And, honestly, she wasn't even sure what her own thoughts about that were—

Marisol slapped her on the arm and pointed down to the road below them.

"Look," she said.

Through the leaves, they could see a dark vehicle moving at speed, down the road, heading toward the lab.

37

THE MAN ON THE FERRY

MOFI STOOD, LOOKING OVER THE RAIL OF THE FERRY, staring down into the white water crashing into the boat's bow several feet below him. The wind was strong against his face. As he looked up, he could see the mountains surrounding the lake.

Lake Volta was long. The result of a flooded river, its length covered nearly half the length of the entire country. This was the second time he'd crossed the lake, though at different points, on the mission Tano had sent him, looking for Paul. And…he was beginning to feel like he was chasing a ghost. Everywhere he'd been, they knew Paul…but he hadn't been there recently…or he's just missed him, a few months back…

The waves and spray were becoming hypnotic. Leaning on the edge of the ferry, he thought again about the look on Tano's face the last time he saw him. The urgency, almost panic in his voice. The image of Tano like that kept replaying in his mind. He'd never seen him like that. All of his life, Tano had been a strong elder in their community, one the rest of them looked up to…

Mofi turned from the edge and moved back across to the other side of the ferry. The lower deck where he now stood was filled with cars. Above, the ferry was filled with people. Several floors. The ride wasn't too long, maybe an hour. And if he didn't buy any food, which he couldn't afford at the price they sold it for on the boat, he could ride for free. Until it docked on the other side, he didn't have anything to do. He walked to ease the anxious feeling. The feeling that kept mounting the longer it took him to find Paul.

As he walked to the other side, moving through the crowds down on the lower level, something caught his eye, between two large trucks. He paused, looking at the spot. An eerie feeling struck him.

The boat rocked, and it was hard to get a clear look. Mofi moved closer, in between the two large trucks.

As he did, he saw it again. Or he thought he did. The same movement, now, again…still. He paused, looking hard in between the large trucks, both under the overhang from the upper floors. He focused his energy on letting his eyes adjust to the darker area. Trying to see.

Was it…the same man? He wondered. The thought, the implications, scared him, though he wasn't exactly sure why.

Mofi moved around the outside of two trucks, between them and the wall of the ferry. Edging along. He slipped around, seeing no one.

Then, over his head, moving up the stairs to an upper floor, he caught the briefest glimpse of a red-checked shirt.

The man from the Nkonya market. The same one he'd also seen the day before. And the same one who stood out… not belonging. *What was he doing here?* he thought.

This was…wrong. Mofi knew something was wrong.

He looked over his shoulder and then back toward the dark stairs, where the man in the red-checked shirt had gone.

Since he started, Mofi had been traveling fast. Looking

for the man, Paul. And not staying anywhere longer than necessary. And his path, as he thought back to his route, made no sense unless you were looking for someone…it wasn't the path another would just happen to take. And so, he thought, to see this same man, several times in the last few days was…he didn't know what it meant, but he had a distinct feeling it wasn't good.

Mofi looked again toward the front of the boat. The shore was closer, he could see it clearer now. He glanced once more into the dark stairwell, before carefully following the inside edge of the boat as close as he could to the front, the exit point. He walked along a route that if anyone were looking down from an upper floor, he'd be hidden from view.

He stayed there, along the edge, waiting for the boat to get close enough to dock. He'd wait, he decided, until everyone exited at the same time, and then he'd blend in with the rest of them.

He leaned against the wall, under cover, and waited.

38

LAB SECURITY

Keeler walked into the control room. In front of him, a large bank of monitors covered the wall.

His security team rotated every hour between watching cameras and walking the facility. The every-hour rotation was for the benefit of those watching the cameras, to keep them from getting bored and forgetting to pay attention.

Like what was happening now.

"Punch in there," Keeler said into the silent room.

The man in the seat in front of him jerked, and he immediately looked up at the screens he was supposed to be monitoring. He clearly hadn't heard Keeler walk in. The Bates GTX boots Keeler wore were known for that. Another reason he liked them.

"Yes…yes, sir," he said, putting his hands quickly on the controls and moving the camera Keeler had pointed to.

"There…," Keeler pointed to a monitor in the upper right bank. "Pull that view and put it on the big screen."

"Yes, sir." He clicked his keyboard in front of him.

The small image moved to the large central screen.

"Zoom," Keeler said. "Stop."

As the man zoomed, Keeler saw what he already knew was there.

"Sir," the man began, looking up at Keeler and immediately diverting his eyes, "I…don't know how they—"

"Shhh," Keeler hissed quietly.

The man turned back around, looking at the screen, and stayed still.

"How long have they been there?"

"I…I don't know, sir," he admitted.

"Play back the recording," Keeler said, in a voice one generally reserves for stupid animals.

"Yes, right, sir," he said, his hands jumping back to the keyboard. The screen flicked as he rewound the video in five-minute bursts.

"There," Keeler said, "stop." He glanced at the timestamp on the screen and looked down at his watch. "Now, play back from there, in 2x time."

The man clicked again. The screen adjusted and started playing.

Keeler stood towering over the man as he looked at the monitor. His six-foot-five, two-fifty-five frame would have towered over him even if the man were standing. Keeler folded his arms as he watched.

"Should I…," the man said quietly, "sound the alarm…sir?"

"No," Keeler said slowly. "I have something else in mind."

INSIDE

The light above the keypad turned from red to green, and the lock on the door clicked.

Keeler pulled the door open and extending an arm the size of a small tree. It was the kind of hospitality that wasn't meant to take care.

Erin and Marisol walked inside, not making eye contact with each other. Erin felt like they were being escorted to the principal's office. She wished it was the principal's office.

"Follow me," he said, walking down an interior hall.

They followed him. Of course, they *had* to follow him, because his girth almost filled the hall.

They walked past doors and some windows, looking into rooms as they did.

"This," he said, "is our facility where we analyze data we collect. And I believe, you, Miss Galli," he said, turning to look at Marisol, "have been here before."

"Uh-huh," she said, not meeting his eye.

They kept walking.

"We saw you out there," he said, "on our cameras."

Cameras, Erin thought. *Of course* there would be cameras. Her inner voice began chiding her for the carelessness. Of course a group this funded would have cameras…

"And we thought," Keeler continued, "why don't we help them out." He turned and gave them a hungry smile. "Why don't we just show them whatever it is they want to see?" he said.

His strides, as he walked down the hall, were so long, it forced Erin and Marisol to walk briskly to keep up.

"By the way," he said, looking forward, "how were the MREs? I never liked them too much, myself."

Neither of them answered. All three kept walking. An employee in a white lab coat, coming from the opposite direction, moved to the side, as Keeler didn't bother to move out of the way.

He took them to the back of the facility and opened up a door to a small warehouse, with a loading dock opening out into the back.

"And this," he said, opening a door into a warehouse area, "is where the truck…," he let the word linger, looking at them as he said it, "loads and unloads."

The stupid, smug grin seemed to be permanently stuck to his face now. This was all just a game. He'd won. And now he was proving it.

Erin felt the heat in her own face. The truck…Mandrell, she thought. He was setting them up.

"We do a lot of," Keeler paused, as if searching for the right word, "*different* kinds of business. And so having the right kinds of…*relationships*," he said, "is critical."

Keeler walked them past the loading dock to another door. He opened it. It led to the outside.

"Out," he said, not smiling.

The two of them walked out, still not looking at each

other. They walked silently back down the long road to where they'd parked the Land Rover. And as they walked, the implications of what had just happened, of their nonexistent upper hand, began to fester.

IT'S READY

Kwami pulled up in his old pickup and parked next to Paul. Gavin sat in the passenger seat next to Kwami.

Paul glanced at them, nodded without saying anything, and resumed staring at the building he'd been watching since he'd called Kwami.

Both vehicles sat parked with their windows down.

"What's it looking like?" Kwami said, looking at the building Paul was looking at.

"About what I expected," Paul said.

"So…you're sure then?"

"Yeah."

They were silent as they all continued to watch the building.

"How long has this been going on?" Kwami said.

That was a good question. Paul and Lee Jun went way back. For most of the time, Paul would bet, Jun was on the straight and narrow. Or, at least, he wasn't actively trying to screw Paul. And there was a time when Lee would have actually risked his own reputation, and maybe his life, for Paul. But that was a long time ago. And a lot had changed since then. Jun, for one, had become political. He'd made allies. And those allies, it turned out, were not Paul's allies.

"I don't know," Paul said. "And, at this point…it doesn't really matter."

"I'm going now," he said, reaching down to turn the ignition in the Land Rover. Its engine hummed to life. "Keep a good distance," he said, looking over at Kwami, "Okay?"

Kwami looked at him and nodded once.

Paul put the truck in drive and pulled out into the street, driving the several hundred feet to the SERA regional office he'd been casing for the last few hours. To where Lee Jun was waiting for him.

He parked out front and walked inside.

BAD NEWS

The mood back at the SERA base camp was sour. Marisol's temper had not cooled. If anything, the long, silent walk back to the Land Rover had only fueled it. She kicked over the fold-up table as she walked by, heading for her trailer. The door didn't immediately open, so she kicked it, too, and walked in.

Erin sat down in one of the folding chairs and went back over it all. The bridge was down. No denying it. She needed another way around. Another way to get something on Lennox, some thread she could pull — something that would push him out from the careful hole he was hiding in. Something, she thought, that would force his hand, and cause him to slip up, make a mistake. And, up to this point, she didn't even have any ideas.

She swore under her breath.

The phone in her bag rang. She reached down, fished it out, and answered it.

It was Waz. "Miss Reed," he said.

"Waz," she said, still distracted with her thoughts, "what's up?"

"I'm afraid," he said, "we will not be able to work together."

She stood up.

"What do you mean?" she said.

"The Minister," he said, "is no longer willing to pursue this case against Mr. Lennox."

"Wait," she said, "what do you mean, what did Lennox say to you?"

"I am sorry," he said, "that is all I can tell you."

The line was dead. She held the phone in her hand, looking at it.

Closing her eyes, she swore under her breath again.

"Bad day?"

She turned, thinking she was still alone. It was Ben.

"I…overheard some of your swearing," he said, sitting down in one of the chairs.

"Oh, yeah," she said, running a hand through her hair. "Bad day."

She sat back down in her chair, still holding the phone in her hand.

The two of them sat there for a while.

She thought about Carl, back in D.C., and Conall at *The Post*. The critical voice her head began talking again. Began telling her—

"Don't think on it," he said.

She looked at him and started to say something back when the phone in her hand rang again. This time it was Carl. Could he have…she wondered. She pushed the button and held it up to her ear.

"Carl," she said.

"Erin…," he said. He sounded like he was— "Erin, I just got a call from Jonah Lennox."

"You're kidding me," she said.

"What's going on over there?"

"Carl—"

"He says you've been working with the government to hold him up."

"I…"

"Erin, that's the exact *opposite* of what I need you there doing," he said with controlled anger, like he was talking to a child.

"Carl, you need to listen to me right now," she said, bracing for his response. But none came. The line was silent.

"Okay," he said, "what."

His response caught her off guard.

"There's something…," she said, "not right here."

Still no response.

"I don't have any proof yet," she said slow and measured, "but…but things are not adding up here."

"Erin," he said in that condescending voice, she could feel her anger rising. She pulled the phone away from her ear, looking away, hearing his tiny voice still coming out.

Marisol walked out of her trailer and around the back.

She held the phone back up to her ear.

"…this really puts me…," she heard him saying, before pulling it away again.

She was purposefully not listening, purposefully trying to keep herself calm. And then she heard something strange. A lawnmower. No, a motorcycle. From behind the trailer, a motorcycle sped off. It was Marisol taking the spare motorcycle…where was she going?

She couldn't hear Ibsen's voice anymore, and she held the phone back to her ear, hearing him say, "…are you still there?"

"Yes," she said, "I'm still here, Carl."

"Good, because this is a delicate situation, one we need to—"

"Carl," she interrupted him, "something's come up. I need to go."

She hung up the phone and sat back down. She looked down in her lap, looked at the phone, and tossed it down into her bag, sick of it being close to her.

"More swearing helps," Ben, still next to her, said. "I mean…I've found."

She looked at him.

She slumped over in her chair, rubbing her eyes.

"What am I missing?" she said.

She sat back up, "where did Marisol go on the motorcycle?"

"Beats me," Ben said.

She was quiet again, thinking. "And what about Paul… where is he?"

"Took off," Ben said, "had something down in Accra. Didn't say what."

Erin stood up and began to pace, but it was short-lived, because at that moment, both of them noticed something quite unusual. Or, rather, *someone*.

And he were running into their camp.

MOFI

ERIN AND BEN WATCHED THE MAN RUN TOWARD THEM.

As he reached them, he bent double to catch his breath.

The two of them looked at each other.

"You okay, mate?" Ben said.

"I need…," he said, with heaving breathes, "…I need to find Paul."

"Paul?" Ben said. "Afraid you've missed him."

The man looked up at both of them.

"But he's…," he started again. He was shaking his head, looking around.

"He'll be back later tonight. Why don't you have a seat," Ben said, motioning to another chair next to him. "Is there something we can do for you?"

In the years Ben had been doing humanitarian aid work, this kind of thing wasn't terribly unusual. People in difficult places will go to great lengths. Once, in Haiti, after the big earthquake, a woman tried to give him her toddler, to take the child back home with him. That kind of thing throws you at first. But after a while, you begin to expect it. Desperate people do desperate things.

"No, there…," the man said, still standing, still looking around, "I think some…" He was talking in frantic bursts that Ben wasn't following. And, judging by the look on her face, Erin wasn't either.

"What's your name?" Erin said, speaking for the first time.

He looked at her, "Mofi," he said.

"Hi Mofi," she said, "I'm Erin, and this," she motioned, "is Ben."

Ben watched this man, Mofi, as Erin was talking to him. Something about him seemed to be calming down, if only a little.

"Why don't you tell us what's wrong," she said.

Mofi nodded, looking at her. Whatever had him riled up a minute ago was beginning to melt, at least a little.

"I know something," he said, "and I must tell Paul. It's important."

"You're at the right place, we work with Paul," Ben said.

"How do you know Paul?" Erin said.

"It's my uncle," Mofi said. "He sent me to find Paul, to tell him what was happening at the lake."

She nodded once, giving him space to keep talking.

He began telling her about the day he heard the noises, the gunshots, and the last day he saw his uncle. And then he told her about the instruction his uncle, Tano, gave him, to find Paul and—

"Wait," Ben interrupted. "Tano?"

"Yes," he said, looking at Ben now.

"Tano from *where*?" Ben said.

"He is from the Jasikan district…"

"Jasikan," Ben repeated to himself.

"He and Paul are brothers," Mofi said.

"Paul did some work years back in a village in the Jasikan district," Ben said. "He's told me about it because there were some government permit issues that came up recently, and…"

"Yes," Mofi said, "with my uncle, Tano."

"Mofi," Erin said, drawing his attention back to her. "What is it you need to tell Paul?"

"Tano sent me, to him, they killed the men at the lake."

"Who are 'they'?" Erin said.

He shook his head, "I don't know. I'd only just started working there. All I knew was they were cutting the trees from under Lake Volta. I helped them, stripping the trees once they were—

"Wait," Erin said, her tone changing. "Are you talking about the twelve loggers that died at Lake Volta?"

"Yes, that's what I'm saying," he said, but now looked confused. "How did you…"

Erin looked at Ben and then back to Mofi.

"Mofi," she said in a voice that sounded like she was choosing her words carefully, "can you tell us exactly what happened?"

He looked down again.

"I don't really know. I was outside, with Tano, when we heard the guns. Tano went to look and came back and told me. And then…"

"Can we talk to Tano?" Erin said.

Mofi was quiet and wouldn't meet their eyes.

After a moment, he looked up again. "I don't know… I have a feeling in me that he…" He was having trouble finishing his thought. And Ben could see him getting anxious again.

"It's okay," Erin began saying, her words coming out steady and even. "Mofi," she said, "can you tell us anything else about the logging business, or what they were doing there?"

He nodded, "That was something Tano told me, before

he…before I left to find Paul. He started talking about the old Ashanti legends. I grew up hearing these stories," Mofi said. "But once I was grown, I knew they were just stories, not real. But…Tano said he saw something that made him think one of the legends was real. And the people we were working for, he told me—that's what they were doing there. They were looking for it. The logging was just so that no one would bother them. Their real purpose was to find the lost Ashanti treasure. And, Tano, at least, thinks they just found it."

"The lost Ashanti treasure," Erin said, "do you know what it was?"

"Yes," he said, looking up at them, "it's what they call the golden chair."

● **43**

THE PATUKA

Keeler's phone beeped. It was the tracker. The Patuka.

About time… he thought. He pushed a button on the phone and held it to his ear.

"I've caught up to him," the voice on the other end said, barely above a whisper.

"Took long enough…," Keeler said. "Where are you now?"

"A few hours walk from Bergora, in a camp. Americans, looks like."

"Describe it."

"Three heavy-duty trailers, two sleepers, one supply. One Land Rover."

"Is the target alone?"

"No," he whispered back, "two others."

"Who?"

"Woman, white. Twenties, maybe thirties. And a man, dark. Not African. Has pink hair. Same age. They're talking to the target now."

"Anyone else?"

"No."

"Are you exposed?"

"No. Want all three?"

Keeler thought about that. He knew the two others. They would be trouble if this went sideways. But he also knew Paul Dannon. And he'd find a way to make trouble if something happened to his team. But...he thought, Dannon might not be an issue after all.

"Do you want me to take all three?" the Patuka asked again.

"No," Keeler said, "just the target. And," he leaned in closer to the phone, "do not be seen by the other two. Clear?"

"Clear," he whispered.

"Call me when it's done."

Keeler ended the call and dialed Lennox.

"What," Lennox said, answering his phone.

"The tracker has found the one who escaped," Keeler said, "He's handling it now."

"Handl-ing or handl-ed," Lennox said.

"It will be finished in a moment."

"And the other thing?"

"It's done."

"Completely?"

"Of course."

Lennox considered this for a moment, the incompetence of force...

"Call me back when this is finished," he said and hung up.

44

NEED TO KNOW

PAUL WALKED INTO LEE JUN'S OFFICE WITHOUT knocking and sat down.

Jun looked up at him. "Thought you weren't coming," Jun said.

Paul sat down in the chair opposite Jun's desk.

"I had to figure out what I was getting myself into first," he said.

Jun sat across the desk, looking at him.

"So," Paul said, "because I'm curious, what does Lee Jun cost?"

Jun let out a breath and looked away, shaking his head. He stood up, walked to the window. He turned back to Paul, "you…," he said, wagging a finger at him. He shook his head and turned away again, apparently trying to find any words that *weren't* incriminating.

"You don't—" he started again. But he didn't get the chance to finish.

Two soldiers opened the door behind Paul and walked into Jun's office. Neither acknowledged Jun. They walked up to Paul, one standing on either side of him, still sitting in his chair.

For Paul's part, he kept his eyes on Jun.

"Come with us," one of them said.

Paul looked up at the one that spoke and then back at Jun. "Well...," he said, slapping his hands onto his knees, almost playfully, "that's it then."

Jun didn't look at him.

Paul stood and walked with the two armed men. Passing through Jun's door, he stopped and turned back to Jun.

"Lee," he said, "this all could have been very different, you know that."

Jun still didn't meet his eye.

⛩

Kwami and Gavin sat in the truck, watching as two armed guards walk out with Paul between them. One opened a car door, while the other stood next to Paul, directing him into the back of the vehicle.

"Whoa," Gavin said, shifting in his seat as he watched the scene. "What's...going on?"

"It's all right," Kwami said, calmly.

Gavin looked at him. "Kwami," he said, pointing at Paul being arrested. "Paul's—"

"Relax," Kwami told him. "We needed everyone to play their hand... We knew this might be necessary."

"*I* didn't," Gavin said, looking between Kwami and the vehicle Paul was now sitting in.

Kwami looked at him. "Sorry about that," he said. "Paul didn't want anyone to accidentally let on that we knew anything, so...it was need-to-know kind of thing."

Gavin looked back at the vehicle as it pulled away.

"So…," he said, "what do we do now?"

"Now," Kwami said, starting the engine, "we follow them."

45

THE GOLDEN CHAIR

"On the first night I was here," Erin said, turning to Ben, "Kwami talked about an old Ashanti legend of a chair like that."

"Yeah," Ben said, "Kwami…he says a lot of things."

"Think about it. Mofi," she said, turning to him, "you said you were working for an underwater logging company, right? Harvesting the hardwood from Lake Volta."

He nodded.

"And Paul's old friend," she said, turning back to Ben, "who hasn't seen him in years, sends Mofi out to find him and tell him all about…what…a bedtime legend?"

"Meanwhile," she continued, "it was the 'pending outbreak,'" — she held up her fingers, making quotes — "that brought me here in the first place. But…what if the outbreak was just a cover?"

"Which is why…," Ben said, picking up her train of thought.

"It's why data wasn't adding up," she finished. "Right. And what if the underwater logging was just a cover to find this…," she motioned to Mofi, "golden chair thing."

Ben began slowly nodding as she talked through it.

"And that would explain," she continued, "why they killed the workers."

"Exactly," Ben said, "because if the rumors got out, they'd be off the charts — you heard Kwami talking about it. That would raise all kinds of attention for Lennox and his operation."

"So," Erin said, "they used the workers until they found what they wanted, and then…killed them, blamed it on some unknown bacterium," she said waving her hand, "which they conveniently had SERA to confirm to the world that it was under control."

The two of them were silent for a moment.

"But there's one thing I don't understand," Erin said. "If all this is right, and if there is such a thing as the golden chair…then what does Lennox want with it? What's his—"

Her words were cut short with a loud crack, splitting the air between them.

For a moment, Erin didn't react.

She heard the loud sound. Felt it, really. But her mind was elsewhere, and it—

Another loud crack. And another after it.

She felt Ben push her down. As he did, she was aware of him pulling the make-shift desk next to them onto its side, papers flopping out into the air.

She was on the ground, sitting behind the table. Ben was beside her, motioning with his hand, *silence*.

She looked around and saw Mofi, dropping down, in the other direction.

"Shooter," Ben called out.

Shooter, she thought, still processing how that could be…

She wanted to turn and look, but all she could manage was to stay completely still, frozen.

Ben moved. He stood up.

Everything in her wanted to pull him back down. But she was stuck. Even her voice was frozen.

As he stood, he jumped over the table. Then he was running. Running toward where the bullets had come from. She pulled herself to the side, looking in the direction he'd gone. As she did, she saw a man drop from a tree, a couple hundred feet away, he was holding something…a gun. As soon as he hit the ground, he began running. Ben was… chasing him.

She watched the two and then remembered Mofi.

Looking over at him, she was surprised to see that he never dove for cover. He was, just, lying there, exposed. And then…she saw it. He was hit.

The shooter hit Mofi.

In a jump-crawl, she was next to him, holding him.

His chest heaved, pulling in hard, shallow breaths. His shirt was full of dark red blood, and she couldn't tell where it was coming from, only that it had hit him, and that he'd bled a lot already.

"Mofi," she said, looking at him. Her hand reached up to touch his face. "Mofi, can you hear me?"

His eyes looked around before finding her. He pulled a hand up, started to speak.

"Shh, shh," she said. "Just be still, okay."

He pulled his head up to look down at the front of him and then let his head fall back. His eyes looked at Erin. "Paul…," he said, wincing, and closing his eyes. His breathing was getting worse. She was wondering if his lung was punctured.

"It's okay," she said, "don't talk right now. We'll tell Paul everything. Just rest right now." She looked up, perhaps for Ben. For some kind of help, or hope.

Erin's arm was under Mofi's head, holding him. Her other hand was holding his. She noticed his breaths were less frequent now. And his eyes, they'd stopped looking around as much.

She watched him as she realized there wasn't anything she could do for him.

Ben came running back, out of breath, and slid down next to Erin and Mofi. He was looking at all that had happened to Mofi.

"The shooter," he said, still assessing Mofi, "he's gone."

Mofi, Erin noticed, had stopped moving.

Ben looked down at Mofi, and then at Erin, who was still holding Mofi's hand.

"Mofi…too," she said, looking up at Ben.

Ben sat back, pressing his fingers into his eyes. He took a deep breath and stood up and started walking.

Erin stayed still. She saw everything clearly. Mofi alive, is now, gone…forever.

But, as she sat there, she wasn't afraid. Nor was she sad. She just…*was*. Was this, she wondered, what shock felt like? She'd never seen someone die before. And certainly not like this.

She pulled her hand out from behind Mofi's head, letting it move gently to the side, away from her. She didn't stand. She just sat. Looking up at Ben. He stopped walking.

She looked down at herself, her hands and shirt were streaked and blotted with Mofi's blood.

"Jonah Lennox did this," she said slowly, looking up at Ben.

Ben looked back at her, but she could tell, he wasn't there yet. The anger that was slowly building in her veins wasn't yet in his.

"Ben," she said, still low, still controlled, "Lennox is behind this. He's behind all of it."

46

THE LOADING

Jonah Lennox stood in linen pants, leather uppers, and his shirt sleeves rolled up. He watched with unblinking eyes. The sun was hot, and the back of his shirt stuck to him. But if he felt it, he didn't let it show.

The off-road forklift carrying the brown wooden box, made tracks in the red dirt as it swiveled. The machine stopped at the back of an eighteen-wheeler, its rear doors open.

"Slowly," he said.

The hydraulics on the forklift hissed as the machine operator positioned the cargo to slide into the back of the truck.

The man standing next to him wore a brown Customs uniform and held a clipboard, which he glanced down at too often. He looked at Lennox without moving his head.

Lennox didn't move as he watched the cargo slide in. The machine operator got out of the forklift and climbed into the back of the truck, tying down the cargo so that it didn't shift in transport.

"Have what you need?" Lennox said to the man next to him, without looking at him. Lennox wasn't a particularly tall man, but he still stood nearly a head above the Customs officer.

"Er," the man said, looking down at the manifest on his clipboard and then back up at the truck, "yes."

The other man jumped down from the back of the truck, brushing his hands as he did.

"Seal it," Lennox told him.

The worker swung the heavy metal doors on the back of the truck until they clanked shut. He clamped a seal on the container, showing the Customs official, who looked at it and made his note. The Customs officer pulled a paper clamp from his pocket and pressed it onto the document, leaving a round perforated mark on the paper.

"Here," he said, handing it Lennox, "you're pre-cleared for export."

Lennox took the paper and looked at the man for the first time. "Are you sure?" he said, continuing to stare at the other man.

"Yes," he said, nodding his head, "just have your trucker show them this paperwork when they enter the port. All is in order."

Lennox walked to the front of the truck, where the truck-driver was sitting, waiting. He hopped, lightly onto the step of the truck, holding on to the rail with one hand, standing at eye-level with the driver. He handed him the paperwork.

"Straight to the port," he said, "It's already Customs cleared. Don't stop. And if anyone tries to stop you, call me before you do anything. Understand?"

The driver nodded, took the paper, and pulled a knob on his dash as Lennox dropped back to the ground. The truck let out a loud hiss. On the other side of the cab, the forklift driver climbed in. The truck drove away.

The Customs man was still standing off to the side.

Lennox looked at him. "You can go." The man moved away to his vehicle and drove away.

Lennox watched him drive away and pulled out his phone. He dialed, waited, pushed a few more buttons and waited again for the click. Secure.

"Loaded and en route," he said and hung up.

47

ANSWERS

"I'm going," Erin said, standing up.

Ben was sitting, his hands holding up his face, staring out at nothing in particular.

"Going…," he said, "going where?"

"The site," she said. "Where Mofi came from and where the loggers were killed."

Now that the adrenaline had worn off, the reality that someone was shot and now lay dead only a few feet from him, was all beginning to settle in. He felt groggy as his mind tried to catch up to what Erin was saying.

"Why?" he said, looking at her.

"Because, that's where answers will be."

"Answers…," he said. His mind was so far from answers. His mind was on solutions. On fall-out. On next steps for what to do when you're operating in a foreign country and a native of that country gets murdered next to you. There aren't guidelines for that sort of thing.

"Answers to what?"

"The people who did this," she said, pointing back to Mofi, "they are trying very hard to hide something. Trying so hard, they're willing to kill for it. Everything they've done has been to keep people away. The new bacterium. Lennox and Keeler collecting data samples directly. And now…now this."

"But why?" Ben said. "Say that's all true, say Jonah Lennox manufactured the outbreak story, fabricated the data, and even," he lowered his voice as he said it, "killed Mofi. Why would he do all of that for this ancient Ashanti artifact?"

Erin shook her head, crossing her arms, "There's something more to it," she said.

"What?" Ben said.

"I don't know yet," she said. "But that's why I need to go there. To find it out."

As much as Ben didn't want to admit it right now, didn't want to deal with this extra layer of complication right now…what she was saying was making sense.

"Fine," Ben said with a sigh, standing up.

"Fine what?" she said. "I'm not asking for your permission."

"I wasn't giving it," he said. "*Fine*, meaning, if you're going," he looked at her directly, "then I'm coming with you."

"Fine," she said, turning and walking to the old yellow Land Rover.

48

GOING NORTH

They turned north onto the main road, leaving the SERA camp.

Up to this point, Erin had only ever gone south. To Accra, to Bergora, even when she and Marisol went to the lab.

North, Erin noticed, was much less cultivated. And soon the road was no longer paved. They drove for a while, not seeing the little towns that dotted the roads south. Occasionally, though, they'd pass a small gas station, planted in the middle of nowhere. Erin assumed they were deserted.

A short while later, Ben stopped at one to get more gas. They were subsidized by the government, he explained. It was similar to the way the government paid for the roads. The rural economy couldn't support these things on their own. But without them, they'd suffer even more, so the government pays for them.

A moment later, they were back on the road. And the regular bumps from the road continued.

"So…you've been to the logging site before?" she said.

"Yeah," he said, looking over at her, "I've got a friend who works for Keeler."

"A friend?" she said, looking at him.

"Not a friend like that," he added. "More of an acquaintance. He works security."

She was still looking at him.

"He's on the level," Ben said. "We swap favors from time to time."

She looked back out her window, watching the trees blur by.

They kept heading north, the road occasionally tossing them inside the Land Rover. The bumps and holes getting bigger. Most of the trip passed in silence. A silence Erin was thankful for. A silence that let her think. And relax.

Ben pulled out his phone, pushed a button, and held it to his ear.

"Who are you calling?" she said.

"Paul," he said. "I tried him earlier, before we left, couldn't get him."

He put the phone back down as another bump rocked them both.

"Still nothing."

"Is that normal?" she said.

"Him not answering?" He shrugged. "Sometimes."

The sun was now coming in sideways through the truck. Filling everything with an orange glow. Up ahead they saw a town. The first since they'd started north. But as they got closer, they noticed, it was empty. The buildings were abandoned. Or, mostly abandoned. The area around didn't look too fertile. Erin figured the town must have failed. Like a ghost town in the American West. Whatever sustained it before was—

"I want you to follow my lead here," Ben said, "and only do what I do." He was looking steadily ahead as he said it.

She looked at him, caught off guard by the sudden seriousness in his voice. She felt their speed begin to decrease.

"What do you…," she started, but then, looking where he was looking, she saw them.

Ahead, men with guns, waving for them to stop.

49

CHICKEN

"How can you eat?" Gavin asked, his knee rocking up and down.

"I'm hungry," Kwami said without looking up at him. "I always eat when I'm hungry."

The noise from Accra was around them, as they sat outside, on a bench next to a chicken-and-rice stand. Across from Kwami, Gavin kept looking around, watching the cars pass by, watching the people pass by, not noticing any of them.

"So…what's next?" Gavin said.

Kwami put his chicken leg down and looked at Gavin.

"You've asked me this same question about forty times."

Gavin's expression didn't seem to register that the answer would be the same. He said nothing in response, just looked at Kwami.

"We wait," Kwami said. "We wait."

"We…*wait*," repeated Gavin. "We wait for what?" he said, raising his voice.

"We wait until he calls."

"How is he going to do that if he's in jail?"

"Don't worry about that," Kwami said, going back to his chicken.

Gavin let out a huff of air and stood up and started pacing.

Kwami looked down at his watch, wiped his hands, and pulled out his phone, dialing.

"Who are you calling?" Gavin asked.

"Ben."

Kwami waited, but there was no answer. He hung up, reached into his pocket for a piece of paper, and dialed another number.

"Who are you calling now," Gavin said, "Paul?"

"No," Kwami said without looking up at him. "Erin. Now sit down and quit asking."

Gavin did not sit down, but folded his arms, and resumed his pacing. He continued to watch Kwami.

Kwami put the phone down. "No answer."

"What does that mean?" Gavin said, stopping his pacing.

"It means…they didn't answer."

"Well, I mean, shouldn't we leave them a message or something?"

"How would that go?" Kwami said, still holding his phone, "Paul's in jail, not sure when he'll be out, hope all's well with you, talk soon?"

Gavin looked at him but didn't reply.

"We wait, and later, we try them again," Kwami said, going back to his chicken. "If I still can't reach them, I'll leave them a message. But for now, most important, we stay calm."

Gavin looked away and started pacing again.

50

THE CHECK POINT

"Step out," the man in fatigues, with a rifle over his shoulder, said.

Ben didn't get out, but instead smiled, like this was all routine.

"Good day, sir," he said, "our papers are all in order." He lifted a laminated badge from a lanyard hanging around his neck.

The soldier did not respond.

"We're here working for the Ministry of Health," he said, still holding up his badge. "Our work is time-sensitive," letting his foot off the brake as he said it, causing the truck to roll forward.

"Step out," the soldier at Ben's window said in a louder voice.

The soldier next to Erin took a step back, pointed his rifle directly at her.

She raised her hands, instinctively. Doing her best to stay still, to not look at the man's eyes — an acknowledgment of her disobedience.

"Alright, alright," Ben said, "no trouble, gov." He reached

his raised hands through his open window and opened his door from the outside. As he did, he looked at Erin and gave her a slight nod to do the same.

She let out the air she didn't realize she was holding and reached her hand down to open the door. As she did, the man with the gun pointed at her, leaned in. He was jumpy, looking down to the hand she'd just put down.

"Just opening the door," she said, making eye contact now.

As the door latch released, the man yanked it open, using his gun to motion her out. She stepped out. The other soldier has already moved Ben away from the Land Rover, searching him for weapons. Erin's soldier looked at her, a few times, but did not touch her.

He flicked his hand, "go there," he said, pointing to where Ben was standing.

She walked over to Ben. A third soldier walked out from the single-story nondescript building next to them. He escorted them inside.

They were put into a windowless room. It had a single, bare fluorescent tube, tied loosely to the ceiling with a metal wire. It filled the room with harsh light. In the center was a table and three chairs. Neither of them sat. The soldier left, shutting the door behind him.

Ben walked to the door and lightly turned the handle.

"Locked…," he said.

Erin sat at the table, leaning her head in her hand. Ben stood next to the door with his back against the wall.

"This kind of stuff happen to you often?" she said, not looking up at him.

"Only on Thursdays," he said.

She looked at him. Making a joke right now… she thought. She felt her head beginning to throb.

"What do they want?" she asked.

"No telling," he said. "They'll probably search the truck, pop the bonnet, do it properly, to see if there's anything good in there. See if they can find any reason to keep us, or fine us, or whatever."

She let out a sigh.

"Do you think this has anything to do with Lennox?"

Ben seemed to consider it for a moment. "How could it?" he said.

That was what she couldn't figure either. It was thin. Conspiracy-theory stuff. And he's a crook, yes. But he's not God, how would he... Then again... what would a road-block like this be doing here in the middle of nowhere? It's like they were waiting for them.

Ben seemed to read her mind.

"Look," he said, "these kinds of things happen out here. We don't actually have anything they can hold us on. They'll soon realize that. And if they hold us too long, they'll be getting a call from our Embassies, which is the very last thing they want. It's just a game. And we have to play it out."

It felt like they'd been in this room for hours when Erin looked down at her watch. *Twenty minutes.* No windows. No visits. Erin stood up and sat back down. Ben was sitting on the floor now, his knees pulled up and his arms resting on them.

The time crept by slowly like this, until, after a couple of hours more, the same soldier opened the door and walked in.

At the sound, Erin pulled her head up and looked at him. Ben, still sitting in the same spot, didn't turn.

"You're free to go," the soldier said, "your paperwork checks out."

"Right...," Ben said in a lazy voice. He stood, and they both followed the man out.

Outside it was dark now. Yellow light from the inside of the building spilled out. And an outdoor light, high on a pole, lit a concrete area off to the side. The Land Rover was there, the keys still in it.

Ben got in, flipped on the dome light and took a brief survey of the inside. As Erin climbed in, she saw where the men had looked through the truck, looked through her bag, too. Everything seemed to be there still.

"Let's get out of here," Ben said, "before they change their mind. …it wouldn't be the first time," he said, backing the Land Rover out and making the tires chirp as he turned hard, bumping back down onto the dirt road.

As they drove, the road was completely dark now. Other than the bumps, the only way they knew they were making progress was from the dirt road zooming under the head-lights in front of them.

"Do you know how to get there in the dark?" Erin said.

"Nope…," he said.

"So then…what…"

"We'll have to camp, but," she saw him glance at her in the dark, "probably not a good idea to do it too close to our friends back there."

The Land Rover bounced for some minutes more.

"There," he said, pointing. "That'll work." He pulled the truck off the road, up a small hill, and down the other side, into a clearing and away from the road.

Best she could tell, they were hidden from the road now, though she still couldn't see much of anything around them.

"We've got some sleeping rolls in the back," he said.

51

NEXT TO THE STARS

"You never really notice how many stars there are…," Ben said, "until you find yourself in the middle of nowhere sleeping on top of a Land Rover."

Erin, below him, didn't respond. For a moment, he thought she'd already fallen asleep. The seats in the back of the Land Rover had long since been removed. And that's where Erin lay, on a sleeping roll, with the tailgate down, next to a small stash of food rations. Ben lay his roll on the roof. It had a small rail around the edge but was otherwise flat. Not, strangely, the first time he'd slept there.

"Do your parents like what you're doing?" she asked.

"What do you mean?"

"This work…with Paul…"

Ben was silent a moment before answering.

"I'm not really sure," he said.

Both of Ben's parents are doctors. And they do a lot of lower-income pro bono work. But they're the kind of people who are building something. Either of them could easily switch to a hospital or a more profitable practice if they wanted. On the other hand, Ben had, at best, a freelancer's resume. On paper it looked like he'd bounced around from job to job. It was the nature of the kind of work he did. But, honestly, he wasn't really sure if his parents did approve.

"I haven't seen them in almost five years," he said.

"Why not?"

"I dunno, just…life, I guess."

"You should go see them."

Ben laid still, his hands behind his head.

"What about your parents," he said, "are they proud of you?"

"I don't know…," she said, almost to herself. "I never met my dad. I was a baby when he left. I'm honestly not sure if he's still alive. And my mom, she died, when I was younger. But I remember her, though. She was always calm. And in control. I liked that."

"I'm sorry, I didn't…"

"It's okay," she said. "It's been a long time. I don't mind talking about it."

"So that's the connection with Paul, then?"

"Yeah. He was my mom's cousin. I met him a few times when I was younger. But he was always off somewhere else. And, so was my mom, for that matter. She was a journalist."

"How did she die?"

Erin was quiet for a moment.

"Someone killed her."

Ben turned on his side, not looking at the stars anymore.

"She was on assignment, in Somalia," Erin said, "in the early nineties, just before Mogadishu fell. She was doing a story on nonprofit corruption. The 'official report' says she was caught in crossfire."

"Official report? But…you believe there's something else there?"

"My mother was a veteran conflict journalist. She was smart. She'd been in a lot of places like that before. I didn't know all that at the time. I was only nine. But later, I started looking into it. And eventually, I became a journalist too. My mom's partner at the time, he thought the same thing."

"Which was?"

"That there was something else there. That she found something…something somebody wanted to stay hidden."

"Do you have any idea who it was?"

"For a long time, I didn't. I only had the case files, her reports. But I knew that she wasn't 'caught in the crossfire.' I knew there had to be something else. And a few years ago, I caught a break. Or I almost did. I found someone who was there at the time, who was working with my mother in Mogadishu. And he was going to talk. But he was pretty scared. So we arranged to meet outside of the U.S., down in Trinidad."

"What happened?"

She was silent again. Ben began to think she might not have heard him.

"He…," she said, "never showed."

"Think he was lying, or…?"

"I think someone got to him," she said. "Anyway, after that, I stepped away from it all for a while. That's when I joined Carl."

"Carl?"

"He's my boss, at R4. I think I was just…afraid, really. I didn't want to go that way."

"Like your mum?"

"Yeah. And then this stuff with the loggers and the pending outbreak started happening. At first, it just seemed like bad reporting. But something was missing, I could feel it. So I started looking into it."

"Over the years," she said, "I kept in touch with my journalism contacts. Mainly, my editor over at *The Post*. He was also my mom's partner years ago. And I still write some for them. Anyway, I reached out to him, I told him what I thought was going on here."

And then…then he found something. He found Jonah Lennox's name in my mom's notes."

"She knew him?" Ben said.

"Apparently. He might have been a source or something. There weren't any details about him in her notes. Just his name. But something about it seemed more than coincidental to me."

"So you came here, because of him."

"In a manner of speaking. I really didn't have anything more than a hunch…until I saw the data from Gavin. There were other little things along the way. And then…Mofi."

"Do you really think Lennox had something to do with your mum's death?"

She was quiet for a long moment.

"I don't know," she said finally. "I don't know what I know anymore… All I know is that he was there. That, and whatever my mother was working on, got her killed. I…don't know how it all fits together yet."

He heard her shift below him.

"Well," he said, "if there's anything dodgy at the logging site, anything we can link to him, then we'll find it."

52

THE SITE

THE NIGHT PASSED QUIETLY. THE MORNING SUN WAS clipping the rim of the windows, passing through and bouncing around inside the back of the Land Rover. Erin sat up, yawned, and slid to the end, sitting on the tailgate, letting her legs hang down.

She saw Ben, already awake and packing his stuff from last night. Moving at full speed already.

She tried to remember what time she'd fallen asleep. Gave a quick attempt at adding up the hours and just as quickly gave it up.

"Here," he tossed her a cellophane-wrapped bar, "breakfast."

She caught it, or rather, her lap did. Her reflexes would be awake later.

Without getting up, she leaned to the other side of the truck, reached her bag and pulled it closer, dropping the bar inside. When she did, she noticed a small red blinking light on her sat phone. She pulled it out and held it to her ear.

"Ben," she said.

"Yeah," he said from somewhere out of sight.

"Have you heard from Kwami recently?"

"Umm, not since he left yesterday, why?"

"He called and left me a message," she said, as she listened to it.

"Uh-huh," he said.

"He says Paul's in jail," she said, putting the phone down.

"Paul's *what?*" he said, coming around to look at her.

"He left me a message. Yesterday. Must have been when we were held up at the checkpoint. I just tried calling him back…no answer."

"Let me listen to it," he said.

She handed him the phone. He stared down at the ground as he listened. He handed the phone back to her without saying anything.

"I was thinking about something," Erin said. "When I first got here, Paul told me he thought there might be a mole in the camp."

"A mole? Like a spy?"

"Yeah. Maybe. Before, in D.C., the night before we left, someone almost ran us over. And it didn't seem like an accident. So I'm thinking he was just telling me to play my cards close."

"Did he say who he thought it was?"

"No. I don't think he knew."

Ben seemed to be thinking about this. He began walking, nodding his head and talking to himself.

"No," he said, stopping. He looked up at her. "No, I'd stake my life on it. We can't have a mole."

"Are you sure?"

"Yes," he said firmly. "Yes, I'm sure." He started walking again. "If he said that, he had to be referring to the Lennox-Keeler situation. That would make sense… He must have been referring to the data tampering," he talked through it.

"Is it weird," she said, "that he wouldn't have mentioned

anything like that to you? You, being his right hand-guy and all."

"No," he let out a little laugh, "not really. Paul doesn't work like that. We work together, yes, and, I think, we make a good team. But we're not *together* like that. He's still very… separate. Nobody ever really knows what's going on in Paul's head."

"So what do we do?" Erin said.

"What, about Paul?"

She nodded.

"Nothing we can do," he said. "If Paul was arrested, it wasn't for something small, he's too careful for that. Which means, even if we could do something, it would take time, days probably. Besides, Paul's got…other measures in place…"

"What do—"

"No," he said, "we keep going. Besides, Kwami's there. Nothing we can do for Paul right now."

Fifteen minutes later, they were back on the road. The drive was easy. It was another hour before Ben started to slow and turned off the road. The road they turned onto was just as large, if not larger. Erin could see in the dirt, wide tracks from large trucks.

They drove slower now, cautiously.

But as they approached, they were surprised to find the site completely abandoned. There was a line of plastic yellow barricade tape covering the entrance. But it had been knocked down and driven over.

They could see the two-story facility, with what looked like a cutting facility below and an office above. Off, on either side, were large stacks of logs and a few large pieces of logging machinery. And then, framing it all was the serene water of Lake Volta, with its low mountains along its edges.

They pulled up to the facility.

"I don't think anyone's here," Ben said.

They parked the truck off to the side, out of sight — just in case — and Ben grabbed his camera. Erin and Ben got out and began walking toward the facility.

"So, this is the place…?" Erin started.

"Where the loggers were killed. Yeah." Ben said.

● 53

TRAITOR

Keeler sat in a twenty-four-hour spot in Accra, a place that saw a mixture of tourists, ex-pats, and locals. Mostly, it was a place he could wait and not be disturbed. And it was public.

That last part, he'd learned over the years, was important.

First-meetings, like this, were precarious. No one really trusted anyone else yet. And so they often had a good chance of falling apart. Public places helped. They were safe.

Or, at least, that's what people thought.

They weren't really safer.

If anything, they were more dangerous. Easier to blend. Easier to get lost. And easier to make diversions.

But today Keeler wouldn't need any of that. It's been said that great empires rise and fall on the strength of their network. Keeler didn't have an empire. But he worked for one. And his job was to—the list of euphemisms was long — 'grease the wheels,' 'encourage under-performing partners,' and, his personal favorite, 'depopulate the threat.'

At the end of the day, most people looked at him as the muscle. But that was wrong. The muscle was simple. Force was only one of the tools in that belt. No, Keeler was a squeezer. Force only got you so far. But to really make things happen, you needed leverage. And sometimes, the best kind of leverage is the kind that kicks them in the balls and then pummels them while they're still down writhing.

In other words, sometimes it's got to be personal.

That's what Keeler was doing here today.

He motioned to the man behind the counter to bring another drink. As he did, a spunky, attractive girl sat down next to him. He let the first few seconds pass without acknowledging her. Then he swiveled on his barstool, leaned back and looked at her. She didn't immediately return the look.

Despite himself, there was something about her he liked.

He, of course, knew who she was. But this side of Marisol was…new…and interesting.

"I wouldn't have pegged you as a traitor," he said.

She didn't respond. Or look at him.

"No, really," he said, reaching to slide the bit of her short hair blocking her eyes.

She grabbed his hand with a force that he enjoyed.

"I guess," she said, looking at him directly now, "we're all full of surprises."

"Speaking of which," he said, pulling his own hand free, "from now on, your job is to make sure there are no surprises coming this way."

She looked away.

"Clear?" he said, going back to his drink.

"Keep up your end, and we'll be fine," she said.

Keeler took another deep drink and put his glass down hard. He slapped both hands down on the counter, got up, and, without another look at Marisol, walked out.

54

CONTROL

IF IT WEREN'T FOR THE STACKS OF LOGS SURROUNDING the place, the facility could pass for a remote lodge. Most of the first floor was open air, like a large carport, extending about fifteen feet high. It had a floor-mounted saw with a small conveyor belt and chipper attached. Everything around the machine was coated in the two-toned tan and red sawdust. The second floor was a series of windowed rooms. And, as is not uncommon in this part of Africa, was a low stone perimeter wall with a large opening in the front and back.

Ben and Erin walked up to the front. It was quiet. Empty feeling.

"Let's do this fast," Erin said.

They opened a door marked 'office' and climbed the steps leading upstairs. Erin went first. Ben followed, his camera slung over his shoulder.

Upstairs had a center hall with a series of rooms on either side. Because of all the windows, the inside was full of natural light. Most of the rooms looked like they were used as office space. One room, in particular, was large, with chairs and a table in the middle. It had a wall of windows and a door leading out to a second-floor veranda that over-looked Lake Volta.

"What exactly are we looking for?" Ben said.

"Anything illegal," Erin said. "And the more it ties directly to Lennox, the better."

Most of the rooms Ben glanced in were sparse, sprinkled with paperwork and office furniture. One room caught his eye. It was the only one that didn't have windows. He walked in and flipped on the lights. The place looked like a cockpit or command center. He heard the soft whir of computer fans and saw a thousand tiny lights dotting the equipment.

In the middle of the main desk was a joystick. He sat down. He put his hand on the joystick, wondering what it controlled. As soon as he touched it, the six monitors in front of him flickered to life.

The center monitor, the one directly in front of him, was still mostly black. But it had a series of green meters on it. It reminded him of looking through the viewfinder of a camera with a lens cap still on. Another monitor, to his left, had a file index with a series of recordings in it. They were ordered by date. He moved the mouse, but nothing happened. Then he noticed the pointer on a different screen off to his right. He slid the mouse across and clicked one of the recordings.

There was no sound, but it was clear right away it was an underwater video. Everything was in shades of green, like the phosphorescent color of night vision goggles. He saw it navigating around what looked like trees.

The lake… he thought. It was somewhere, here, under the lake outside. Lake Volta was known for its underwater forest, with its eerie bald trees, sticking up from the water, still preserved since it was flooded fifty-something years ago.

He watched another video. More of the same. He kept watching videos. In another, the video showed an underwater cave. As he watched it, the screen went dark and then bright green again as its exposure was adjusting, all captured in the recording. He kept watching as it—

The screens flickered, then died.

Ben looked around. The power was still on in the building. But he noticed, the computer-fan hum he'd heard since he walked in this room, it had also died. It's as if the entire system just shut itself off.

A small light off to the right, about eye level, glowed red for a brief moment. He looked to see what it was and then it began flashing brightly, like a strobe. Bright and red. And then, like the rest of the equipment, it went off, too.

He shook the mouse. Nothing. Tapped the joystick. Still nothing. He didn't like the feel of it. But it wasn't a normal-looking computer. He didn't even know how to turn it on. Or reset it. He pulled his camera off his shoulder and took a few pictures of the room. Just in case.

55

GL-013V

Erin sat at a desk, in a featureless room, surrounded by stacks of dot-matrix printouts. It was the only office room with any paperwork in it.

She'd intended to start with the computer. But it was locked with a password other than 'password' or 'password1234.' She tried a few more guesses before moving on to the stacks of paperwork. They were grouped by date. She started with the middle stack. It was from around a month ago.

When she picked up a page, the next page came with it, and so did the one after it. The entire report appeared to be connected.

GL-008V. The entire stack of paper had this code on it. She skimmed it, a series of progress reports. Mostly coordinates she didn't understand, concluding with a "negative" report.

She moved on to the next stack, older. She put it down and picked up another stack, three weeks ago. Getting closer. She noticed the code at the top was getting higher, too. GL-009V, GL-010V, GL-011V.

But as she skimmed the body and the progress reports at the bottom, they too were all "negative reports." They were looking for something, and, it appeared, they were trying different spots and still not finding it.

Sitting here in this room alone, staring at the same endless white and gray paperwork had a hypnotic effect. She looked down at her watch. Had she really only been in here twenty minutes? It felt more like a few hours. She looked up, noticing she couldn't hear Ben. He must be elsewhere. She looked back down and kept working. She'd made it up to last week's reports now.

GL-013V. By now, she started with the report summary at the end. This was the first one they'd finally found something. *A potential target,* read the report, *was located via sonar in an interior cave. The structure of the cave appears to predate the lake itself, making it a high-value property.*

Erin skimmed further down.

DGT2-R visual inspection confirmed target is intact... DGT2-R was familiar. She looked back through a different stack, keeping her finger in the current one. She found the reference. The DGT2-R was a submersible, 'modified for underwater exploration.' There was a small stencil drawing of it. Looked like an eyeball with arms.

Database modeling confirmed, object size is within range... the report continued.

She flipped to the end, realizing she was already at the bottom of the stack — the top of it being in a mess on the floor beside her. The report wasn't conclusive. They'd found something, but not yet extracted it. She looked around for the next report.

But everything else she found was old. Past dates.

"This wasn't much on its own," she said to herself. "But...if the story about the Ashanti artifact checks out, it sounds an awful lot like we've just found the documentation of them stealing it…"

She reached down and began putting the report she'd been reading back in order. In the U.S., using something like this without first getting a court order would be illegal, not submittable in a court of law. But here…she hoped…this might slide. She'd take it. Just in case.

As she picked up about four inches of report, the most recent ones, she heard Ben call from a room down the hall.

"Erin," he said. "You should come see this…"

56

VISITORS

"Ben?" Erin said, walking down the hall.

"In here," he said.

"I found a bunch of reports…," she said. "Might be able to use them…they look like automatic printouts. At first, I thought they were nothing," she said, walking into the room where Ben was. "And then, as I started reading, I fou—"

She stopped mid-sentence, taking in the room. She'd glanced at the room when they first walked in. But now it was— "What did you…," she said.

"Look here," he said, pointing.

He had pulled large swaths of wood paneling off the walls. "This," he waved a hand, "is all new."

"Okay…," she said.

He was on his knees, feeling something on the wall.

"But right here," he said, looking over his shoulder at her. "Come here, look."

She walked to him and leaned down to where he was.

He showed her the pitting of the old wood underneath the paneling he'd pulled off.

"This," he said, "is not natural."

"What, the holes?"

"Yeah. There's one here," he pointed, "and here…here…
and here," he said, pointing to other places on the wall.
"Now," he said, "step back and…what does it look like?"

Erin walked to the other side of the room and looked
back to where he was pointing. Her back was to the large
windows overlooking the lake.

"See the pattern?" he said.

"Er…no," she said, shaking her head.

"They're bullets."

"What?"

"Don't you watch the tele?"

She looked at him with a not-time-for-jokes face.

"No, seriously," he said. "Pretend you're holding a
machine gun. Then pretend this room is full of a bunch of
blokes. Now just unload your gun on them."

"Come on…"

He walked along the wall, not deterred, and traced points
with his finger. "Bullets would spill over and hit along here…
and here," he kept moving as he talked, following the holes
he'd found under the paneling he'd just removed.

"And what's more," he said, "this stuff, the paneling I
pulled off, wasn't hard to pull off."

"Meaning?"

"Meaning it was probably put up in a hurry."

"I don't know," Erin said, shaking her head, "it seems
kind of…"

"Look down," he said.

She did, the floor under her feet was darker.

"And here," he pointed to another place, "and there, too,"
pointing to a third.

She looked at the spots and then back at him.

"What?"

"It's blood," he said.

She immediately stepped off the spot, looking at it again.

"Are you…sure?" she said.

"What else woul—" Ben started.

"Shhh," Erin hissed, holding up a hand.

Ben froze, hearing it, too.

"Was that a car door?"

57

THE VERANDA

BEN MOVED QUICKLY TO THE DOOR, WALKING OUT ON to the balcony that surrounded the back of the facility. He went to the far end and looked around the edge. She walked outside, still holding the computer printouts in her hand.

He looked back at Erin, and held up four fingers, "four men," he mouthed. He looked back around the corner, kept watching.

Erin heard a noise downstairs. She motioned silently to Ben and nodded her head in the direction of the conference room they'd just walked out of. "Downstairs," she mouthed.

He looked around the corner again and came back, going past her into the conference room, picking up his camera. Before he came back out, he bent down and opened one of the windows only a few inches. Outside, he shut the door slowly without a sound.

"Two are still out front," he said, turning to her, "which means we can't climb down and get to the truck." He looked over the edge. "We're going to have to hide," he said.

Ben put his leg over the two-story balcony, putting his weight on the frame on the outside.

"It'll hold," he whispered.

Erin followed him over, still holding the stack of paper-work. The two of them sat crouched on the outer side of the half-wall that surrounded the upstairs balcony. His camera hung on his shoulder. The paperwork under her arm flipped lightly in the wind. They waited, not speaking.

Erin looked down, praying the two guards at the front didn't walk to the back. From the ground, their hiding spot was laughably vulnerable.

She heard a radio scratch close by.

"They were here," a voice said.

They must be in the room, she thought.

"Look at this place…," another said.

"Check the other rooms," the first one said. "I'll call Keeler and report in."

Erin could feel the lactic acid building up in her legs, burning, as she crouched on the ledge, waiting.

"We're at the site," she heard the first man say again. "They were definitely here," he continued. "Tore off the paneling in the conference room. And—" He stopped talk-ing. "Yes, yes sir," he said, pausing again. "Right away, sir."

"They're still here," the first man called out in a loud voice, "stay sharp." A radio scratched, and the same man spoke again, "Fan out, they're still here."

58

CAPTURED

"We need to move. Now," Ben said.

Erin was thinking the same thing. But there were four men now looking for them. And, other than the stacks of logs around them, the only other hiding place was the woods, and it was quite a good stretch before they could get to the tree line. None of their options looked good.

Ben looked down at the ground and silently dropped from the second-story ledge. He hit the ground in a crouch, moving only his head to look around. Then he motioned to Erin. She dropped silently next to him.

From the ground, they moved to the short perimeter wall around the lodge and slipped over the short wall. Following it along the outside, they made their way to a long stack of logs a few yards away from the facility. The logs were organized in stacks, about fifty feet long, with narrow aisles in between. The logs made for a good cover. But only briefly. If someone were to look down their row, which Erin figured would happen soon, their hiding spot would be blown. Not to mention, their truck was hidden on the opposite side of the compound. With four men searching, it wouldn't be long before they found the truck either. Whatever they were going to do, they needed to do it soon.

"Okay," said Ben. "We need to split up."

As he said it, she knew where this was going.

"We *what?* No," she said, shaking her head, "not an option."

"We don't *have* another option," he said, pulling the memory card out of his camera and holding it up for her.

"Everything in there," he said, motioning to the facility, "is on here."

She held up her hands, shaking her head.

"Here's the plan," he said, moving closer and sliding the card into her hip pocket. "I'm going to make a run for those trees over there."

"They'll shoot—"

"No," he said.

"Ben…"

"Listen, I'll surrender before I get there. It's a distraction. I'll let them get me. Plus," he said, smiling, "I've got a friend who works for them. Best case, he can vouch for me and they'll have to let me go. Worse case, he'll find a way for me to get out.

"But you said—"

"*Trust* me on this one."

She started to argue, but he kept talking.

"Meanwhile, when you hear the commotion, once they've realized I'm running, you get to the car. It's important that you don't wait," he said almost clinically now. "You'll need the diversion so that they don't see you. And then — and this part is key — don't leave until *after* they do. They need to think I was the only one here."

"Okay," Erin said, "say we go with that. What's the *rest* of your plan? What if their instructions are to…*kill* on sight whoever they find?"

"They won't. At least not right away. They'll need leverage. Hostages."

"Hostages? What could they possibly — this won't…"

"Don't worry, we don't have another play right now," he said. "They know we're here. Lennox has had the upper hand since he's been here. And what we just saw in there is that he's responsible for this."

"Plus," he said, "I told you…Paul's connected. Which means one of the first things you need to do when you get out of here is to get in touch with Kwami. He'll be able to get word to Paul."

"Paul…? Paul's in jail right now. What's he going to do?"

"Don't worry about that. If Paul's in jail, it's because he's got some plan."

Some plan… This was a bizarrely optimistic position to be taking right now, Erin thought. Her mind was racing forward. Besides her own objections, she was trying to find a world where this could all actually work. But — the objections continued to mount — even if Paul *could* somehow do something, she didn't even know where they would take Ben. What would she tell Paul? And, come to think of it, if Paul was so 'in control,' why was he sitting in a jail—

Ben put his arms on her shoulders, breaking into her deluge of thoughts.

She looked back at him.

"Remember," he said, "I'm going that way," he pointed with his head, "so when they notice me," you go toward the truck."

Everything in her wanted to object and tell him this was a bad idea. That with just a few more seconds, they'd think of a better plan. That even some kind of peaceful negotiation would be better than this. But nothing came out.

Instead, she just nodded.

Somewhere inside of her, she was ashamed of the

thought. She knew this was a zero-sum game. If they were going to get proof about Lennox, proof about the loggers' death, even proof about this Ashanti artifact, she was the better of the two to do it. And now…she had everything she needed to blow the whistle. It was the right play. Still, she hated herself for not finding a better way.

"It's time," he said.

He hiked the camera farther up on his shoulder, turned and jogged down the aisle. He turned at an opening and disappeared.

Erin moved to see better. On and off, she could still see him.

Then, she could hear *them*.

They'd found him.

And then, a shot.

And another.

She couldn't see him anymore.

Did they… she wondered, before stopping herself. *Forcing* herself to focus.

It's time.

She reached down and felt the card Ben put in her pocket. She adjusted her grip on the papers still in her hand, took a controlled breath.

It's time to move, she told herself. *Now.*

59

WHAT COMES NATURALLY

Erin sat behind the wheel, both hands on the steering wheel. Her forehead rested on the wheel, and her lungs filled with quick, rapid breaths.

She was doing her best to control her breathing, to keep her focus, to remember what she needed to do right now…to not lose sight of what mattered. That Ben was still alive… The thought turned into a question. No, Ben *was* still alive. She forced herself to believe it, despite the fact that his plan was terrible, that she'd heard the shots, and that she hadn't —

"No," she said again, this time out loud. The forcefulness of her own voice startled her. "No," she said, calmer now. "Breath, focus, drive."

It took the rest of her willpower, but she managed six deep, controlled breaths. The oxygen was strangely hypnotic. And, despite herself, she started to feel good. Not naive as if everything was going to be okay. But energized. As in, there was still work to do, and not everything was lost.

She turned the ignition and the old truck's engine revved to life. She put her hand on the shifter and moved it into gear. As she did, she pushed down on the accelerator. Harder than she meant. But still not letting up. Behind her, the back wheels kicked up dust, and it covered her rear view.

The thought hadn't occurred to her until she was back on the main road: she wasn't entirely sure where the turnoff to SERA's camp was. Each time she'd gone there, she'd been with Paul or Marisol or Ben.

She was driving fast now. Fast enough that the truck seemed to glide over the bumps on the old road. In the back of her mind, she registered, this probably wasn't good for the truck, not in the long-run. *The long-run…*an idea that seemed—

Something captured her attention. Ahead, in the road.

She was being flagged down. Then she realized where she was. She was approaching the outpost where they were stopped last night. It seemed an eternity longer than the fifteen or so hours it had been since they were last here.

The guards, maybe the same ones, were there, waving for her to stop.

She felt a dryness in her throat. Then she made a decision. She pushed the accelerator down, harder. The truck was already moving fast. But she felt the RPMs increase, and the speed began to creep higher.

She didn't bother steering around the soldiers flagging her down. They would move. They would move *if they wanted to.* Her inner voice began rationalizing her dangerous actions, in a way she'd never heard before. It was as if she were listening to someone else inside her head. And then, her inner critic, the one she knew so well, began criticizing the new, reckless voice. For the briefest moment, she contemplated a new set of consequences.

She hushed it all. It was too late now.

The men jumped out of the way, yelling at her as she raced past. One shot his rifle into the air a few times. The sounds were already muffled and small.

Her eyes stayed in her rearview mirror until she couldn't see them. Just like that, they seemed not to care that she'd almost run them over. No pursuit. She looked forward again.

It was a gamble, what she did. Not to mention completely out of character in just about every way. A small smile came to the corner of her mouth as she thought about it. Her heart still thumping from the adrenaline. It was a gamble, but it worked.

She reached into the bag in the seat next to her, pulled out her phone and tried Paul. A recorded voice told her his phone was disconnected. She thumbed to her recent calls list and dialed Kwami's number. She let it ring. No answer. She tossed the phone back into the seat. She'd try again when she got closer to the camp.

60

THE TURN

ERIN TOOK THE TURN, FASTER THAN SHE SHOULD HAVE, and the truck slid into a tree.

Once she saw the turnoff for SERA, she recognized it. That was the good news. She had been afraid she might not recognize it. But that old fear was now replaced with a new one: what had she'd just done to the truck? In the three and a half decades she'd been alive, the only time she'd ever been in a car wreck was when someone rear-ended her aunt. She wasn't even driving the car then.

She looked around now, taking stock.

The engine was quiet.

The truck was still the right way, sitting on all four wheels, though it was leaning at an angle.

A few trees were flat against her door. She'd slid into them. Her window had already been down. But, she thought, it probably wouldn't go back up after this.

She considered getting out to check for any other damage. But whether it was the urgency of her situation…or just her own fear of what she might find, she decided to stay. She reached down and turned the ignition.

Nothing happened.

The truck didn't start.

She was close to SERA. She thought about walking the rest of the way, but then what? She was here alone. Paul was in a jail somewhere. Kwami and Gavin were hours away in Accra. Marisol was elsewhere doing who-knows-what. And Ben…

She didn't want to think about Ben.

And she didn't want to think about all that was riding on *her* right now, either. The lives, and…

Something about those thoughts narrowed her mind. Like a sharp jab, warning her to keep focus.

She turned the key again.

This time, the engine made a noise. It was trying.

She kept forcing the ignition, pushing it harder. She pushed the pedals now, all of them. Not letting go of the ignition, hearing the engine whine. Forcing the machine with every stimulus she could. It sounded like it was choking on itself. Erin pushed it harder. Banging her palm on the steering wheel, letting her own anger come out, yelling.

She heard the engine yell back. It roared to life, the RPM gauge racing to catch up to the gas she'd been forcing down into it. She let off the pedals and it slowed to a steady hum.

She slumped back, closing her eyes and catching her breath. She let the engine do the same.

Then she put it in gear and inched it forward, slowly. The trees next to her squeaked and ripped just outside her window as she pulled away from them. The side mirror, she noticed, was no longer there.

She moved cautiously down the tire path that led to the SERA camp. The old truck was holding its own. Building confidence with each new meter it rolled forward.

A moment later, she saw the clearing. And the trailers.

Parked in the same horseshoe pattern they'd been in when she first arrived.

Except…now, something was different.

It was all wrong.

61

THE CAMP

Erin stopped the Land Rover, and it took a moment before she realized what was wrong with the scene in front of her.

"What in the…" she said, stepping down out of the truck. She left the door open behind her as she walked slowly forward, looking out over the campsite as she did.

The place had been ransacked.

One of the trailer doors was open, and another looked like it had been kicked in, hanging diagonally by its top hinge. And the third trailer, their heavy-duty supply trailer, looked like it had nearly been knocked off its wheels. It had large crumple marks in the center.

She walked, listening, looking. No sign of anyone else around. Whoever did this, they seemed to be gone now.

Her mind was taking in the scene as she walked through it, brushing her hand over the table she'd sat at yesterday, now knocked on its side. Who would have done this? And *why* would they have done this? Clearly, she thought, someone was looking for something. But what did SERA have?

She walked into her own trailer, pushing the door aside. The place was a mess. Everything pulled out. Dumped out. The cabinet doors were left open. Her bag had been emptied onto her bed. Marisol's, too. She looked through her stuff.

She picked up her computer and pulled her hand away. It was coated in dark ash. It looked like they'd set off a firecracker in the middle of it. She didn't try to turn it on.

Other than her now-fried computer, everything else seemed to be still there.

She stepped out of her trailer and walked to the supply trailer, the one that looked like a large truck had rammed it. Upon closer inspection, she thought that description might be right. The door had been ripped clean off. She walked in. The equipment inside also looked like it had been torched. Whoever had come was clearly intent on destroying their electronics.

Their computers…all of the models Gavin had shown her…all the data SERA had collected independently…

She walked outside again and picked up a chair and sat, to think.

It all felt so surreal. Like a strange, weird dream.

Then…sitting there, she saw him. Still laying there. Still covered where they'd left him. Where he'd been shot, and… A twist of guilt went through her middle. Not that his death had been their fault. It was just that…that she'd forgotten him so quickly. That she and Ben had run off, leaving Mofi here. And now she was back, here with him. She kept her distance from his covered body.

She put her head down in her hands, not sure if it was fatigue catching up to her, or just the exhaustion of the world she'd stepped into a few days ago. A few days… *Had it really only been a few days? How many?* she wondered. *Three…four?* It seemed like months and months since she and Paul were in a pub in downtown D.C., feeling the cold night air as they walked. And then, she remembered the van. The one that mounted the curb, almost running them over. That did seem like an eternity ago. A time when her life was anything but out of order.

Paul…, she thought, *what is going on…*

She stood and walked back to the Land Rover to see if she could reach Kwami on the sat phone. She couldn't imagine what the point was. She reached into her bag and pulled out the phone. Ben had been overly optimistic. Even if she could reach Kwami, what would he do? Break Paul out? And then what…

The phone in her hand began to beep. It was a moment before she realized someone was calling her. She pushed the green button, holding it to her ear.

"Hello?"

"Where are you?"

The voice was hard to make out, but it was quick, and quiet.

"Hello?" Erin said again, wondering if it might be a wrong number.

"*Erin.*"

"Marisol…is that you?"

A wave of static came through Erin's ear. She thought she might lose the connection.

"Marisol," Erin said again. "I'm at the camp, and it's been—"

"Erin, stop," Marisol cut in, "listen." The static was gone, but her voice was still low, hard to hear. "I already know about the camp," she said.

"They — you do? What happ—"

"No time. I…," she hesitated. "I need you to listen to me," she finished, as if she were forcing her voice to be steady.

"Okay…"

"Wait," Marisol said. "Stay on the line. Don't hang up."

"Marisol?"

She heard another voice. And then nothing.

MARISOL

Erin pulled the phone away from her ear and looked down at the screen. The numbers were still counting, the line was still connected. She put the phone back to her ear, listening. She could hear movement. Muffled voices she couldn't make out. And she could hear a slow, plodding *whump, whump* sound from somewhere in the background.

"Marisol," Erin said, "can you hear me?"

Still no answer, just the low thumping noise.

"Erin," Marisol said, back on the line now. Her voice was low now, like a whisper, "are you still there?"

"Yes. Marisol, yes, where are you?"

"Accra," she said quickly.

"What—"

"Listen very carefully. I'm with Keeler. I made a deal—"

"Keeler?" Erin said. "What do you mean *with him*? And what kind of…"

"It doesn't matter. You need to get in touch with Paul."

"I can't, Paul's in—" Erin started, but Marisol was talking over her.

"The chair is in one of ITG's shipping containers on a

vessel called *The Mariner*. It's scheduled to leave in five hours."

"ITG…," Erin said. "What do they…"

"*The Mariner* is sailing under a Panama flag," Marisol was talking in a rapid whisper now. "Panama doesn't enforce extradition, so once the vessel leaves, we won't be able to get it back. The chair," she said, "it is in an ITG shipping container. I don't have the container number. But it'll be on the manifest. And, Erin, you'll need to look for 'cocoa beans.'"

Cocoa beans…what was she…?

"It's the only ITG container with 'cocoa beans.'"

"ITG doesn't ship cocoa beans," Erin said. And she knew this for a fact. In West Africa, ITG only dealt in raw minerals and other nonperishables.

"I know," Marisol said, "that's why it will be easy to find. You just need to stop the vessel."

Erin was trying unsuccessfully to piece this together. ITG, one of her company's main clients, was *smuggling* this ancient Ashanti artifact out of the country in a container of cocoa beans…and Marisol had somehow found out about all of this. And then, in the process, Marisol had made some kind of deal with Keeler…So much of this sounded bizarre.

"Marisol, why would ITG…"

"It's Lennox," she said. "He's working with them. No time to explain. The chair's already loaded. I couldn't stop it."

Marisol said other things, but Erin didn't hear them. *It's Lennox*…she said. Lennox is working with ITG…it was unreal in a kind of movie-conspiracy plot.

"Why," she said, "how is Lennox working with…"

"No time to explain. Erin, you need to—"

"Marisol," Erin said, she could feel the urgency as it came out. "Where are you right now?"

"Port. Now, Erin, listen," she said, "You need to get Paul.

Five. Hours," she stressed. "Then it's in international waters. And we can't touch it. Five hours." She said again. "Call Paul's number."

Call Paul was exactly what she'd been trying to do. And exactly what she'd been failing at. Whatever was going to happen was going to happen without Paul.

"Wait," Erin said, "I can't get to Paul. There's got to be another—"

"I've got to go," Marisol cut in. "Get to Paul."

Erin could hear someone else with Marisol. She couldn't make out the other voice. In the background, she could still hear the low rhythmic whumping sound. She listened hard, trying to make out the words. *Fought...* or... *pill...* The conversation was getting louder. "Feel," she heard Marisol say, not to her. No, *Keel*er, she was talking to Keeler. Marisol's voice was louder now. But not angry. Erin still couldn't make out the words, but she could hear the tones, the emotions. Marisol was worried, or scared, she thought.

Then, distinctly, as if Marisol had put the phone back to her mouth, she heard her clearly say, no yell, "no."

"Marisol," Erin said into the phone, "Marisol, tell me where you are. I can come to get you."

Erin's hands were sweating. If only Marisol would give her a hint. Some direction. Marisol was in trouble. Erin could hear it. She'd gotten in over her head with Keeler. *What was she doing with Keeler?* Whatever it was, it was going wrong. Erin was listening to it all happening. And there was nothing she could do.

"Marisol," she yelled into the phone again.

She could hear Marisol, talking fast, panicked, and rushed sounding. She could hear the other voice — Keeler's voice, but he was calm, controlled. The voices were punctuated by the rhythmic *whumping* in the background. Erin wished it would stop so that she could hear better.

Then, without warning, the phone sounded loudly in Erin's ear.

The voices stopped.

"Marisol," she yelled.

Nothing.

She pulled the phone away and looked down at the screen. The numbers were still counting. That meant the phone was still connected. The noise wasn't from the phone. It was on the other side of the phone.

She put the phone back to her ear, pushing it hard, "Marisol," she said again, still straining to hear any detail, any clue from the other end that would tell her Marisol was still okay.

Then she heard it.

It was a small sound. It was like a small animal, like a dog. No, it was crying. It was Marisol.

"Marisol, talk to me. Sweetie, I need you to tell me where you are. Tell me so that I can come and get you."

She could still hear Marisol. But she wasn't responding.

"Marisol," she said again.

Erin heard another wave of static pass over the phone, and then two more deafening explosions. Shots. They were shots she was hearing. *Keeler.*

"MARISOL!" Erin yelled.

And then…the line went completely quiet, no more static, no more low rhythmic whumping…just quiet.

Erin pulled the phone away again, quickly looking at the screen, not wanting to miss anything Marisol might say. But…the counter had stopped.

The line was disconnected.

She pushed the menu button, harder than she needed to, trying to find the recent calls. She found it. The phone almost slipped out her hands. Sweaty. She selected the top incoming call and pushed redial. Erin put the phone back to her ear.

A recorded voice answered, telling her the number had been disconnected.

She hung up, tried again.

Same message.

She dropped the phone.

She didn't notice her own movements, what her body was doing. She was on the ground now. On her knees. She bent over forward. Her head in the red dirt. Pushing it with her hands. Grabbing and pushing. A tear hit the ground and almost just as quickly faded into the dirt.

Her mind was not ready to accept it. Not yet. That would be giving up. Erin still needed to help Marisol. But right now, her body wasn't responding. Marisol wasn't gone…not like that. More tears were coming now. She kept saying it over and over in her mind, *Marisol's not gone, Marisol's not gone.* And as she cried, saying the words out loud now, or trying to, because the only words that would come out were, "gone…gone…"

Marisol was gone.

Somewhere inside, she knew that.

PAUL SAT IN A MOSTLY DARK CELL ON THE EDGE OF HIS bunk. He was hunched forward, his elbows rested on his knees, while his fingers formed a point in front of his mouth.

A clank on the bars next to him.

He didn't respond.

"Hey," said the man on the other side.

Paul continued to ignore him. His face was mostly dark. He could have fallen asleep in that position. But he wasn't asleep. He was far from asleep.

"Hey," came the voice again. "You uh, you gonna eat this?"

The guard was referring to a tray he'd left two hours ago.

Paul turned his head to look at the man.

The man was looking at Paul. He opened his mouth to say something, but instead just squinted his eyes. "So…," he said finally, "that's a…no?"

Paul shook his head slightly and looked back ahead.

He heard the heavy clink of the man unlocking the jail cell.

"Okay," the guard said, "just you stay where you are, right."

Paul had no intention of moving.

The metal-bar door moved open a few feet, and the man picked up the tray, holding a rifle lazily in the other hand. He put the tray outside and pulled the door shut again, with the same hand. It locked automatically.

Unlike American jails, Ghanaian jails put you in the cell with most of what you came in with. No change of clothes. The only thing the jailer had taken from him was his phone, which was now somewhere out of sight. Probably gone. But it was a cheap phone he'd picked up in one of the local markets.

Across from Paul was a seatless toilet. It was so dirty it looked like an exaggerated movie prop. And beyond that, the cell next to him was empty. The cell behind him had a man who'd been here before Paul arrived yesterday. He was sleeping now. He'd tried to talk to Paul earlier. But Paul hadn't responded.

Paul continued to sit still. He'd moved in the last few hours, but it wasn't to eat, it was to check his watch. He was keenly aware of what time it was. Because timing would be everything.

The guard was at the cell door again. "I'm going to bring this back later, right," he said, motioning to the tray of food.

"Mm-hmm," Paul said, not looking at him.

He wanted something. Maybe a bribe to slip Paul his phone. Maybe a bigger bribe to turn the other way so he could take a trip outside. Or sneak a girl in.

Paul didn't want any of that.

As the guard lingered, Paul moved his hands back up to his mouth, resting his elbows on his knees, and formed a little tent with his fingers. Waiting.

THE NUMBER

Erin felt herself crumbling. That was the only description that seemed accurate. For as much as she was here to help, everything she touched — whether it was her fault or not — it was all falling apart. And here she was, watching it happen and unable to stop any of it.

It had been tough enough, having Mofi dying right next to her. She'd never seen anyone die before. Much less from a gunshot wound like that.

And then, just after she and Ben found the hard evidence they needed to expose the coverup, and to bring the people who killed Mofi and the loggers to justice, they took Ben. Or, rather, Ben sacrificed himself so that she could escape. So that she could get their proof into the world.

That still didn't sit well with her. No matter what they were accomplishing, getting the story into the open…at what cost?

And now…now it was Marisol. Erin was still holding onto the phone where she'd last heard Marisol, as if letting go of it would somehow let go of her…of her memory…as if it would somehow make it all unmistakably real. *How could everything have fallen apart so fast?*

The proof, she thought…exposing some corporation's greed. Stealing some culture's heritage…those loggers who died…it had seemed so distant before. So clinical. It was an injustice, for sure. But it wasn't personal. Not like…not like it was now.

Erin was still on the ground. Sitting now, with her knee propped up and her arm and head resting on it.

She thought about Ben. He could still be alive. If he was right, they'd want him for leverage. But she didn't want to think about that. Because when she did, a rational little voice in the back of her mind told her there was a good chance that time had passed, that they'd…she had trouble even forming the thought.

It was that same rational voice that told her to keep moving. That was, after all, the whole point of what Ben had done. To give her the chance to escape. To give her the chance to get the proof — the story — out, so that those responsible would be exposed.

She looked around and reached for her phone. It had fallen when she did.

For the third time, she called Kwami's phone and, again, it rang.

"An-swer…," she said, through gritted teeth. "Come on…pick up."

She put the phone down, not bothering to hang it up. No one was answering.

Paul…she thought, *what do I do…*

As she sat there, she felt the small memory card in her pocket. Ben's pictures. And then, from out of nowhere, she remembered something Marisol had said. She said, "Call Paul's *number*." Paul gave her a number to call when she'd first arrived. It was at the same time he'd given her that fake badge. She'd completely forgotten about it.

She got off of the ground and went back to her trailer. She was rummaging through the already wrecked trailer. Making the scene even more of a mess. *Found them.* The shorts she was wearing on the first day. She turned out the pockets and found the wrinkled paper. *Paul's number.* Her phone…she ran back outside and picked up the phone she'd left on the ground, and, looking down at the crumpled piece of paper, she began dialing.

She put the phone to her ear, listening. But there was no sound.

She pulled it away and looked at the screen. A faint battery icon flashed and faded.

The phone's battery was dead.

She swore loudly.

"Think…think," she said to no one. She went to the supply trailer. All of the large computer equipment was completely demolished. Whoever did this was focused. But they weren't particularly thorough. She looked on one of the shelves in the back. She remembered Gavin mentioning something in passing. He'd occasionally needed to use his laptop for extended periods in remote areas. And so he was set up to work completely out of the truck. He had a way to convert the DC power from the truck to the AC power his laptop needed. Which was, as it would have it, exactly what Erin needed right now.

She moved things around until she found what she was looking for. She pulled down a small hardshell case and opened it. Spare laptop batteries. Extra cables. And…an AC/DC inverter. It was a small red box with a fan inside. It had a couple of AC plugs on one side, and a DC cord hanging out the other side, which fit into a cigarette lighter in a vehicle.

She pulled it out, spilling a few other supplies off the shelf and ran back to the Land Rover. Starting the engine, she shoved the DC plug into the old cigarette lighter. The small fans inside the red box whirled, and a little green LED light lit up. She reached into her bag and pulled out the plug for her phone and plugged it in.

She pushed the power button on her phone and stared at the dark screen.

The triangle logo appeared. It was coming on. She let out a breath she didn't realize she was holding.

The phone was back on now. She pulled out the crumpled paper from her pocket and dialed it again. She put the phone to her ear, leaning down slightly, so as not to pull the power cord out, and listened.

It was silent, but she could hear something, like it was working.

Then, a low-toned beep. And then another.

But it wasn't a ring.

And then the phone stopped making any sounds. She pulled the phone away and saw the numbers still counting. It was still connected. Maybe, she thought, it had to re-route. The number wasn't a Ghanaian number. So maybe that was it.

She put the phone back to her ear and heard two more low beeps. It almost sounded like an automated system. As if she were calling some customer service line.

Another low beep, and then, nothing. Silence. The call had ended.

She pulled the phone away, wondering if her signal had been weak. Maybe it had dropped. She looked down at her paper and dialed the number again.

This time, nothing. No low beeps. No connection sounds. Nothing. It just immediately disconnected.

And then…like an old movie that had run off of its reel,

all of the last few moments energy, all of the hope of remembering there was still a chance…all of it had just…disappeared.

Just like that, she realized, there was no one else. There really was no one left to call. No one to come and save them. It was her.

Just her.

The words echoed for a moment in her mind.

And the only thing she could do was run away. No, not away. But back to home. Where she could break the story. It would be a blow to everyone responsible. A win. …if you could call it that.

But, she heard a different voice in her head now, a quieter voice…*running back home wouldn't save anyone. Not anyone who still needed saving… Not Paul… and,* she tried to swallow, though her throat was too dry now …*and not Ben.*

65

BEN

THE RADIO IN THE FRONT OF THE TRUCK SCRATCHED AS
the truck hit a bump. Ben's head thumped the side wall of
the truck, adding to his already throbbing pain.

But there wasn't much he could do about that. His arms
were pinned behind him, tied.

He tried to see where they were going. He was facing
forward, but his left eye was swollen shut, and his right one
was struggling now. He didn't put up a fight when they
caught him. But that didn't seem to matter much to them.
He'd worked in these kinds of places long enough to spot
mercenaries when he saw them. They were paid. But they
weren't here for the money. They were here for the sport.
Which is what he'd become when they caught him.

He twisted himself, and pain shot through his back and
arm. He looked behind him, through the rear window.

The best he could tell they were in Accra now. It was
either Accra or Kumasi, the regional capital farther north, in
the opposite direction. Both big cities. And both about the
same distance from the logging site.

He twisted again, looking forward, angling his head

lower so that he could see up through the front. As he did, the man in the front passenger seat turned back to him. Smiling.

"Bryan, your friend, he's not, uh…with us anymore," he said with a laugh. He blew cigarette smoke down in Ben's face as he did. Ben could smell the acrid imported tobacco.

He closed his eyes, letting out a deep sigh as he did.

The truck continued to rock forward.

Ben opened his eyes again and caught a glimpse of something he hadn't noticed before. A series of towering cranes. They must be in Accra. Near the port.

The truck slowed at a guard stop.

Ben's heart thumped, a moment of hope. This meant one of two things. Either the guard would inspect and see him, and, maybe, he'd be able to go free. Perhaps, at least, buy some time. Or — the truck lurched forward, moving again — or they'd already paid off the guards and no help was coming from them.

The man in the passenger seat took a deep drag on his cigarette and picked up his radio.

"We're here," he said into it, "and we've got the one you saw."

"Is he still alive?" came a rough voice from the radio.

The smoking man looked back at him, with a grin that almost bordered on joy. "Enough," he said, back into the radio.

Ben closed his eyes. Which really meant he stopped struggling to keep his right eye open. And rested his head back on the wall of the truck, letting out a low labored sigh as he did.

66

ERIN

The story.

That's what was in front of her.

That's what *needed* to be in front of her. She needed to take the evidence in hand, write it up, and get it to McGillis. This would easily headline the International section. Maybe even make A1.

She stood up and started to pace. Walking back and forth, not conscious of what she was doing.

Putting the implications for her own career aside for a moment, *this*, she reasoned, was the right thing to do. After all, the ones responsible need to be exposed. It was the greater good. And, she continued, it was the very reason Ben did what he did. He knew the risk… He would *want* her to leave, to focus on getting the story out.

Yet…still…

There was something gnawing at her, somewhere just below the surface she couldn't quite put her finger on. Something she didn't yet understand.

Then, as if from another planet, she heard a small bird. It was in a tree somewhere behind her, or in front of her. And it was chirping constantly. It must have been doing this for a while, but it was the first time she'd noticed it.

Next, something strange happened.

The jungle around her came alive. It wasn't just that little bird, it was a cacophony of sound. Of crickets, singing in waves. Of some small animal running through the branches high above her. And even the wind, too, was constantly in motion.

For the first time since she'd been in this world, she'd noticed how much was going on without her. Without her problems. And no matter what happened to her, or what she did, it would all continue on without her.

Instead of making her feel less significant, this all had a calming, subliminal effect. It was as if, in that moment, everything was right. Everything was okay. And what she should do became as clear to her as the world living and breathing in front of her.

The sun was now falling, not yet low, but not high anymore. She could feel it soaking into her bones. Waking her up. And filling her with life.

Now, finally, she understood the difference between what was good for her to do, and what was *right* for her to do. Finally…she understood why she was here.

THE PORT

Erin got into the Land Rover, started it, and felt the calm hum of the motor in front of her. The sun shone into the back of the truck, filling the inside with yellow.

She pulled off, heading to the port in Accra to find Ben.

She knew it would take her to Keeler. The man who killed Marisol. And, she knew, he might kill her before it was all over with.

She knew all of this. And yet, as she pushed on the accelerator, and as the tires below her gripped the dry dirt and threw up a cloud of red dust, she was okay with it.

68

IBSEN

CARL IBSEN PICKED UP HIS PHONE AND DIALED.

"Erin," he said, hearing the static on the other end, "can you hear me?"

"Barely," she said. "I'm on the road, it's a bit remote."

Another wave of static came over the line before it cleared.

"But Carl," she said, "I'm glad you called. A lot's happened. I'm headed to the port now and —"

"I know," Ibsen said. "I…know."

"You know?"

"Erin…I have to…" he said, with a heavy sigh, as he sat behind his deep mahogany desk in R4's headquarters.

Behind him, the large windows looked down on Washington D.C.'s busy K Street. People walking by dressed in their dark business attire, the uniform of D.C. How many of these people were instrumental in deals being made all over the world at this moment? New York, Los Angeles, even San Fransisco are cultural centers. But it's D.C., where the real power brokers are. It's not about volume. Or even about commerce. It's about leverage. Power. That's what a city like D.C. really translates in to.

Ibsen sat with the windows behind him. His elbows were propped on his desk, one hand massaging his forehead, with the other holding the phone to his ear. He was deciding on what — no, *how* — to say this next part.

"Carl," Erin said, slower now, "how did you know I was heading to the port?"

"A few…" he hesitated. "A few developments have happened here."

As he said the words, he felt his own fatigue catching up with him. He was good at walking the political line. It was an intuition he'd developed over the years. He could read the situation and react, almost at an instinct-level.

But he wasn't good at doing it on behalf of others.

He wasn't good at helping others survive.

"Erin," he said, "I'm going to cut to the chase here. Don't go to the port."

"I have to. They have Ben, and —"

"Who's Ben?"

"He works with Paul. Doesn't matter. But Paul's been arrested. And I have proof of the…"

"Erin," he stopped her. "Forget the proof, the story. And forget whoever else is wrapped up in this."

The line was silent for a moment.

"Erin, I need you to do this."

"Tell me why, Carl," she said.

"It's a setup," he said, lowering his voice. "If you go to the port, you're not going to come out."

"You mean Jonah Lennox is going to have me killed."

"Yes. Something like that."

"How long have you known about this, Carl?"

She kept saying his name. And she was doing it in that

calm voice. Not the voice of someone who just heard they were about to be ambushed and killed.

"It's not that simple," he said, resting heavier on his hands now.

"How long," she repeated in a measured tone.

Ibsen closed his eyes.

"The van was Plan A."

"Back in D.C.? The one that almost ran over Paul and me?"

"I fought against it," he told her, beginning to talk faster now. "I told them you wouldn't be a problem."

"A problem…for what?"

For what…he thought. Her world is still black and white. The cowboys and Indians of childhood. The real world doesn't work like that. It never did. Everything is a compromise. Everything.

"Ghana," he said, not answering her question, "was Plan B."

She didn't respond this time.

Static again washed over the connection.

"Like I said, I wanted to find…another way," Ibsen said, trailing off.

What else was there to say? The irony was that it really was this simple. In the end, his decision really was a black and white one. You could move forward and adapt…or you could tie yourself to the weaker ones, and then go down with them.

"So," she said finally, "what it really comes down to is, you sent me here to get wrapped up in whatever this is Lennox and his thug Keeler are into. And, in the process, they just take care of me. Do I have that right?"

Yes. That was exactly right. But he couldn't bring himself to say those words. Whether it was to her, or just to himself… But, it didn't matter much now.

"I want to know why, Carl. After all these years…why you couldn't have trusted me."

"Don't go to the port," he said, quietly.

"And then what, Carl?" her voice was louder now. "I just…come back and pretend nothing happened? And *they* pretend nothing happened, too? Come on, you know it doesn't work like that."

"If you go," he said, still quiet, "I can't help you."

"*You* can't help me?" she said. "Carl, you're the one who sent me into this. Don't pretend like you didn't have a choice. You always had a choice."

There was, Ibsen realized, nothing else left to say.

In fact, he'd said too much already. If they were listening in — his heart sunk at the thought — he shook his head… she didn't realize the risk he was taking in just calling her right now. Much less warning her.

But she wouldn't change. He could see that now.

"Okay," he said. "Erin…"

"Goodbye, Carl," she said.

The line went dead. He looked down at his cell phone and then set it quietly on his desk.

A knock on his door.

His assistant, Julia. She opened it slightly, poking her head into the crack.

"It's Eli Bren."

How did he…

"He's on the line for you."

Ibsen let out a long sigh.

"Okay, tell him—"

"He said it was urgent," she said, somehow knowing he was about to make an excuse.

"Alright," he said, "Put him through."

69

THE HIGH VIEW

THE PORT, FROM THE OUTSIDE, WAS A LONG CONCRETE wall. Over the wall, Erin could see cranes jutting up into the sky, with large metal shipping containers stacked around them.

She passed by the port entrance and kept driving. Two blocks away was a three-story parking garage. She drove to the top and parked at the edge.

She got out of the Land Rover and walked to the edge of the parking garage, looking over the port. From here, she could see its entire layout. She walked back around and without opening the passenger door, reaching into the open window and pulled out her sat phone. Looking out over the port, she thumbed through her contacts and dialed Conall McGillis at the *Washington Post*. She held the phone to her ear, waiting for it to connect.

"Hey kid, how's Africa?" McGillis said.

"It's...," she trailed off.

What *was* it? she thought. The whole experience has felt so surreal. Like being in a movie and simultaneously watching it play out.

"Conall," she said, "this whole thing is bigger than I thought."

"What, the story about the loggers?"

"Yeah. The loggers…and…"

She replayed in her head, everything that had happened over the last few days, trying even to find a place to start. It all sounded like the conspiracy she'd been looking for.

Except, now that she'd found it, it was the last thing she wanted to be true.

"The bacterium," she said, "it was a fake."

"Fake?"

"Yeah, I've got proof."

"Wait, weren't Paul and his guys all working on this together? Were they in on this?"

"No, well…not Paul's team. But there's more."

"Okay…"

"The loggers who died, it was murder."

"Murder?" She could hear his chair squeak, as he said it. "How do you—"

"I've got proof of that, too. And get this, it's all connected to InTrans Global — ITG."

"The client you work for over at R4?"

"Right," she said.

"This proof…," he said, "can we print it?"

"Conall, there's more. You're not going to believe this, but…"

"Erin," he started, "if this is about —"

"Just listen to me. It's not *about* that. I mean, I think it's connected, but I… What I mean is, I've got proof they killed thirteen loggers, then covered it up with a fake bacterium, and — and this next bit is the weird part."

"What."

"I don't know why yet, but, apparently this has all been

so that they could smuggle an ancient Ashanti artifact out of the country."

"Ashanti?"

"They were a tribe that ruled this part of —"

"I know who they were, but what do they have to do with any of this?"

"Best I can tell, Jonah Lennox has been looking for this artifact for a while now. And then finally he found it in an underwater cave. Then…he killed all the witnesses — the workers — and covered it all up with a story about a small bacterial outbreak. He's a chemist by trade. And so it makes sense that he could pull it off. The idea is, it would get mild press and create enough of a distraction while he smuggled the artifact out of the country."

"So how does this connect back to ITG?"

"It's Lennox."

"Lennox?" he snorted. "Because he was in your mother's file?"

"No, *not* because of that. Because he's the liaison between SERA and ITG. *Officially*, he's here doing research for ITG. But he's *really* been leading the underwater expeditions to find the Ashanti artifact, the golden chair."

"What's Lennox's relationship to Paul?"

"None, other than giving them data to analyze."

"Why didn't SERA do that themselves?"

"This is not unusual for ITG," Erin said. "They do this kind of thing all the time. For them, it's the intellectual property they're after. The data.

"One of the ways they capitalize on this is by leveraging the nonprofit work for their own PR. Because ITG needs to appear to be *supporting* and not controlling the nonprofits they work with, they don't technically own them. But they still control them indirectly through grants and other donations. But legally, they're separate.

"And so ITG's interest is data collection?" McGillis said.

"Right. Data is expensive to collect. And so in this case, they're the ones feeding SERA the data they need. SERA then takes it, compares it against WHO or CDC data to then make a recommendation to the local government on how to handle any new developments."

McGillis was quiet. She could tell he was thinking, piecing it together. In the journalism business, the process of a story started with a reporter or field investigator who'd pitch a story to an editor. Like what Erin had been doing. The editor then had to pitch it — in a different way — to management. Management in the newspaper business was most interested in placement. How would this be received? Who'd be interested in reading it? And is it strong enough, or should something else go there instead? No matter how good it was from a journalistic point of view, if it wasn't set up to get eyeballs, it wouldn't make the cut.

But there was something else in all of this.

This was political. ITG was a large conglomerate. And, as Erin could personally attest — being her client — they'd cultivated a savvy media position with their various nonprofit support. If the *Post* ran this, they'd have to contend with heavy blowback. A company like ITG wouldn't be accused of corruption and *murder* without swinging, and probably landing, a few heavy punches in return.

All of this added up to a highly charged situation. One that McGillis now needed to walk carefully through.

"Okay," he said finally. "Say all that is true. Say ITG really does want this ancient Ashanti artifact, and say they've found it and even gone to the extreme of killing people to smuggle it out of the country. Putting aside their motivation for a moment, which still isn't clear, what actual, printable proof do you have to back any of this up?"

"Internal reports, where they recorded their progress of

finding and excavating the artifact. And then we've got pictures of the bullet holes and bloodstains of the location where the loggers were killed. Plus," she said, "one of the guys on the SERA team did an analysis of the bacteria-data Lennox's team gave them, and it shows clearly it was manipulated from the start."

"And…," McGillis said.

"And what?"

"And what else do you have? That's all good, but each of those can be turned around — explained in a different way. A better way, if they're clever enough."

"I…," she said, biting her lip and letting out a breath, "I've got an eyewitness."

"An eyewitness? One who will go on record?"

"Well…no," she said. "That's part of the problem. He was killed.

"Killed?" he huffed. "You mean you *had* an eyewitness. What's that do?"

"I mean," she said, "before he died, he told me what he knew. And, Conall, he was killed by a sniper."

"I'm really sorry about that, but…so what?"

"So — we were in the middle of *nowhere*. Someone tracked him. And then, they took a shot from, I dunno, a really long distance away. It was clearly a professional job."

McGillis was silent.

"So," Erin said, "tell me, why would someone expend all that effort on keeping someone quiet who didn't have anything important to say?"

"And you can *prove* it was ITG who did this, who sent this sniper?"

Erin felt her heart thump in her chest, thinking about the answer to this question. "I…," she started. "I will."

"You will? What do you mean 'you will'?"

"I mean…I'll have that proof soon enough."

And that was true. If she could find Ben, she'd find Lennox. She wasn't exactly sure how she'd extract something as helpful as a confession out of Jonah Lennox. But it was a detail. Lennox was the one who had Mofi killed. There was no doubt of that. And combined with the rest of the story, that put ITG in a vulnerable position.

Her own death was a thought that was becoming more and more common in her mind. She hadn't, she could firmly attest, become okay with it. But the more she felt herself getting pulled into this thing, the more that end became a real possibility.

"Okay…okay…" he said. "InTrans Global, ITG, wants this artifact, this, eh…"

"Golden chair."

"Right, they want this golden chair. And why…? We don't know yet. But…" he continued, working out the narrative. Erin was used to this. He wasn't talking to her anymore, he was walking through the story, out loud, trying out how the pitch felt.

"But," he continued, "we know they've been searching for it for some time. And then they found it. And, presumably, because it was a cultural artifact, they couldn't just export it. Also, knowing word would get out about finding such a special thing, they killed the workers and quietly hushed the piece out of the country," he said. "That about the sum of it?"

"Yes," she said. As contrived and bizarre as it all sounded, yes…that was it.

"We're going to have to play this one close, you know?"

She did. All that mess from Trinidad all those years ago — if it taught her anything, it was who to trust. Or…

"Conall… there's one more thing."

"There's more?" he snorted.

"I'm going to send you what I've got," looking down over

the port as she said it. "For safekeeping. The pictures, I'll email to you. And the reports, I'm going to fax them over. You still have a fax, right?"

"Eh, yeah, but —"

"After I hang up, I'm going to go to an Internet cafe. You should be getting something from me within the hour."

"We'll need to move on this fast. I'm going to need your story soon. If this is happening, I'm going to need it, like, as soon as possible."

"I know. But…there's one more thing I need to do here."

"Lennox," he said.

She didn't respond.

"Look," he said, "we've got the story already. There can be more, later. But this is enough to run, as is."

"I know," she said, "I've just got to go do this."

"If all that stuff, the stuff with your mother. If it's connected to him and if he was the one who…"

"I know," she said. It didn't help to hear the odds. Reality, for what it was worth, wasn't always helpful. Right now, she needed all the courage she could find.

70

ENTRANCE

Erin pulled the Land Rover into the queue to get into the port.

There were three vehicles in front of her. They looked like official work vehicles. The one directly in front of her was for a chemical survey company. As they waited, a man in a tan uniform at the guard shack ahead was stopping each vehicle and checking credentials before letting them proceed.

Credentials, she thought. She'd been so obsessed with finding Lennox, finding what she needed to prove his and ITG's involvement, that she hadn't even considered the detail of *how* she'd get into the port.

For a moment she considered pulling out of line and turning around. She didn't have another plan, there was no other entrance that she knew of. And if there was, they would surely be checking ID. All she knew right now was she didn't have an ID that would let her…*wait*. She did have…

She began rummaging in her bag in the seat beside her.

"Got you," she said, pulling out an ID badge. The one Paul gave her just after she'd arrived.

She glanced up at the pickup truck in front of her. It had moved ahead, leaving a space. She let off of her brake, moving the Land Rover forward.

She looked back down at the badge Paul made for her. She hadn't bothered reading it until now. She had no intention of using it before now. It said she was a member of SERA, working in conjunction with the American Embassy. *I guess*, she thought, *that could…kind of…be true.*

She looked up again the truck was gone. She pulled up to the uniformed man standing next to the guardhouse.

"ID," he said.

She handed it to him.

He looked down at it, reading the label. Looking at it.

"What's your business?" he said, without looking up at her.

"I'm…here," she said, "to…"

The man looked up at her. His face was blank. Was he seeing through this? Could he tell the badge was a fake?

"To…?" he said.

Focus.

"I'm a journalist," she said flatly, pulling out her other badge, the one from the *Washington Post* that she always carried.

He took both badges without responding and walked back into the booth. She looked straight ahead, watching him out of the corner of her eye. He was looking through a clipboard. He put it down and picked up the phone. He said something into the phone, but he was talking low and she couldn't make out any of it. He stopped talking, still with the phone to his ear. "Okay," she heard him say, as he glanced her way. "Okay," he said again and hung up the phone.

He walked back out.

"We don't have any media personnel scheduled for

today," he said, handing the badges back to her. He began pointing, for her to u-turn, already looking at the vehicle behind her.

She didn't take the badges. Or move the truck.

"I'm with the Embassy," she said.

He paused and looked at her again.

"My visit won't be on your lists," she began inventing. "The *Washington Post* and the U.S. Embassy are doing a joint project, and it's been authorized by the Accra Port Authority" — she saw that title as she was driving in and wished now she could remember the official's name in charge of it. Vice Admiral Something-or-other — "he's cleared it all. It's an unscheduled inspection, for all American facilities in the port, to make sure they're…er, up to code."

She stopped talking but kept looking at him.

He looked at her for a moment and then walked back to his booth and reached for the phone again.

"It's a visual inspection," she called out to him.

"A what?" he said.

She pointed up to the sky. "We've only got a short time before our window closes. Your Vice Admiral asked us to come as close to closing time as we could. To make sure no one was cutting corners at the end of the day."

With that, he stood up a little straighter.

"Wants to make sure the Americans aren't taking advantage of the Ghanaian facilities."

He began nodding. He began to hand her ID badges back and then hesitated.

"I haven't seen you here before," he said.

"It's my first time," she said without hesitation. Which, she noted with a sense of irony, happened to be true. "Everyone has a first day on the job, right?"

Something in there seemed to satisfy him.

"In that case, you'll need to check in first at Building Four," he said, handing her credentials back to her.

"Building Four."

"First on the left," he said, pointing forward. He took a step back and reached for something in his booth. As he did, he motioned her forward. The bar in front of her car lifted, and he waved the vehicle behind her forward.

She drove forward slowly, trying to find some indication of where to go next. She was looking around so intensely that she had to slam on her brakes. There was a man standing directly in front of her. If she were going any faster, she would have run him over.

He was dressed in the same tan uniform as the entrance guard, but he held an automatic rifle over his shoulder. He stood, looking directly at her, not speaking.

She waited for him to move, as he was clearly standing in the middle of the road. He continued to stand, squared off to her vehicle, not saying anything.

Seeing he wasn't going to move, she opened her door to get out and see why he was standing here and maybe ask for direc—

"Do not exit," he barked at her, as soon as she'd opened her door. "No vehicles beyond this point," he said.

She shut her door again and leaned out the window. "I'm looking for Building Four," she said, realizing she'd have to at least pretend she was going to follow the instructions the last guard gave her.

He pointed to his right, her left. In block letters, painted on the front of a one-story building, she saw the embarrassingly large words, "BUILDING 4." It was thirty feet away from her.

She glanced back at him. But he seemed only interested in standing stock still and making sure no vehicles got past him.

"Thanks," she said, though he probably didn't hear her. Or he didn't react if he did. She turned her truck and drove to Building Four, parked out front, and then walked inside.

71

BUILDING FOUR

Erin pulled open the glass door of Building Four and walked inside. The inside was a typical non-descript government building. A few pictures of officials on the wall and a Ghanaian flag in the corner. Directly in front of her was a man sitting behind a desk, looking at her. He wore a tan uniform, like the one who checked her ID at the gate. But he didn't have a gun, not that she could see.

"Sign in here, please," he said.

Erin walked to the counter, scribbled something illegible. She dropped the pen and looked around, trying not to appear out of place. The make-it-up-as-you-go approach was a lot harder in real life than in the movies. In real life, people paid attention. And there were checks and balances in place.

The man, she noticed, didn't seem to care much about what she was here for.

She walked to the far wall where she saw an electronic board, like in airports that showed flight statuses. Except, this one appeared to be for shipping vessels. It was split into five columns: Vessel name, ETA, ATA, ETD, and ATD.

She studied it. ETA, she knew, stood for estimated time

of arrival. That means ETD is probably estimated time of departure. She looked at the other two columns, ATA and ATD. They all had times in them, too. Some were the same as their corresponding ETA and ETD column. But others were different. Some were flashing. The A must be actual. This board is showing her the port at a glance: all the vessels, their scheduled times in and out, and then their actual times.

That means…she did the calculation in her head, backing up to the time Marisol had called her. Marisol kept repeating, five hours left. That means, with the drive down to Accra, the time it took her once she arrived here, and then…how long had it been between the time Marisol called and she left? Best she could tell, five hours put the departure time between 6:00 and 6:30, which was, she looked down at her watch, between thirty to sixty minutes from now.

She scanned down the ETD, estimated time of departure, column. Which vessel leaves at —

"What are you doing?" The voice came from behind, causing her to jump.

She turned around. The voice belonged to the man sitting behind the counter. In all of her thinking, she'd forgotten she wasn't alone.

"I'm, uh," she said, turning back to the board, maintaining her inspector-character — in case she needed to use that again. "I'm just looking for —" *Forget it*, she thought, turning back around.

"I'm new here," she smiled.

"Yes," he said, as if he was thinking the same thing.

"And," she went on, "I work with the American embassy, who is partnering with the Ghana Department of Agriculture"—*why was she changing her story?*—"and I have to sign some paperwork for the vessel leaving at, er, 6:15 today," she said, splitting the difference on her estimate.

He walked around the counter without responding. He walked up next to her and pointed directly at the board.

"You've got two," he said. "One leaves at 6:10 and the other at 6:22. But," he gave a quick look over the board. "None at 6:15."

"Okay," she said, "well…I'll just…check on them both then," she smiled.

"Don't you have a manifest, telling you what the vessel name is?" he said.

"A manifest…" she said. "Yes…I do." She didn't. "It's… eh," her eyes darted to the door, "it's in my truck. Outside. The manifest is in my truck outside. So I'll just…go…check it when I go out there."

He looked at her.

"Okay," he shrugged and turned to walk back to sit behind his desk.

She started to walk out of the door.

"And," he said, before she could reach the door. "Don't forget, since you're new, you can't drive any farther at this point."

"Right," she said.

"So…," he said, "you'll want to get the manifest before you go down that way."

"Oh, yes. Right."

She put her hand on the door.

She looked back at him, "you wouldn't happen to know which direction the 6:10 and 6:22 are, would you? I mean, I'll just get directions for both, depending which is on my manifest, then I won't have to come back in, and bother you," she finished lamely.

He squinted back at the board. "6:10's at Berth 1, in the north quay," he pointed, "and the other," he said, still looking at the board, "is down near the warehouses, in the south quay." He looked back down at his desk.

"Thanks."

"Mm-hmm," he said, not looking up at her.

She walked out, immediately holding her hand up to cover her eyes. The sun was falling and was now directly in front of her. It would be dark soon.

South quay, she thought, looking around. The sun was setting in front of her. Which means, south was to her left. She turned and began to walk.

The port felt a bit like a long tarmac. Wide and expansive. Off to the side was buildings. And instead of walking past planes, she'd walk past large stacks of shipping containers.

Ahead of her, about a mile down the port, she could see a series of warehouses.

She thought back to her call with Marisol. It didn't sound like she was outside when she called. And it sounded like she was hiding, at least part of the time. A warehouse could fit that description. And if they took Ben here — which she realized was really no more than a guess at this point — then holding him in a warehouse would probably be the easiest way to stay under the radar.

She tried not to think about the odds. The chance that she was going to the right place was disparagingly small. But what else did she have?

She picked up her pace, walking faster.

72

LOOSE ENDS

THREE LIABILITIES. THREE ASSETS. AND THIRTY-ONE minutes.

"Check it," Jonah Lennox said.

"We've *just* checked," Keeler said, in a tone that would suggest he was responding to an insubordinate toddler.

Lennox paced, hands behind his back. "Check it again," he said without looking up at Keeler.

Keeler motioned to the two men under his control and they both walked out the door.

Lennox stopped walking and looked at the Customs official, standing against the wall. The man was staring at him but immediately looked away. Lennox looked back down and resumed his pacing.

"What are you going to do with the girl's body?" Lennox said.

Keeler was looking out of the warehouse window, and he didn't immediately respond.

Lennox looked up, toward Keeler, while continuing to pace. "Keeler…the girl," he repeated.

"How many years have we been doing this, Jonah?" Keeler said with a sigh.

The problem with guns, Lennox thought, was the level of confidence they inspired. Or, rather, the level of *false* confidence. You have a gun and all of a sudden you're an optimist. Or lazy. Neither was acceptable.

"What if someone finds the body and makes the connection to us?"

"They won't," Keeler said.

"They won't?" Lennox stopped walking. "How do you *know* they won't?"

"Because John and I," he said, nodding to the Customs official standing off to the side, whose name was clearly not John, "we have it worked out." He looked to the Customs official, "Right?"

The man's eyes darted from Keeler to the girl's lifeless body. Lenox looked at the Customs official now. Then the Customs official nodded, understanding.

"Keeler…" Jonah said, "if you…"

"You handle your part," Keeler said, forcefully, "and I'll handle mine. Like always."

Lennox turned away and continued his pacing.

"And what about him," he said, without motioning, referring to the man they'd captured at the logging site.

Keeler looked down at him.

"I don't think he'll make it."

73

THE SOUND

THE SIZE OF THE PORT WAS WEIGHING ON ERIN'S MIND as she kept walking.

To her right was a wall of shipping containers arranged in rows, with streets in-between, like a small city. Towering above them all was a seventy-foot high machine, shaped like a giant staple with a crane hanging down in the center, which she watched lift and stack containers, building the container-city. Beyond the containers, she could see the ocean vessels, docked. She caught a glimpse of one through a space between containers, and it was easily three football fields long.

The distant metallic clanks of the port followed her as far as she went. She continued walking. On her left now was a long series of nondescript buildings. It was a moment before she realized it was all the same building. It seemed to stretch on forever.

She looked down at her watch. 5:55 p.m. She had as little as fifteen minutes, and she still wasn't close to finding out which vessel the smuggled golden chair was on. And even if she did find it, she didn't have the slightest idea about how to stall an entire vessel. Add to all that, finding Ben in the process…if he was even here, or — it hurt to think it — if he was still alive.

Erin was moving forward now, not because it was the logical thing to do. She was doing it simply because something inside of her wouldn't let her do anything else.

The sun was fading fast now. The only thing she could really say confidently about her trek was that she was heading south. The number of workers didn't seem to be dwindling with the sun, however. It looked like the port would continue working into the night. She kept walking.

Then she heard it.

What was that sound? It was hauntingly familiar, but she couldn't place it. Like a word she knew but couldn't recall.

She kept walking, thinking about it.

Then, *that's it.* The low thumping. It was the sound she'd heard when she was talking to Marisol. When Marisol was… a feeling like a bucket of ice water came over her, causing her to stumble as she walked. *Focus,* she told herself.

She looked around for the sound. Above her, thirty feet up, a large fan built into the side of the wall was making a *whump…whump…*sound. The blades on the fan must be ten feet long.

She looked down at the building. It was mostly a brick building. Probably another warehouse. And it had a series of panel windows. The only entry point was a door, about forty feet away. She moved closer to the brick wall, staying low enough so that anyone inside would not be able to see her through the windows.

The sun was almost gone now.

Whump…whump… The low bass sound was immediately above her. This was the place, she was sure of it. This was the place where Marisol was when she called her. As she stood there, a surreal feeling came over her. And then, another completely different emotion. Not sadness. Not fear. Rage. Pure rage at the people responsible.

Erin didn't try to control the emotion. Instead, she let it flow through her. She let it fill her up, because she would need it for what she was about to do.

74

OUT

Three American soldiers entered the building, not acknowledging the jailer behind his desk reading his magazine.

They walked directly to Paul Dannon's cell.

By the time the jailer started paying attention, the three were already standing in front of Paul's cell.

"Open it," said the older soldier, standing behind the other two.

The soldier closest to Paul's cell door reached down and put a key in the lock and, with a metallic click, turned it.

The jailer stood up, looking at the three men. He looked like he wanted to say something, but couldn't seem to get the words out.

The soldier who unlocked the cell grabbed the bars with one hand and swung it open.

"Hey," came the wobbly voice of the jailer standing behind them. None of them turned to look at him.

Paul stood from his bed and walked out, as if this were normally how a person leaves a Ghanaian jail.

"Good to see you, Bill," Paul said, reaching out to shake hands with the older soldier in the back.

The other two soldiers stood to the side, looking ahead not making eye contact with Paul or Bill.

"Tell me," Paul said to Bill, "what's the latest?"

"We have their location," Bill said.

None of the four men had yet acknowledged the jailer. And the jailer, for his part, hadn't said anything else. Probably deciding whether he should push the issue. After all, three armed men had just walked in with keys to the cells he was responsible for.

"The team is mobilizing now," Bill said. "Be ready in…," he looked down at his watch, "six minutes. Then another fourteen, fifteen until we're in position."

The four men began walking to the exit. Bill and Paul walked first, and the other two followed.

"Uh…," the jailer said, apparently beginning to find his courage, "you, er…" he stumbled for what to say as he made eye contact with Paul.

Paul's look was not unkind. "It's okay," he said. "Call your superior. Tell him exactly what happened. He knows I'm leaving."

The jailer stared at Paul and then looked to where the other men had just been standing. Paul nodded to him, signaling the exchange was over, and walked out of the building.

Outside waiting for them was a large black humvee. The two soldiers climbed into the back. Paul opened the front passenger door, resting a leg on the step up, getting ready to hoist himself in. As he did, he looked over his shoulder and saw Kwami's truck still sitting a few hundred yards down the street. He couldn't see him inside of it from this distance. But he knew he was in there. He also noticed that his own truck was not where he left it. *Good man*, Paul smiled. He pulled himself in the large vehicle and shut the door behind him.

Across from him, Bill was in the driver seat. He cranked the humvee's diesel and it bubbled to life.

"What about the object?" Paul said, continuing his previous debriefing. "Do you know where it is?"

"Still narrowing it down," Bill said.

The humvee backed out into the street and drove down the road.

"Bill," Paul said, looking over at him, "I'm going in with your team."

"Paul…," Bill said.

"Non-negotiable, Bill," he said, looking straight ahead, "you know what's at stake."

They were moving along Accra backroads, and so there were not many other cars. The humvee's tires gripped the pavement as Bill took a corner at speed. Humvees don't have air condition, so all of the windows were down. Paul could feel the hot coastal wind coming in as Bill drove through the city.

"Fine," Bill said. "But," he looked at Paul, "it's my command. Understand? You come with me, you do what I say."

Paul nodded, "I got it, Bill."

The humvee pulled up to a steel gate. From the road, all that could be seen was the large metal perimeter wall. An American soldier, from the inside, walked the gate open. The humvee drove forward.

"You've got eight minutes," Bill said to Paul, "to suit up before we leave."

75

BY THE DRUM

ERIN CROUCHED DOWN NEXT TO THE ENDLESS WALL OF the warehouse.

Above her, the wall-mounted fan, the one she'd heard in the background when Marisol called her, continued to thump.

Apart from the windowless door near her, she couldn't see any other entrance. Along the warehouse's brick wall was a series of square-paned glass windows — windows she'd be careful to stay away from. But none of them looked like they could be opened. Getting in there was only an option if she broke the glass. And she wasn't ready to make that kind of noise yet.

She looked over her shoulder toward the water. The sun had just dipped below the horizon, and an orange light flickered to life high above her.

She looked at the door again. She wondered if it had any kind of alarm on it. She couldn't see any wires or magnetic clips nears the edge. If it was unlocked, and if there was no alarm…then she may be able to quietly slip in. But…she didn't know what was on the other side of it. And, if this really was the place they killed Marisol, then would they still be here? Probably, as she reached her hand up to turn the handle, and make a quick, quiet entrance, they'd already —

Click.

Her heart flubbed and her hand stopped in mid-air.

She knew the sound.

And she knew the feeling. The same distinct feeling that you're not alone. No longer alone, in her case.

"Stand up slowly," said a dark voice from behind her.

Erin stood. She put her hands up instinctively and slowly turned around.

"I was wondering," said the man, "if we'd see *you* again."

Keeler.

Erin had never stood this close to him before. He was easily a foot taller than her. And his shoulders were more than twice as broad as hers. He wore dark tactical gear, the kind with pockets all over. And he had a dirty smirk on his face. Like this was a game, and he was winning.

Then, in the middle of his bulk was a black pistol, its dark hole aligned with Erin's stomach.

With his free hand, he reached for the door she'd been about to open a few seconds ago, and pulled it open. "Let me get that for you," he said. Then, he flicked his gun. "In."

Erin turned and walked slowly inside. As she did, Keeler pushed her roughly.

Inside it was a large warehouse, with an open floor and fluorescent strip-lighting high above her.

"Over there," he said, motioning to a stack of fifty-five-gallon drums. Someone was already there, sitting. Her heart jumped with recognition as she looked to where Keeler pointed.

Ben.

He was sitting, propped against a scratched fifty-five-gallon drum.

Keeler grabbed a handful of her shirt from the back and walked her over to him. She couldn't tell if Ben saw her yet. As she got closer, he looked like he might be unconscious.

Keeler shoved her down next to him.

Then, leaving them, he walked to the other side of the cavernous room.

"Ben," she said, moving to him.

His face was badly bruised. And one of his eyes was swollen shut. But he was awake, and he looked at her.

"I…thought, you were…," she said.

"Not yet," he said, trying weakly for a smile, "but…we might both be soon."

"Are you okay?"

He was having trouble keeping his head up, she noticed. He shifted his weight. But as he did, his face went rigid and he grabbed his ribs, groaning in pain.

"Only when I don't move," he said, offering another weak smile.

"What did they do to you?"

"Nothing that won't heal," he said, not meeting her eye that time.

She noticed he was having a hard time breathing. Probably broken ribs, she thought, and a concussion.

He closed his eyes again.

"Ben," she said, "keep your eyes open. Okay?"

"I'm more concerned," he said, through a wince of pain, "with getting out of here."

"I'll worry about that," she said, looking around.

Keeler was across the room talking to another man who's back was to her. There were a lot of barrels, like the one Ben was propped against, stacked around the inside. And near them, they created a kind of false wall.

Behind them, into the depths of the warehouse, were

rows and rows of cargo stacked high. Erin couldn't see the end of it. She imagined it must go on for a mile or so.

She looked back at Ben. Any chance of getting out of here would require fast, agile movement. And Ben wasn't in any shape for moving…much less 'fast' and 'agile.' Erin's mind began searching, planning… If there was a way they could find a hiding place, she looked around, and then maybe create a diversion. It could appear they escaped, giving her time to actually move Ben—

She saw something.

Something she hadn't seen before.

No *someone*.

A frigid shock leapt through her body.

Behind the row of barrels Ben was propped against, a person was lying, face down. Not moving. She hadn't noticed them before. And as she looked at the person now, they still seemed more like a flop of blankets than an actual person.

Erin leaned forward on her hands, moving to get a closer look, to see the face. *Her* face…

Short, dark hair, flung haphazardly, covering the face that lay statue still. Erin reached a hand forward to pull the hair back. But even as she did, she already knew who it was.

Leaning forward, on one hand, she softly moved the hair out of Marisol's eyes, seeing her vivacious face, now asleep. Forever.

Erin sat back, closing her eyes tightly.

She opened them again and looked at Ben. He was still struggling to stay awake.

"She was already like that when I got here," he said. He leaned his head back again the drum and closed the one eye that wasn't already swollen shut.

Erin looked at Marisol again, taking in the shape of her still body. Her shirt, stained. A small puddle under the side of her. Erin couldn't stop looking at her. At the way one of her arms was folded unnaturally under her body, causing the middle of her back to bend up a little.

Keeler must have dumped her here, she thought.

After he'd killed her.

She felt the same rage coming back, not far from the surface. But now it was tempered with something else. Something heavier and more stable. A kind of deep sadness.

Erin reached to straighten Marisol's shirt. A pointless act. The kind of reverent thing people do to dead bodies, and, as she did, she felt something solid. She lifted her shirt, and clipped in the small of her back was the tiny black pistol Marisol carried, still clipped to her. The whole thing was only a few inches long in total, and barely a half-inch thick. Easy to hide.

It was ironic, she thought. The only one of them who actually carried some kind of protection, the only one of them who had the right view of the situation…was the only one of them who wound up dead.

"HEY," she jumped at the sound.

It was Keeler.

She slid back to where Ben was. Across the warehouse, she glanced in Keeler's direction, and she could see him standing still, looking at her.

He'd clearly overlooked Marisol's little gun before. Did he suspect something now? Keeler looked at her for a moment longer before turning back to what he was doing.

Her mind was on the gun. But until Keeler moved somewhere else, where he couldn't look at any moment and see her, it would have to wait.

She moved to sit next to Ben. Against the wall of barrels where he sat propped. From this angle, she couldn't see Marisol's body. But she could see Keeler. The two of them sat there, next to each other, for what felt like a long time.

"I'm sorry," she said after a while.

"Sorry…" he said. "For what?"

"I…," she started but didn't finish.

The truth was, she didn't know *what* she was sorry for. Only that she felt all of this was connected to her. Maybe if she hadn't pushed to uncover what Lennox was doing. Maybe if she would have just stayed home and let things take their natural course…maybe it would have been better that way.

"There's nothing to be sorry for," Ben said quietly. "You didn't do this. They did," he said, motioning with his head to Keeler and the other man, on the other end of the large room.

Ben moved his hand, resting on the floor beside him, and put it on top of hers, wrapping his fingers around hers.

She turned her head, looking at him. But his head was back against the barrel, eyes closed.

"Don't think about it," he said, still with his eyes closed. "If you want to dwell on something, dwell on getting us out of this mess."

The two of them sat there like that, not talking.

Keeler, she saw from a distance, looked out the windows on the far side. She hadn't noticed it yet, but there was a third man. He was dressed like one of the port employees she'd run into earlier.

But that other man…he was still sitting there, at that table, his back to her.

"Ben," she said.

He breathed in sharply, opening his eyes and wincing as he did. He picked his hand up and held his ribs, breathing in carefully.

"Yeah," he said with some effort.

"Who's that guy over there, with Keeler?"

He moved his head slightly in that direction.

"I don't know who the guy in the tan uniform is, but the other guy's Lennox."

"Lennox…?" she said.

It occurred to her for the first time…she'd never actually seen Jonah Lennox before.

When he'd delivered the fabricated data to the SERA team, it was via Keeler. And when she and Marisol went to his lab, it was Keeler who found them. In all of the cases, she'd somehow missed him. She didn't doubt he was real. But now, seeing him for the first time, in person…

She stood to get a better look at him. The man who'd shown up in her mother's notes 26 years ago. The man who'd mysteriously appeared just before she turned up dead. Now he was standing fifty feet away from her. Now…after all these years…he was this close to her.

"Erin," Ben said, with some effort, "where are you going?"

76

MOVE IN

Fifty yards ahead, Paul was watching their target. A nondescript warehouse building. He was leaning against the open door of the humvee, using it as cover. Bill stood on the other side, doing the same.

"Sound off," Bill said into his radio.

They were in the port now, and two other teams were out of sight, getting ready.

This was as close as they'd been able to get without risking being spotted.

The radio scratched. "Unit two is in place," it said.

Unit two was the extraction team. They'd be the first ones in. They'd move in, blow the door, and take out any hostiles. Unit three, also on-site, was the outer perimeter. It consisted of two sets of snipers. One positioned on an adjacent warehouse building, and the other just above ground level around the corner.

Bill — and now, Paul — consisted of unit one. Their primary role in this operation was to give direction. They stayed far enough back so that they could see everything, but were still close enough to interact if needed.

And, for Paul, this was almost too much. He was good at strategy. But he was better at hands-dirty work. Something Bill moved out of as soon as he could.

"Unit three," the radio said, "we'll be in place in one minute."

Though, if Paul were being honest, it had been a while since he'd been in the kind of situation where he needed tactical gear. He pulled at his vest, repositioning it. Either this stuff had gotten more uncomfortable over the years, or it really had been that long.

Bill looked over him, "it's been a while…you ready for this?"

Paul didn't take his eyes off the warehouse.

"Do you have eyes inside yet?" Paul said.

"Only thermal," Bill said, "but we have a contact who's been keeping tabs for us. He discretely tracked Lennox here. And they've been here for the last hour or so."

"They?" Paul said.

"Three hostiles, including Lennox, and maybe another."

"Another…" Paul said, looking at Bill now, "you mean a hostage."

"We don't know," Bill said, not meeting his gaze. "Could be anyone."

Paul shook his head and looked back into his binoculars.

"How well do you trust your informant?"

"Let's just say…," Bill said, "it's in his best interest to cooperate."

Paul understood the meaning. Bill, or somebody, leaned on this guy. Probably threatened him. Or maybe just bribed him. Didn't matter, it was the same thing. Paul never liked coercion. It was a weak force. To break it, all the other side needed was *greater* coercion. It wasn't like loyalty. Or aligning values. Working for the same thing. Those kinds of forces were strong. But…people like this never understood that.

"We'll blow the door first," Bill said, "then smoke the inside and be ready to take them out before they know what hit them."

"Take them *alive,* you mean."

Bill was looking through his binoculars. "Uh huh, that's…what I said."

"Bill, if this is what we think it is —"

"We know, Paul," he said curtly. "My men all know what's at stake here."

"Because if this gets—"

"Paul," Bill said, putting down his binoculars and looking at him, "it's beginning to sound like you don't trust me."

Paul *didn't* trust him.

Which was exactly the point.

But people like Bill had moved up, not by being good at their job, but by being political. And Paul would know, he and Bill started at the same time.

"Bill, you know that better than anyone…we don't trust anybody."

The radio scratched.

"Unit three is in place, sir. All is clear."

Bill raised the radio and looked at Paul. "Remember what I said, Paul, you're with me, and it's my command out here."

Bill looked back at the warehouse and pushed the button on the radio.

"Unit two," he said, "move in."

VILLAINS

"Lennox," Erin yelled, with a volume that surprised herself.

As she walked toward him, Keeler turned and began walking toward her, to intercept her.

Lennox sat unmoving, with his back to her.

"Get back over there," Keeler said, pointing past her.

"No," she said. Her words sounded braver than she felt. "Not until he explains."

Keeler stepped forward.

Lennox raised his hand, just slightly. Still sitting, still with his back to Erin.

Keeler saw the motion and hesitated. He appeared to be conflicted by it, but in the end, he didn't challenge it.

Lennox stood and turned, looking at her directly for the first time.

She felt, as he did, he was somehow channeling more energy than was possible for a single person. He was barreling into her, his pale green eyes, with their unblinking stare. Cutting all the way to the inside of her.

"Who are you that *I* would owe *you* any kind of explanation?"

His words were smooth, and measured. Not threatening in the way Keeler's were.

No…Lennox's words were much worse.

Erin felt a muscle in her leg spasm as she stood there. She'd forgotten Ben was behind her. She'd forgotten the entire world was still alive and moving outside the walls of this warehouse. In that moment, she'd even forgotten about Keeler, looming behind Lennox. Right then, she was his captive.

"Well," he said.

"I know," she said, pushing the word out of her mouth, "who you are."

"Oh?" he said, not interested, not bored, not…anything.

"Somalia," she continued, "1993."

Lennox looked at her, waiting. Or maybe he was thinking, she couldn't tell.

"Gillian Reed," she said.

At those two words, something in his expression changed. Something she wouldn't have noticed if he hadn't already locked her down with that stare.

"She was my mother," Erin said. "You wer—"

"She was careless," he said plainly.

Erin stood, not knowing what to say next.

"You don't know why she died," Lennox said. "You couldn't know, because you're the same as her. Coming in here, like you have some divine right to do so."

"But," Erin said, "you killed those people. The loggers, and…"

"I didn't *kill* them, as if that matters. I used them to open a new way. A better way. Life is only as significant as the value it brings."

"You believe, like your mother, in a one-to-one world. Where there are good things, and there are bad things. But you have no concept of the aggregate," he said, his voice almost medicinal as he spoke. "You don't pull your head back far enough to see the bigger picture, because you can't. You're incapable of understanding that the basic building blocks that we use to construct our world, the cement and brick, that these are the result of other, *lesser* things that were crushed. They were crushed so that something bigger could be made."

"That's why you betrayed her?" Erin said.

"You're asking the wrong question," he said in his placid, monotone voice. "I didn't *betray* her. I was never beholden to her in the first place. She and I wanted different things."

"And she was too foolish to see that," he said, turning away, as if he had merely been thinking out loud this entire time.

He turned to Keeler, but didn't look at him.

"It's time," Lennox said. "Radio when you're through."

With that, Lennox walked out the back door of the warehouse.

Erin watched him go. She wanted to call out after him. She wanted to say all of the things she'd planned. But all of those things had dried up in her throat the moment he started talking. Part of her just wanted him to continue talking, as strange as that sounded. Not because she liked what he was saying. She didn't. But because what he was saying was…somehow…singular. In a bizarre way, she felt a kind of lulling comfort around him. It wasn't a feeling of safety. No. Quite the opposite. But when he was there…she felt insulated from everything else. Even…from Keeler. Like he was a drug.

She didn't say anything else. She just watched him disappear.

Keeler walked up to her. And with some effort, she pulled her eyes from the door where Lennox disappeared.

He was standing over her now, his large frame towering over her's. Reality was here again. And it was hungry.

"What are you going to do?" she said to him.

He smiled. But even as he did, she couldn't help comparing his presence to Lennox's. Keeler was his own brand of evil.

But he was different.

"What are you going to do?" she repeated, taking a step back as she did.

"All in due time," Keeler said, continuing to advance on her.

78

BLOW IT

PAUL WATCHED THROUGH HIS BINOCULARS AS TWO MEN moved carefully up to the warehouse door.

One attached thin strips, which adhered to the edges of the door, around the hinges and the doorknob. The other attached wires and carefully walked it backward, each of them, all the while making sure to stay below the window line so that no one inside would see them.

As those two men backed off, two more holding body shields crept up and stood on either side of the door. They each held automatic rifles and were prepared to rush the room as soon as the explosions opened the door.

"On my mark," Bill said into his radio.

Paul watched through his binoculars, digging with his eyes into the clouded windows, trying to gain some understanding of what was happening inside.

"Three…," Bill said into the radio.

The snipers were positioned on the front and back, to take down anyone who made a run for it. But that's not what Paul was worried about…

"Two…"

In a case like this, he'd prefer nobody died, the risk was just too great. What mattered more was…

"One…

His mind stopped thinking. He watched. What happened next would be critical…

"*Blow it*," Bill said.

FRIENDS

BANG.

A loud noise came from the door behind Erin.

Keeler's eyes flicked to the direction of the sound.

And Erin, despite her every instinct telling her not to turn her back on Keeler, turned her head to do the same.

The door, she saw, was standing open, and a figure filled the frame, silhouetted by the overhead lights outside. It was the same door she'd been crouched down next to when Keeler found her.

He was dressed like Keeler and crossed the distance between the door and where Keeler stood, with military precision. Or ex-military, she figured. He walked up to Keeler, ignoring her completely. Up close she could see that he was nearly as broad as Keeler, though not as tall.

"It's done," he said to Keeler.

"Any trouble?" Keeler said.

"No. Nothing that couldn't be…handled," he said, holding out a black radio.

"Good," Keeler said, taking the radio.

He looked at Erin with a face somewhere between a

scowl and a smile. Keeping his eyes on hers, he twisted the knob on the top of the radio, like he was putting on a show. Though, any significance was lost on Erin.

The radio scratched and started spitting out voices.

"We've finished the search," it said.

"Exits?" said a different voice.

"No sign anyone's been here recently," the first voice responded.

The man who'd delivered the radio, stood like a statue, feet apart, hands behind his back, not reacting to any of it.

"Hear that?" Keeler said, still looking at Erin. "Your friends," he nodded at the radio.

My friends…, she thought.

"Minus one," he said, waving the radio and doing what looked like it was meant to be a smile.

"Two, sir," added the man who'd delivered the radio.

"Two," Keeler said, raising his eyebrows in mock surprise. "I guess it's minus *two* friends."

Erin understood exactly what he was saying. But she couldn't figure out *who* he was talking about.

Keeler looked back at the man who'd delivered the radio. "Begin the exit protocol," he said, all pretense of humor gone.

"Sir," the man nodded, promptly leaving.

"You," he said, turning back to Erin, "you're coming with me. We need to go on a little…field trip."

He grabbed her under the arm with one hand, lifting her shoulder almost to her ear. He pulled out his pistol as he did and walked her to the door, taking her with him out of the warehouse.

80

GONE

Paul held onto the strap above his head as the humvee came to a hard stop. Its headlights shone through the empty warehouse windows and reflecting back everywhere.

A man in tactical gear walked out of the warehouse, shielding his eyes from the headlights. Another man stood outside against the wall, not looking at the new arrivals.

Bill jumped out. Paul opened his door and stepped down.

"No one's been here," the unit two leader said, shaking his head, as he walked up to Bill.

Paul peeled off his vest. He looked over at Bill as he did.

Bill turned but didn't look at Paul. He didn't get it yet. He was still looking, as if the men had just missed their target. He squeezed his radio and yelled something into it.

"Bill," Paul said, tired, "the intel was bad."

"They're here," Bill hissed.

"They probably were," Paul said, tossing his vest into the humvee. "Lennox is careful. He's gone now, Bill. We missed him."

The men from unit three had come back from their perches, and walked up, long guns over their shoulders.

Bill continued to bark orders. He was making plans to regroup, to reform.

"Bill," Paul said, standing close to him now, talking low so that the others couldn't hear. "There's more to this. We have another—"

"No," Bill snapped, "no, this is still *here*. This is still in play."

"Not," Paul said calmly, "if your informant was lying."

Bill seemed to be considering this. He threw another quick glance at the scene. He looked at Paul, and then he closed his eyes.

81

TWO CATS

"You make a sound," he said, pressing the short barrel of his gun into her ribs, "and I pull the trigger." Erin and Keeler were outside, walking.

Keeler held her close to him. His arm was thick and sweaty. The size of his upper arm was almost as big as her waist. It seemed almost effortless, the amount of force with which he held her close to him. Her body was forced to mold to his, while his gun continued to jab into her ribs.

He twisted sharply, looking behind them. It hurt. Her body wasn't made to move like this. He turned again and pressed himself flat against the wall, making her push up on the balls of her feet to relieve some of the pain from his hold on her.

The night was in full force now. From where they were, the only light came from the port's street lights. It was like walking through a small city. Except it was made of warehouses. And where they were, it was empty.

Apparently satisfied, not staying still for more than a few seconds, they were moving again. She could hear his breath. Feel it, occasionally, rippling down her shirt. Each step seemed to be more dangerous than the one before it. Keeler was moving with purpose. But it was a frenzied purpose. There was blood in the water, and it was drawing him.

"We're just…," he said to her as his head continued to dart around looking. Or maybe he was talking to himself, "…two little cats…" He was talking in a rhythmic, sing-song voice. "…moving through the moonlight…slinking through the shadows…"

That picture, Keeler talking in a way that made him sound more unhinged than ever, scared Erin more than anything else she'd seen him do.

"No one can see us…" he continued in that strange voice, "as long as we just…," he stopped talking. The muscle in his arm flinched, squeezing her chest, causing her to wince. His arm was slick and specks of dirt were in his sweat.

"Shh, shh, shhhh," he said. But she hadn't said anything. He wasn't talking to her.

They were at the edge of a building. Around the corner ahead of them was a large open area and another warehouse farther away. In the open area, near the other warehouse were a group of military men. She couldn't tell from this distance who they represented, but they were white, so probably not Ghanaian. They were standing next to several humvees, each with a tall, floppy antenna sticking up.

Keeler hoisted Erin up, adjusting his position. She let out a small groan from the pain of the motion. The gun he was holding was now down lower, pushing into her kidneys, and the feeling was making her sick.

She looked out across the space now, to the men Keeler had clearly come to see.

"Your friends," he said.

Erin looked harder at the men standing, trying to recognize any…why he would, wait—

It was… she looked harder, squinting to see from this

distance. She didn't know how, but…it was Paul. *Paul* was over there with those men. A feeling of warmth filled her. Hope was flooding her inside. And she knew this whole thing would pull up. Paul was here, and he could—

Keeler tightened his arm painfully around her chest, as if he was reading her mind. He simultaneously pushed the gun further into her kidneys, causing her vision to momentarily go black with stars.

"Verrry quiet," he said.

Erin looked at Paul again, forcing her eyes to focus again.

She felt so helpless, so close to those men, but not able to do anything. A group of men that size —and she could see from here, they were armed, with guns — they were a clear match for Keeler and his other guy. If only they would…

As those thoughts passed through her head, she saw the men moving. They were climbing into their vehicles. They were…driving away.

Keeler let out a *humph* of satisfaction.

And as she stared in disbelief at the red lights of the vehicles driving away, she heard Keeler say something.

Her vision was jerked into the darkness as Keeler pulled her away. He'd turned back to where they'd come from, and she, forcefully, with him.

For the first time since he'd taken her out on this 'field trip,' she began to struggle. Not a struggle from the pain. And not a struggle of hope, because she somehow thought Paul could help her…he clearly couldn't. She didn't know why she was fighting him now, why she was rallying her energy, whipping her body, trying to twist out of his grip. But she felt a fight deep inside of her, coming out now.

And then, without warning, his large arm, that had tirelessly pinned her to him for the last half-hour, had simply let her go. And she was free.

82

GILLIAN REED

Erin dropped to her knees, partly from the surprise of Keeler letting her go, and partly because the muscles she normally used to keep her body vertical had begun to go numb from the way he'd been holding her.

Keeler reached down, grabbing her under her arm with one of his hands and lifted her too high. She stood on her own, shakily.

"Keep moving," he said.

The threat, she thought, must have passed. He'd seen what he came to see. And now, she wasn't a risk to him. Though, she noticed, he still held his gun in his hand.

"Walk," he said.

The walk back felt miles longer than when she'd done it moments ago. Maybe it was the adrenaline, again washing out of her system. Or maybe it was just her mind, slowly giving up, letting go of hope once and for all.

As she walked, she realized Keeler was talking to her.

"…I guess you didn't know that," she heard him say.

She looked at him slowly, as they continued to walk. He was watching her as he talked.

"…that I was there, too," he said.

"There…" she said.

"Somalia. With the SEALs."

A pinch of his smugness flickered away when he said that. "Part of DEVGRU. Then."

This guy was a Navy SEAL? she thought. *It makes sense…if Navy SEALs recruited psychos…*

"In the nineties," he said, letting the words linger, "I was there."

She looked at him again. It was as if he'd tossed a cup of ice into her face.

"And yeah," his face crumpled in what was probably meant to be a smile, "I met your mother."

At that last word, Erin stopped walking. It was an involuntary motion on her part, as if it took all her concentration to process the words he'd said. That…*he knew mom.*

Keeler stopped walking but continued to talk. He reached out a hand, casually, like he was picking up something he dropped, and he grabbed her behind her neck, shoving her forward.

"Deployed at the time," he said, "but I'd done a few jobs for Bren by that time. Always through Lennox," he made a face that wasn't a smile. "Lennox *was* there, but…"

He interrupted himself with a bark, or a laugh. It was the kind of noise that was loud enough, that if there were anyone around, which there weren't, they would have heard it.

"But," he continued, "it wasn't that coward *Lennox* who killed your mother."

Erin didn't know what to think about what Keeler was saying. He was talking in a way that made her think he'd never told anyone these things before…or that no one else had cared to listen. As if she were somehow the first one who'd heard all of this.

Despite that — despite how strange this entire exchange had been — she was listening completely.

"What do mean?" she said.

He seemed to like that he had her attention. That she was listening to him.

"He never does that kind of stuff," he said with a huff. "Doesn't have the stomach for it."

His mouth opened like he was going to say something else, but he didn't. "I do it…," he said without emotion or pride or pain, "and I'm good at it."

He was walking again. And for the first time, he didn't bother to force Erin. She walked on her own.

As they walked, and as he talked, there was something else she was beginning to see in him. A quiet rage, something that had been waiting, patiently, behind all that other stuff. It wasn't a soldier's machismo. No, it was something else.

He turned, locking his clear eyes onto hers.

And then a new flash hit her.

He wasn't bragging. Talking about Lennox. About her mother. No, he was confessing.

"You…," she said slowly.

She'd stopped walking again. And this time, he did, too. The two of them stood, looking at the other. Whatever pity had been forming in her mind around him was gone now.

"You…did…," she said, not able to finish the rest of it.

"Yeah," he said, finishing her unspoken accusation, "*I* did." And with the kind of demonic pride, he said, "I was the one who killed your mother."

The words hit her like a hollow pipe.

83

ONE DOWN

THE LIGHTS FROM THE WINDOWS BLENDED INTO A swirl, a swirl that started channeling toward him. Squares, glowing and turning into a kind of vortex that seemed to be…looking for him, no…looking *at* him. They were moving toward him, toward his—

No, that's not right.

He closed his eyes. Squeezed them until he saw stars.

He opened them again. His breathing was shallow.

Still not right… he thought. He rocked his head back, letting his eyes close themselves.

He'd been having these bizarre visions since…well, he couldn't tell how long. Keeping time had been one of his many new challenges recently.

The warehouse was empty except for Ben. Sometime earlier, after Keeler and Erin had left, he saw the tan-uniformed man, who apparently, on discovering his own new-found freedom, took his leave and slipped out the back. If only he could just stand up straight, Ben thought, now would have been a really good time to do the same thing. He could at least have followed Erin and Keeler and…

The thought was cut short. His eyes darted to the front door as it opened again.

Keeler was back. And Erin with him.

Her features, though, were muted. He thought for a moment it might be more visions, but it wasn't weird like that. It was just her, there. But something, he noticed, was…off.

Keeler began walking Erin forward, to where Ben was.

Ben rolled over on his knees, to stand up. But the pain put him back down.

"Don't get up for us," Keeler said, as he walked past him.

Ben lifted his finger above his head, though it hurt every inch of him to do it.

Keeler kept walking, taking Erin with him, behind the wall of metal barrels. To where Marisol's body was…

Ben knew what that meant. He forced himself, pushing through the pain. He propped himself on all fours. *A start*, he thought. His head was swimming. And with each movement, the darkness that kept threatening to take him out cold kept flooding back into his vision. *Slow…*he thought to himself…*steady…*

He raised his head, still on all fours, and he could see Keeler standing with his back to him. He saw him toss Erin down, and she landed on top of Marisol's body. Erin let out a sound as she landed, either from the fall or just from being tossed on top of Marisol.

Ben shifted, but his eyes started blacking out again, like when you've been lying down and stand up too fast. He forced himself to stay still, to let the blood move back in place. Given his condition, staying still wasn't hard. In addition to fighting off the blackouts — which staying still helped with — every move he made was painful. He wasn't sure the extent of the damage, but with each movement, he felt a lightning storm of pain in his torso.

"Where are you going?" he heard Keeler say in a playful tone. He was still looking at Erin.

Ben looked up, and he saw Erin scrambling away. It was as if she was trying to pick up Marisol's body, or hide under her, or something.

Ben pushed his eyes shut and began hoisting himself up. He was on one knee now, with a foot under him. That hurt. It was all he could do not to yell out, to give himself away.

He looked at Keeler again. But he could only see Erin's legs.

Keeler was pointing his gun down at Erin now.

Seconds left, Ben thought.

Ben looked around. He couldn't see anything he could use. Anything he could throw or…

He heard Keeler say something else and noticed the tone of surprise in his voice. But he couldn't make out the words. To say he was having trouble focusing right now was a bit of an understatement.

Ben was on both of his feet now.

Keeler was ten feet away.

Ben breathed deep, feeling the spidering pain as he did. He'd run, knock him over. It may only buy a second or two, but—

BANG.

The sound froze him to the spot. All of his thoughts were gone.

Keeler had done it.

He'd shot her.

And Ben…

…he was too late.

Ben continued to stand there, staring at Keeler's back. The scene in front of him, frozen in his mind, frozen for all of time.

He didn't think anymore.

He didn't fall down because of the pain. He didn't even feel the pain. Ben just…stood there. Disbelieving.

84

DOUBLETAP

Erin lay there in disbelief.

The loud sound took place in only a fraction of a second. But it filled the space around her, lingering like a stain.

Keeler stood there, still hovering over her, not moving, and with a protruding look on his face.

She watched him watching her, not quite sure what would happen next.

And then, as if someone else had entered her, she felt her hand squeeze the trigger again. Another violent *BANG*. And just as it had before, the small gun recoiled, and she thought it might come out of her hand.

Keeler, still standing over her, jerked slightly. A delayed reaction. As if his body were still deciding if it were really hit or not.

And then, without any more words, he tumbled lifelessly forward.

His two-hundred-something pounds landed squarely on her, smothering her and knocking the wind out of her. She tried to breathe, but his sweaty deadweight body covered her face.

She pushed, and it was like he was tied down on top of her. She realized, with some dread, that she might not be able to push him off of her. Her body completely depleted of strength. She couldn't get a proper breath in her lungs.

And then…to her relief and horror, Keeler rolled off of her.

She breathed deep, knowing it might now be her last. The little gun only had two bullets and she'd used them both. She really didn't have any other plays at this point.

Except, it wasn't Keeler…

He was as still and dead as ever.

The strip-lighting on the warehouse ceiling shown down into her eyes. She blinked, trying to look, and then her eyes came into focus on Ben. He'd pulled Keeler's body off of her.

Without saying anything, he was down on his knees next to her, touching her, inspecting her.

His face was tense.

He put his hands on her middle. Pressing, looking. It was clinical, like an EMT responding to an accident.

She looked down at herself and saw his cause for alarm. She was covered in dark, wet blood.

"It's not…," she said, reaching for his hand, "it's not mine."

He stopped inspecting her and looked up, meeting her eyes for the first time. And then he glanced over at Keeler, who was laying on his side. Dark, thick blood was draining out of a small hole at the edge of his torso.

"You…," Ben said, putting together for the first time what had happened.

Erin looked at Keeler, and then down at Marisol's small gun, still in her hand.

She held it up, showing it to Ben.

"It was Marisol's," she said. "She always carried it with

her. And…I guess it was so small Keeler didn't notice it when he dumped her over here."

Ben was still on his knees, next to her. His face a mixture of relief, more-questions, and awe.

"I saw it on her earlier…but," she said, "it never occurred to me to take it, that I'd be able to use it. I didn't think I could ever do something like that," she trailed off.

Ben was silent, watching her and listening.

"And then, now," she said, motioning to Keeler, "it wasn't even, really, a decision…," she shrugged, "it just happened so fast."

Ben slumped back down.

Erin put the gun down on the hard floor.

After a moment, she leaned over on her knees, and reaching out to Keeler's body, she unclipped the radio on his belt. The same one the man had brought him earlier. She pushed the button on the side of it, and said, in a tired voice, "Paul…" She pushed the button again, "Can you hear me, Paul?"

And with that, she dropped the radio, feeling her own consciousness slipping. The day had finally taken all she had to give.

85

THE GOLDEN CHAIR

ERIN WOKE UP TO SEE PAUL, CROUCHING DOWN NEXT to her.

She lifted her head but immediately regretted it. She dropped her head back and closed her eyes, to soothe the throbbing.

"Take it easy," Paul said.

Her senses began filling her in on what was going on around her. The shuffle of people moving around them, voices casual. She opened her eyes again. Men in black field gear were in the warehouse now. She was still on the floor, but propped against someone's jacket.

The rest of her thoughts began coming back to her.

"Lennox," she said, trying to get up. "He was…," she paused as a wave of dizziness passed over her.

"It's okay," Paul said, resting a hand on her, "we know all about it."

She looked at him.

"We didn't get him," Paul said, "but we know where he's going."

She rested her head back against her makeshift pillow before trying to sit up again, remembering Ben.

"Where's Ben?" she said.

"He'll be fine," Paul said. "They're looking at him now. A few broken ribs. Probably a concussion. But, he's had worse."

There was a lot she wanted to fill Paul in on. A lot that had happened while he was away, while he was…in jail. She remembered that now. But as she saw him now, dressed like this, in those dark tactical clothes, she had the feeling he knew a bit more about what had happened than he'd let on.

Paul looked over his shoulder at some men walking by. She looked in that direction. But it was just more people doing clean up. Keeler's body was gone, too.

"It's good to see you, Paul," she said. "What…happened to you?"

"That's a long story," he said, sitting next to her. "Lee and I — the guy who runs SERA's head office in Ghana — we go way back. But Lee made some bad choices. And I needed to see how far those choices went. Sorry I kept you in the dark on all that."

"I called that number you gave me, after…," her mind began to flood with thoughts of Marisol. She turned to look behind her…where Marisol was…

Paul must have seen what she was thinking, his eyes looked down for a moment.

"She was working for us," he said.

"Us?"

"Yeah, that's…another long story. She was a CIA recruit."

The letters almost didn't register.

"Wait…," Erin said, "CIA?"

Her thoughts were still swimming.

"I've been on loan with them for some time," Paul said. "Not full-time, though; my work with SERA was all legit. But the two were…working toward the same end. And

Marisol, they'd recruited her about eighteen months ago. She was working undercover for them."

"Marisol…was…," the ideas just seemed too far out… too bizarre. But at the same time, it didn't. It explained some things, like how eager she was to help Erin find something on Lennox…and why she carried a gun with her…and even why she'd come up here on her own…

Paul glanced at where her body had been. "She was a good one, but…," he said quietly, "it was too soon."

The two of them sat there for a while as the other men walked around, cleaning the scene.

"Was there anyone else?" she said.

"Anyone else?"

"At SERA, who was…CIA?"

"No," he said.

The two of them sat and talked more. Erin continued to have more questions, and Paul patiently answered them. Or, most of them. Kwami and Gavin, she learned, were safe. And SERA was probably done-for in Ghana for a while. The other offices in West Africa would lend a hand as needed. But there was one more thing she hadn't heard about…

"What happened to the chair?" she said.

Paul looked at her for a long moment. She couldn't quite place his hesitation. It didn't look like distrust…almost as if he was trying to decide how much to tell her.

"You want the truth?" he said finally.

"Of course," she said, wondering what he wouldn't want to tell her at this point.

"The artifact itself," he said, "sailed. Officially, we did everything we could to stop it. But unofficially, we let it go."

"You *let* it go?"

He looked at her again, with that look.

"What," she said.

"We let it go, because we know where it's going. And,

more importantly…we know who it's going to," he said. "Sometimes you have to let little fish go to catch the big ones."

At this point, she was too tired to keep pressing. A medic was by her side now, helping her up, taking her out.

"When you get back home, and settled," Paul said, "we'll talk more."

86

WASHINGTON DC

Erin's doorbell rang again, just as she pulled the door open.

"Paul," she said, hugging him. "I didn't expect you to actually drop by."

"I know," he said. "How are you doing?"

"I'm, pretty good," she said. "Still officially on leave from R4 while they do the investigation. They've arrested Carl. Conspiracy to murder…*me*."

"So I heard. Think the company's going to survive?"

"I don't know," she said.

"Speaking of which, I saw your article in *The Post*."

"Yeah, apparently everyone has. I've been getting calls almost nonstop."

"How's Ben?"

"He's doing better. Been sleeping on my couch until he figures out what's next. Come on in," she said, turning to walk back to the living room.

"I can't," he said. "Got a flight to catch."

"Where to?"

"That's why I stopped by."

"Yeah?"

"Yeah," he said, his tone a touch more serious now than a moment before. "The golden chair, it's heading to Cartagena. Colombia."

"Okay…"

"I've got some contacts down there, from previous work I've done. They'll be able to help us, so I'm going to be heading down there to lead one of the teams."

"For the CIA?"

"Sort of…in conjunction with the CIA. I'll still have a cover, like before."

"Uh-huh," she said. "And that's what you wanted to stop by to tell me?"

"Not exactly," he said. He looked at a picture on the table in the hall. "That's Gillian," he said.

"Yeah," Erin said. "Paul? What's up?"

"The thing is, Erin. I…wanted you to hear it from me first…"

"What is it."

"It's… The person we're looking at, the person who was the master-mind behind the golden chair — behind a lot of stuff really, he…," Paul glanced around the room, before looking at her, "he's your father."

The words almost didn't register.

Erin didn't *have* a father. Well, she did…but he was long gone. A deadbeat who left when she was a baby. A guy who her mother had never talked about and who her aunt had always changed the subject about when she'd brought it up. And now…this. What Paul was saying — it couldn't be right. Erin had tried to find him in college, but it was a dead-end. She found a guy who she was pretty sure was him, but he'd died some years back.

Now…all she could do was look at Paul…who was looking at her…who was talking to her…

"…been for it," he'd said.

"Wait…," she said, not hearing any of that, "you know my dad, and…he's alive?"

Even saying the words out loud was surreal. Like a weird trick her mind was playing on her, one she knew couldn't be real, but still…a trick every one of her senses seemed to be confirming.

"…he's more than alive," Paul said. "The Agency has had a file on him for several decades. But, he's been careful. And they haven't been able to touch him. Until now. That's why I'm going down to Colombia. They're pulling out all the stops."

"Paul," she said, calmly, pushing all of the rest aside. "What's his name?"

He looked at her, this time with pity, a look she hated.

"I can't tell you that. Not yet. It's still classified." He sighed, as if he hated to say it. "But if what we do down there is successful, then you'll know soon enough. I just didn't want you to hear about it first in the news."

He looked at her. "You going to be okay?"

She looked at him, barely registering the question. She nodded.

"Listen," he said, "I've got to go. Cab's outside waiting."

He leaned over and kissed her on the cheek, then he turned and left.

She continued to stand there, not watching him, not watching…anything. The cold air from outside was coming in, but she didn't feel it.

"Was that Paul I heard?" said a voice from behind her.

She turned and looked at him and turned away. For the briefest of moments, she'd forgotten she wasn't the only one left in the world.

"Yeah," she said to Ben, "…that was Paul."

"What did he want? And, why didn't he stay?"

"He told me he was catching a flight to Colombia, because…my *father* is there," she said, looking at him again.

"Your father? I thought he was…"

"I know, I…thought that, too," she said.

She leaned against the wall, letting herself slide down to the floor.

Ben, with some effort — and a wince he did his best to hide from her — sat down beside her.

"He said," she stared at a spot on the floor in front of her, "my *father* was the one who stole the golden chair, and that the CIA had been on him for a long time…decades."

"I thought Jonah Lennox was behind that?"

"I…dunno," she said, shaking her head. "I don't really know much of anything."

"So, what are you going to do?"

That thought hadn't occurred to her until now. What *was* she going to do? Even more, that thought, as it began to blossom in her mind — as it began, like a hot sun, to burn away the fog that had been clinging to her thoughts — actually gave her…hope. Hope that, maybe this was the link she'd been waiting for.

"I…," she said, looking at him with a newfound clarity, "I'm going to go find him."

87

THE CENTURY MAN

THE STORY PICKS UP AGAIN IN THE NEXT BOOK, *THE Century Man*.

Erin investigates the conspiracy her father is involved in… Ben has a secret… And Jonah Lennox has a plan that forces Erin and Ben to team up with him…

The mysterious golden chair was only the beginning of something much more sinister, and bigger.

Don't miss *The Century Man*, the second part of the Erin Reed Trilogy! Sign up at ajfontenot.com so you don't miss it when it comes out.

And if you liked *The Golden Chair*, please leave a **review** for it wherever you bought it.

Thanks! -Joe.

ACKNOWLEDGMENTS

To my early readers, Stacey (aka Mom), Marilyn Stewart, and Joe Waller, you were invaluable in helping me work through plot and structure. And to Kristin, for always keeping me from saying dumb things.

Thanks to Elena at L1graphics for making a cover that makes me want to pick up my own book and read it. And thanks to Paige from RedPenEdits for all your editing.

Want to connect? Find me online and let me know what you thought of the book. twitter.com/aJoeFontenot.